MW00912396

TOXIC

LEGACY

An anthology of dark fiction and verse
collected by W.A. Grüppe.

Contents

Introduction

Dear Reader,

It is with pleasure I bring you my latest collection of dark stories and verse, purloined from the hidden recesses of humanity.

With this latest batch you can travel into the past, the id and the near and far futures. You will experience psychopaths and killers from fiction, those that sanction death from reality, and every graduated level of malfeasance in between.

I know you will enjoy, as much as I did, reading these dark tales and hope they gladden your heart as deeply as they did mine.

Sincerely Yours,

W.A. Grüppe

I Go Back To '82

By Nicolette Coleman

I watch the young girl
Tiny, slender, hair crimped like Toyah.
She's nervous, worried,
Having second thoughts.
I wish I could call to her, shout,
Say: "Don't do it!
Don't marry him!
He'll cheat on you, hurt you,
Isolate you from your friends,
Destroy your confidence and sense of self.
And in the end he'll leave you for another woman
When you're in labour with your second child.
He'll send you to hell and back during the divorce,
Lying, making you doubt yourself and worry you're going mad.
Run while you can!"
But I don't do it.
Wouldn't if I could.
I know what will happen you see.
She'll suffer for sure.
But along the way she'll learn self-worth.
She'll learn forgiveness and peace.
Her daughters will grow beautiful, strong and intelligent.
She'll marry again and have another child.

She'll become a better, stronger person.
It will be worth it in the end.
And somewhere along that journey
She will turn into me.

On the Road to Hell

By Paul Bunn

Chapter 1

Tapping on the steering wheel to the music of "*Uptown Girl*" by Billy Joel, Stuart couldn't have been happier.

The sun had just peeked its nose over the horizon introducing what he was sure would be a hot, sticky day. Summer had been long this year, with very little interruption by rain. The grassy fields that bordered his route had turned from the lush green of spring to dead and lifeless brown. Barely a breath of air stirred its spindly stunted growth.

He chewed a piece of gum slowly as he pondered his night's work. It had been easy.

Leaving his house at seven o'clock the previous evening, he had already decided on the area he would drive towards, just a few minutes from the squalid bedsit that was his latest home. He spent the next hour "on the hunt" as he called it; watching and waiting, he was good at that. Patience was something he had always prided himself in ever since his childhood. He shivered as he remembered the dark days of his youth, when to fight his way out of any trouble had always been his only form of defence. If someone did him wrong, he always got his own back eventually, no matter how long he had to wait.

Sensing the dark clouds encroaching on his mood, he forcibly pushed those images away. He didn't want to spoil what he was sure would be a perfect day.

Chapter 2

Seeing the "Services - 2 miles" sign at the side of the motorway, Stuart decided to have a break. Although he was quite early, there were still a few cars in the car park, most of which were congregated nearest the café area. Pulling up near (but not too close, that wouldn't do!) to a Ford KA, he switched off the engine and sat there for a few moments.

As usual when completing one of these "trips," he was careful to ensure nothing out of the ordinary was going on, particularly anything to do with the police. Scanning the car park, he saw no police cars or any other sign that they were around.

"Time for a sandwich, me thinks." He climbed from the car being careful to lock up after him.

"You can't be too sure of thieves," he murmured, with a satisfied grin on his face.

The café, like the car park, was virtually devoid of life with very few seats taken. There was some mind numbing *musak* being piped from hidden speakers, not quite loud enough to grate on you. The woman at the cash desk was plump and middle-aged, staring into the middle distance thoroughly bored, probably thinking of her daily diet of soaps she would watch when she got home.

Stuart grabbed a tuna sandwich, a Danish and an orange juice. He paid the woman, not giving her a second glance. Someone as ugly as her didn't even deserve a "good morning." He made a beeline for a seat by the window, so he could keep an eye on his car.

Tearing open the packaging of his sandwich, he didn't realise how hungry he was. Taking large bites, he wolfed it down in no time at all. A woman sitting a few tables away gave him a disapproving look so he smiled sweetly back at her.

"Stupid bitch," he thought. "What's she staring at? A man's got to eat."

The woman finished her tea and hurriedly left without a backward glance. He watched her as she headed towards her car, she must have been in her mid-thirties with short brown hair grown into a bob. His chewing on the Danish slowed as his imagination conjured up pictures of her slender body crushed against his.

"Have you finished, sir?"

Startled, he looked up into the spotty features of a teenage boy who was clearing the tables.

"What?"

"The sandwich wrapper, sir?" The boy pointed at the empty carton.

"Yes, yes take it," he said dismissively.

He hated being interrupted when his mind wandered like that; the pleasure he'd been feeling, gone in an instant. By the time he looked back outside, she had already driven off.

Gulping his orange juice down, he made his way to the toilet, weaving between the tables, towards the "Gents", which was on the far side of the café. The teenager who'd cleared his table was standing by the service counter talking to Mrs. Blobby. They were both doing their best to ignore Stuart, which was fine by him.

A car alarm going off stopped him in his tracks: It took him only a few seconds to realise it was his.

With his heart now racing he flew out of the café to his car, the hazard lights flashing back at him mockingly. A quick run around to the other side of the vehicle showed no attempted break in, with everything seemingly intact.

Switching the alarm off he took a few deep breaths, regaining his composure. Jesus, if someone had stolen his precious cargo…

He shook his head, trying to dispel the notion but it wouldn't go that quickly. Taking one final look around he climbed into his car and accelerated away, not wanting to spend any more time at the service station.

Chapter 3

Feeling at ease after a few miles, he began to enjoy the day again, switching on the radio for some easy listening music. The alarm sounding had given him a fright; the last thing he wanted to do was attract any attention.

Glancing in the rear view mirror, he saw the sweat still glistening on his forehead. His shock of jet-black hair was still brushed back over his head and perfectly in place; he liked to be clean-shaven and well groomed.

"Soon baby," he said smiling, turning off at the next junction and heading for a place he knew very well indeed.

Chapter 4

The day became hotter with very little breeze and the car warmed up very quickly. Starting to feel sticky, Stuart put the air conditioning on, directing the flow onto his face. The cooling effect helped clear his mind for the task ahead. He had done this four times before and knew the routine: go to his favourite secluded spot, wait until dusk and then row his dinghy out into the middle of the lake before reverentially dropping the load he had in the boot of his car into the water.

This one had been a fighter compared to the first three; after he had grabbed her from behind and clasped his giant hand around her mouth, she had bitten his index finger, drawing blood. Rather than making him angry the pain from the bite only spurred him on, increasing his excitement. He could tell that, although light in weight, she was fit, probably worked out in the gym.

"Naughty, naughty," he had whispered softly in her ear, before dragging her behind a hedgerow.

He remembered, as he forced himself on her, how, as well as fear in her deep brown eyes, there was something else and only now did he realise what it was – hatred. She did not plead with him to let her go, only re-doubled her efforts to try and escape. Eventually he had to slap her viciously around the face twice to make her comply. Even then she didn't turn away, watching him with fury in her eyes as he enjoyed her body for the first and last time.

The difficulty, as always, was getting the body to the car. He liked to park as near as possible to his hunting ground to minimise the chances of being seen, whilst also using the cover of darkness, which was usually enough: Usually.

The previous episode had almost been his last. He'd been waiting nearly an hour before anyone suitable had turned up; a young woman in her mid-twenties – Julia Smalling had been her name, according to the newspapers. The snatch had gone like clockwork, with the woman being brought under control quickly. He had been about to transport her to his car, when the dog arrived. It took him completely by surprise as the mutt, a cocker spaniel, appeared out of nowhere just a few yards from where he squatted with the girl. Stuart and the girl were hidden from the dog by a thin screen of bushes but he felt it would spot them at any moment. Keeping perfectly still, he held his breath as the dog buried its nose in the leaf litter, sniffing loudly as it absorbed the various scents in its immediate locality. Stuart was sure it would spot him, so looked around for a weapon to eliminate this nuisance.

"Alfie!" A shout from the pathway a dozen yards away stopped the dog in its tracks. Raising its head the dog began to wag its tail and bounded off in the direction of its master's voice.

He shook his head at the memory; it had been close but with this one he hadn't taken any chances – making sure he was well hidden in the undergrowth and moved at least a hundred yards from the path when he carried out his attack. More importantly in his now meticulous planning, the car had to be as close as possible.

This time it had gone like clockwork and he smiled at his ability to avoid police detection. He felt most of them were useless anyway with little or no detection skills; look at the crime rate for Christ sake!

Turning the car down the now familiar gravel covered road, he smiled, "Nearly home now, love," he called to his unresponsive passenger. "Nearly home."

Chapter 5

The gravel road ended after half a mile, becoming tarmac again, although this had obviously seen better days. There were a number of large potholes that had to be negotiated if you didn't want to get a broken axle, so his speed was restricted to five miles per hour in places. However, as he knew where they were off by heart, it didn't concern him too much.

The land either side of this track was barren and featureless and you could see for quite some distance all around. After a further mile, the track sloped away at a gentle gradient heading towards his destination: a large reservoir that provided water to some of the surrounding towns. Like the day, the water was still and calm, barely a ripple disturbing its surface. At the end of the track it widened into a space where there was just enough room to turn the car around to return to the main road. Gently coming to a stop a few yards from the water's edge he switched the engine off and leant back in his seat sighing. This was his favourite spot in the whole world, its peacefulness in stark contrast to the mad world just a couple of miles away. To him it also brought closure; just like a cemetery, this is where he gave his final respects to his victims. They had given him a few minutes of real pleasure, so this was the least he could do for them. Holding that thought in his mind, he climbed from the car to begin his last task of the day.

Chapter 6

A few yards further down the bank of the reservoir hidden in some thick reeds was a small rowing boat. It was Stuart's own vessel, something he had brought here before embarking on this "journey" as he called it. It was beginning to show its age as some of the paint was flaking off and the wood was splintering in some places.

"The hearse," he whispered as he spotted it with oars folded neatly inside, exactly as he'd left it last time. There was a puddle of blackened rainwater in the bottom but barely enough to cause him any concern.

The day had passed its zenith but the air remained hot and sticky. Loosening his shirt, he made his way back to his vehicle. Something in the water caused him to pause and take a second look; he couldn't quite put his finger on it but it didn't seem to be sparkling the way it usually did in bright sunlight.

"Strange," he said, wiping his sleeve across his brow.

As he drew nearer the edge, he noticed the water had a darker tinge to it with the tiny wavelets moving listlessly as they lapped against the bank. Curious now, he crouched down touching the water with his outstretched hand, his task temporarily forgotten.

His first reaction was to draw his hand away; the water had a viscosity to it, which was alien to him. There was also an aroma that couldn't be mistaken.

"It's bloody oil," he said with incredulity, his eyes widening.

He pulled his hand from the water and stood, unconsciously wiping his hands on his jeans.

He now saw that what was once a beautiful living, breathing reservoir was now unfit for any life. Racking his brains he wondered where this could have come from before remembering the large oil refinery not far from there. How the hell had the oil got here though, it wasn't on the banks of the reservoir? Shaking his head, he sighed. It wasn't his problem; he had far more important things to concern himself with.

Lifting the girl from the boot of his car was easy, he prided himself on his level of fitness. Putting her over his shoulder he glided across the uneven terrain and placed her gently into his boat. He had already wrapped her in black bin liners from head to toe, held down with brown tape with arms and legs kept in place by her sides.

"A work of art in its own way," he thought, appraising his handiwork with great satisfaction.

A loud splash from the water caused him to jump and almost fall over backwards as he spun round to investigate. He noticed a large ripple spreading out across the lake just a few yards offshore with no sign as to what had caused it. Regaining control quickly, he presumed a fish had leapt out, probably trying to escape the crappy water it was swimming in. Still, he waited for a few moments in case there was any further disturbance from the deep. The lake returned to its murky, flat calmness, so he returned his attention to the boat and his prize.

He brought the boat nearer to his car along the shore and lifted it onto the bank just enough to stop it drifting away.

In the boot of his car he had two pieces of heavy netting, some rope and two large rocks, bringing them one item at a time to his boat. Pushing off from the shore, he climbed onto the seat and began to row.

The only sound was the gentle splatter his oars made as they cut into the water. Stuart's mind soaked up the atmosphere of the place; it was truly beautiful. As a boy he had lived near a lake and had spent many a hot summer's day either playing by it or on it in a boat not dissimilar to the one he had now. Fishing had been a favourite pastime of his as it had allowed him to be lost in his own world, just stirring when a fish was hooked. When the fish was reeled in he would be fascinated as he watched it die; its mouth gulping, trying to force non-existent water across its gills, and eyes staring helplessly with its swishing tail movements becoming weaker and weaker until its last gulp when it suddenly stopped, giving up the struggle.

This fight for life against the odds had always made him spellbound; from the spider ensnaring a fly to a lion burying its teeth into the neck of an antelope.

Stuart shivered with pleasure as the thoughts flowed through him like a wave.

Reluctantly, he pushed his dreams aside as he approached his normal spot in the centre of the reservoir. Bringing the oars on board and laying them in the bottom of the boat he began his work. The netting had been made into a two drawstring sacks; a piece of handiwork he had completed at home. He gently rolled each boulder into a sack and pulled the drawstring tight to ensure they wouldn't fall out. At the top of the sack was a loop where he fed the rope before tying one end around the girl's neck with rock attached, and the other around her feet, ensuring it was as tight as possible.

He was sweating with effort now, breathing hard and, combined with the stillness and heat of the air, he was feeling uncomfortable in his sticky clothing. Leaning over the edge, he gazed down into the depths of the water seeing nothing through the oil, which still covered the surface, even out here. There was also an odour coming from it that was faintly disturbing, something he hadn't noticed on the shore: a faint fetid smell as if something had gone off.

"Perhaps something has died," he mumbled to himself before bursting out with laughter at the unintentional slip of the tongue. The noise from his outburst echoed off the surrounding hills, creating a weird maniacal sound that cut through the sleepy silence.

Wiping away a tear, he glanced at his watch - already three o'clock. He needed to get a move on. With little ceremony, he dumped the body over the side watching her at first float for a few seconds before slipping silently beneath the blackened surface.

"So long, little lady," Stuart gave a mocking salute. "It was good while it lasted."

Not wanting to delay any further, he made his way back to the shore, turning his thoughts to dinner that night.

Chapter 7

Once ashore, he hid his boat back in the reeds, ready for his next visit. The smell hit him as he made his way back to the car; doubling over with his eyes stinging, he almost vomited on the spot. It had been like walking into a wall of stench, cloying at the back of his throat and invading his airways.

He desperately pulled a handkerchief from his pocket and covered his mouth and nose, which eased the sensation a little.

A spray of water and a giant splash caused him to look back out over the reservoir. His heart nearly stopped with fright. Standing at the water's edge stood three figures covered from head to toe in the same oil that floated on the water's surface. Despite the black oily covering, he could see they were in an advanced state of decomposition – he knew immediately they were his first three girlfriends.

Stuart couldn't think straight – was he going mad? Had the oil in the water got into his body causing him to hallucinate? He didn't think so.

A second splash behind these first three drew his attention and that's when his mind cracked. Standing with her eyes boring into him in defiance was girlfriend number four, the bin lining and rocks gone from her body.

His throat was dry as he backed slowly away trying to get as far away from these abominations as he could. Considering these women were dead it didn't seem to affect their movement, which was surprisingly fluid. They approached him, moving with menace, which shocked Stuart into action.

With panic setting in, he turned and rushed over to his car, slamming and locking the door behind him. Reaching into his pocket, his shaking hand found the key, pulling it out and forcing it into the ignition. The engine caught first time and his relief was almost palpable.

Looking through the windscreen he stopped in shock; the women were gone. The lake was as calm as it had been when he'd rowed on it earlier but there was no sign of them. He felt the tension ease from his body as he slumped behind the wheel. Maybe it had been the heat of the day that was giving him these hallucinations or was he just tired? After all, it had been a long day.

Putting the car into reverse gear, he glanced at his rear view mirror. The horror of what he saw caused his foot to slide off the clutch pedal and stall, the engine shuddering to a halt. In the back seat of the car sat his first three girlfriends, their maniacal grins driving him to the edge of insanity.

The smell of them almost overwhelmed him and he began to cough and splutter, his eyes watering. He looked wildly around, grabbing at the door handle, pulling at it to escape the awful stench. It held fast, he'd forgotten it was locked.

"Shit, the key, the key," his voice almost hysterical now.

A cold hand gripped his wrist in a vice like grip before he could reach the ignition. His final girlfriend stared at him directly, her face just a few inches away

"You took my life," she whispered, a tear rolling down her face. "Now you must pay." Her fetid breath was overpowering as her grip tightened further.

Stuart began to laugh and didn't stop until his is head had been ripped from his body by a rotting blackened hand.

My True Love

By Colin Butler

I did love her, I really did
It had been love at first sight,
I could not stop touching her
Or keep my eyes off her, day or night.

We went everywhere together
She became truly and totally mine,
As the years went by, my passion cooled
And our love was really in decline.

Then that fateful day in June,
I saw this French model, proud and vain,
She had a lovely body – really gorgeous,
Racy and loving life in the fast lane.

How to dispose of my first love, now past her prime,
If she went to another, it would be bizarre,
But I still felt guilty as the Crusher engulfed her,
For she had been such a really wonderful car.

With Best Endeavour

By David Shaer

Chapter 1

If I consider it honestly, I suppose my marriage has had its good points.

As a cook, my wife is termed "creative", although nobody has ever had the nerve to tell her that. Third World nations are today trying to destroy people by using nuclear weapons. They could have saved a fortune in research time and money by using my wife's cooking. Coley poisoning saw off my only true mate, the cat with an attitude. E-Coli is harmless by comparison.

We used to have friends of mine round for "Evenings of Compromise" – they produced Fine Wines, provided I paid for the Take-Away cuisine. Fine wines, good conversation and an assortment of splendid Thai or Indian dishes went well together. And then, one day, she just decided to cook. Immediately after, the so-called friends moved away, allegedly. I still think I see them occasionally, but they're always on the other side of some obstruction, apparently hiding nervously and then running. At least they're keeping fit.

Consequently, I've learned to cook. But too late. My "friends" have moved on.

I have put on weight. Not just slightly but substantially. Every meal is like a banquet, to which a coach load of diners have failed to turn up. Rather than waste the food, my wife and I eat it. The food is good but I just can't get the volumes right. My wife has blossomed. People ask when the baby is due. She gets upset. They have also stopped coming round.

We even had friends with whom we used to go on holiday. We rented villas in Florida with pools. But the gargantuan sizes we became put people off joining us in the pool area. One night we had some Californian wine that was almost palatable. We had more of it, and then some more.

Then my wife decided that we should skinny dip. Even with the pool lights turned out, and despite our being only in our late twenties, the friends got called mysteriously away to a sick relative whom nobody knew was in Florida at the time. We didn't see them again until they sat next to us on the flight home, although one of them apparently became ill during the flight and had to be moved into business class.

Before we landed at Gatwick the friends announced they'd be separating and getting divorced. All rather quickly, I thought, but it stopped all subsequent contact.

Until recently we had other hobbies and pastimes which included gliding and soaring up high with the birds. The birds now seem to have migrated permanently as well.

Paranoid? Moi?

Well, the gliding club called a meeting one day and produced a copy of a set of rules of which I had never even heard before, let alone seen, relating to weight, size and inadequate insurance cover. We were asked to stand down and, even more humiliatingly, a cheque for a pro-rata refund of our annual subscriptions had already been prepared and signed, and this was presented, with a smile, to us. My request to attend the AGM a week later was turned down, on the basis that we were no longer members.

We were, I thought, at least welcome in my rugby club, where, having lost some weight, I was still playing and held the position of captain of the 3rd XV. Or so I thought.

One evening, after an away game, I left the club earlyish and nipped home to pick up my wife for a quick beer in the club before dinner. She was cooking again, from a new recipe and just for the two of us. We strolled into the club as though we owned the place which, considering how much I have spent over the bar in the years, I thought we probably did. Conversation stopped instantly and everybody looked embarrassed. Nobody spoke or even looked directly towards us, until the door of the gents' toilet opened and out came the 4th XV captain, an old, well early thirties, buddy of mine. His eyes flickered nervously between me and my wife, back and forth, hesitating and looking for an escape.

The rest of the club members turned their backs on the three of us and re-started their conversations, although not, I suspect, at the point or on the subjects in which they had been involved prior to our entry.

Bugger. Bastard. I had no idea. And he a mate, or so I thought.

Jason, for that was the name of the figure facing me, went bright red and shrugged his shoulders. He turned away and went back into the gents' toilet, Shortly after, I could hear the sound of somebody throwing up violently.

What the hell? I was not just the 3rd XV captain of the club, but also already a life-long vice-president. I strode to the bar and watched both of the bar staff scatter. Neither could deal with me. I turned back to my wife and just caught her backside, disappearing homewards out of the clubhouse door. It was still bigger than I remembered it being.

Nobody behind the bar could talk to me and none of the remaining members present was waiting to be engaged in conversation with me. I had only two choices, and I wasn't leaving.

So I opened the doorway into the gents' toilet and reeled backwards from the stench. Whoever was in the first cubicle probably needed hospital treatment, he smelled so unwell.

"Jason. Is that you in there?" I asked rhetorically.

"Leave me alone," came the groan from within. "I wanna die."

"Well let me help you," I threatened. "Just get your untrustworthy arse out here, so called buddy, and I'll help you."

Another groan emanated from within and a further round of vomiting sound effects without any issuance followed.

"Jason – arse out here before I come in there and get ugly."

"Wait," came the nervous reply.

I shoved the door which, I discovered, wasn't locked and there kneeling in front of me, engaged in deep prayer, was Jason Horton, looking white, sweaty and terrified. His arms rose instantly, trying to protect his head from a feared attacker.

"Aw, Christ man. Get up off your knees. Stand up and look at me." His body-language froze and he ducked as he turned around, still on his knees. His clothes were covered in vomit, his mouth dribbling the stuff and the fear in his eyes was a picture to behold. I dragged him up to his feet, shut the toilet lid, sat him down on it and looked at him. He flinched again and I couldn't tell he was either about to throw up again, or cry.

"Jesus, Jason. What sort of a bloody fullback are you? You know that involves you going one way and the ball and twenty nine players coming towards you from the other way. Just bloody look at you! I've never trained you to fall apart like this. Stand up for yourself. Be a man. Where's your confidence?" I moved – he flinched again and raised his arms to protect his head. I lent to his side and pulled a roll of about a dozen sheets of toilet paper off the roll-holder and started to wipe his hand, which was covered in puke. I then grasped it and hauled him back up to his feet.

I shook his hand violently and the rest of his body flapped around attached to it. He was truly spineless.

"For Chris'sake, man, she's yours. I hope you'll both be very happy. Now come outside with me and let me buy you a bloody beer. Come on, you stupid sod.

"I knew she was playing away and I just hoped it was with someone who could handle her. You won't believe this, and I'm sure this won't help you at all, but I am just so pleased that it's you. At least you've got some spunk in you – well I thought so, anyway. Look man, she and me – our time is over. We had about ten good years but the last two have been purgatory. We've outgrown each other but neither of us has had the balls to do anything about it. You are my feckin' hero and today I'm going to get you totally battered. You are my bestest mate and what do you want? Brewmaster or Spitfire? Kronenbourg? Whisky? Champagne? Come on man, let's get out there and show all those pathetic arseholes they need to grow up and accept it. I have. What say you?"

He turned and threw up again, but this time it was controlled and he was already wiping his mouth as he stopped and turned back.

"Are you sure, Ted?" I could see the fear in his eyes and the total lack of trust.

I hugged him, wiped the debris off my sweatshirt and then started to open the door out of the gents back into the bar. Yes, I'd had a few beers both before the game – and after, but I was in control of myself.

The whole room plunged into silence again, as now, with my arm around Jason's shoulder, I led him straight to the bar and ordered, for everybody to hear, "Two pints of Brewmaster, please," and opened my wallet to produce a ten pound note.

The silence around us was deafening. Everybody was staring at us and I'd never really understood the expression "their jaws dropped open" until that moment.

Chapter 2

"Oh, come on, Guys. You all know the expression 'All wives are lovely, provided they're somebody else's', well Jason and I have today negotiated a guilt edge asset transfer and shaken pukey hands on a deal that makes us both happy. It doesn't matter a jot what you guys think with your dropped jaws, we're being totally open and honest about this and it will make both of us and woss'ername happy ever after."

I slapped Jason on the back, half expecting him to throw up again but he turned towards me and smiled. He tentatively offered me his hand again, so I shook it and heard the sharp intake of breath all around us.

We turned our backs on the narrow-minded, blinkered-visioned masses, and faced the bar where our beers awaited, somewhat ironically side by side.

"Five pounds exactly, please, Ted," asked the club barman and Jason said, "No, no, no – I'll get these. It's the very least I can do."

I thought, "*Big mistake, old chap, you're gonna need every penny you've got to support my wife – no, my soon-to-be ex-wife, but thanks, buddy – although the price you'll pay will end up being much higher than a bloody fiver before it's all over*", but was about to say something far more conciliatory. However, I may have thought much louder than

I realised because Jason said, "Maybe, but she's worth it – shame you never noticed. Your loss, my gain, old chap."

My turn for my jaw to drop but it was only momentarily as I converted it into a mild snort and a quick smile with raised eyebrows. Both of us leant forward, picked up our beers and raised our glasses to each other, clinked them and supped. Deal complete – well, apart from the formalities.

The first pint didn't touch the sides, as we both poured the beers down in seconds. The second wasn't much longer and then I thought that maybe we should invite my soon-to-be ex-wife to join us, so that at least she would know that I wasn't beating the crap out of Jason, or he out of me. She could relax, be happy and start to move out – no rush, but tomorrow would be good, before Jason changes his mind.

Jason thinks it might be better if we have another couple first, because he hasn't quite got all of his confidence back yet.

My plan is much simpler. Get Christine, on my side and then make her believe that she has lost it. That way, she might feel guilty of violating any marriage vow, which might mean that any misdemeanours on my part might also get overlooked – yeah, right! The problem with my plan is that it isn't a plan. It has no theme or aim. It just makes me feel better. Apart from which, where am I going? My only ambition seems to be stepping away from the problem, rather than addressing it.

Jason, by comparison, has a whole new, exciting life ahead of him. I've absolutely no idea what his current life involves but I suspect that he probably lives at home with his mum and has been a good, clean-living man until he met my wife. She would have seduced him, probably unwittingly, and then held his hand while he cried.

He's no idea what he's taking on and it's not my intention to dissuade him. Stupidly, I offer to give him her telephone number, at which he merely shrugs and starts to walk outside, obviously knowing it better than I do. Maybe I'm getting pissed, although I haven't really had that much.

Jason says that he should ring Christine, if he can find her, and persuade her to come back. He won't be long. That sounds a good idea to me, apart from which I have finished my pint and am looking for a top up. I get us both another Brewmaster and wait.

After about twenty minutes, I've finished mine and think it only sensible to drink Jason's before it goes too flat. I can always buy him another one when they return.

The club TV has been turned on for Rugby Special, so I take up my position on a bar stool and order two pints. The first match involves London Irish and Toulon, a captivating match that just takes my attention totally. By the time it's finished, I've either mislaid Jason's replacement beer, or drunk it. As I contemplate ordering another one, my mobile phone starts to ring. I don't recognise the number and am about to avoid the call when it dawns on me that I've already done that a couple of times before, during the televised match, so whoever is ringing probably needs me to answer. I change my instinct and answer the call.

"Ted Johnson," I greet, in my usual way, and am surprised to hear a rather distraught female voice.

"Edward? Is that you? It's Carole, next door – you know, Carole and Tony. I've been trying to get you for some time now but you've been busy – constantly engaged."

"Yes, sorry," I reply, wondering what could be so pressing.

"I'm sorry, so, so sorry. There was absolutely nothing we could do. I tried calling you but we saw you leave and just assumed you were en route to somewhere and couldn't talk while you were driving. Where are you now? In France? There's not much point in coming back now – it can wait until your holiday is over – no point in spoiling that too, is there?"

"What?" I say. "Carole, slow down, I don't understand what you're saying. What are you sorry about? What holiday? What do you mean – leaving?"

Carol takes a deep breath and then starts up again. "Look – about an hour or so ago, when you and Chrissie put all the cases in your car and drove off, Tony and I just assumed you were going away for a weekend again. We thought it was a bit funny that you didn't wave at me when you drove out but I suppose it was dark and perhaps you didn't see me. Chrissie waved at Tony but you just didn't seem to see me. Anyway, it's of no consequence now but if you do decide to come back tonight, you'll be very welcome to sleep in our spare bedroom – it's only got twin beds but, in the circumstances, I'm sure you won't mind."

Suddenly I start to add two and two together. Bloody Jason. No wonder he hasn't come back, he wasn't ringing Christine, he's gone round to my house and collected her.

"The Fire Brigade have left now but there was absolutely nothing they could do – the fire took hold immediately after the explosion......"

"Whoa, hang on, Carole," I interrupt, "what explosion, what Fire Brigade? What are you telling me? Can I speak to Tony? Calm down, please."

"No, Tony's gone in the ambulance but he's alright, it's just a breathing thing, he got out OK though – well, one of the firemen got him out – but he'll be fine."

Now I'm frightened. I interrupt Carole again. "Look hang on there, I'll get a cab and be with you in a minute, just calm down and I'll be there soon."

I ring one of the local firms I use and eventually get through.

"Oh hi, Mr Johnson. Glad you're OK. Look we can get a cab to the club in minutes but your road is closed because of the fire. We'll drop you as close as we can but you'll have to walk the last bit to have a look. I'm so sorry but at least you're OK."

"Look, Hazel," I say, "I'm sorry to sound stupid but what are you talking about? I don't have a clue."

"Oh, shit. You really don't know, do you? There's been a dreadful accident and your house is gutted. First rumours are that there was a gas explosion and the whole house blew up but it seems that it may have just been a dreadful fire, you know, like a kitchen or electrical fire or something. But as long as you're OK, then that's alright, isn't it? We've already ordered you a cab and it should be at the rugby club any second now. Good luck," and she rings off before I can ask anything else.

It takes me no time at all to collect together my belongings, which consist of a light leather jacket, a wallet, a phone and my front door keys – I leave the remaining dribble of beer – and I slide out of the club front door, where I find the said cab waiting for me.

"I'm very sorry," says the driver. It seems that everybody knows what's going on, apart from me. "I can take you to the end of Park Road but it's all sealed off from there. You'll have to speak to the security force on duty after that."

"Security Force? What the hell does that mean? It's my bloody house we're talking about here."

"Were, mate, were! There's buggerall left now – just a thin layer of rubble."

I sit in the cab in silence, trying to regain control of myself. What the hell's all this about? The driver's plunged into silence and even those indecipherable code messages they talk in (you know –

"Diamond four, seven, three, Crowstone" and the like) remain silent as we crawl our way the mile and a half to my home. Or, to be more precise, to the end of my road, where the driver stops. "Sorry, mate. This is as far as I can go," and pulls up next to an enormous, unwelcoming military vehicle and a group of soldiers with flat hats who look terribly professional and nervous. I pay and creep out of the cab onto the pavement at the corner of Park Road and shiver. The whole area is sealed off and I feel very much alone.

One of the flat-hatted army guys walks over and stops in front of me with an apparent sense of purpose.

"You are?" he asks.

"Well I'm not sure," I reply, "I thought I used to live down here but I'm not so certain anymore," and stand there looking, and sounding, pretty stupid.

"That may be so, but I need your name, sir," the soldier states, fairly abruptly, I think.

"Edward Keith Johnson," I say. "I live at number 27."

"Not any more, you don't, sir. It's been destroyed and there appear to be suspicious circumstances involved. I need to ask you to come with me – we have some questions to ask you."

I almost put my hands forward, expecting to be handcuffed, when the soldier spins on his heels and turns his back to me. Glancing over his shoulder, he says, "Follow me," and starts to stride off. I suppose he expects me to follow, so I fall into step behind him and do just that. Each of his steps is about ten inches longer than I can reach and within seconds I'm dragging behind, having to run occasionally to keep up.

We march and sprint down Park Road towards where I live but the soldier wheels right and we turn down a cul-de-sac where I notice an enormous articulated truck and trailer parked. The trailer is silver and unmarked, apart from a military plate, and has steps coming down from a door in its side. I'm ushered inside, where I find myself confronted by three military and two police "presences." For a moment, I feel a panic attack looming, but I don't get those, so I dismiss it.

I'm waved into a seat in front of the interrogators to which I foolishly respond and sit down. The more senior looking policeman wants to know why they've not been able to contact me and where my wife is, whom they've also been unable to contact. My gut reaction is anger but then it dawns on me that it won't help my case. Whatever my emotions portray could be dangerous, particularly since I still feel anger and frustration towards the people in front of me.

"I think my wife has left me," I say. "Apparently she packed cases into our car and drove off perhaps a few hours ago, possibly with another man."

"Sir, with all due respect, how do you know that?" asks one of the policemen.

"Hearsay, doubt and a gut feel. Hell, I don't know. I am trying to find out what's been going on. It seems that one of my colleagues from the rugby club left me at the club and came here to collect my wife and take her back to the club. According to a neighbour who rang me, she packed cases into our car and has now gone, along with our car and my so-called buddy. Can you tell me anything else?"

"Sir, we're here to ask you questions. What makes you think that your wife has gone and where do you think she might be headed?" The policeman is not being very sympathetic to my cause.

"Officer. As I already said, I just received a phone call from my neighbour who wound me up with a story of cunning and deceit, then managed to convince me that all was not right but I haven't been able to reach her yet to find out what she meant. I was at the rugby club and met a colleague who was going to run off with my wife. I bought him a beer and he was going to invite my wife to the club to join us for a drink. However, I sort of lost track of time and then my neighbour rang to tell me about the fire and my wife's apparent departure. Apart from the fact that the neighbour thinks I helped my wife to pack the car, her phone call has merely confused me more, so I should like to go and talk to her."

"In the fullness of time, sir. First I need to put down a few details – like yours and your neighbour's particulars, where you met, how often you meet, why, where, and so on. We need to know all about you because, sir, there are so many aspects of your story that don't ring true. The fact that your house has been destroyed by an explosion, your wife is missing, you have turned up so soon after the explosion, but, most of all, I need you to talk me through the material changes in your insurance coverages in the last few days. So sit down and start thinking clearly, because, Mr Johnson, we have a large number of questions to ask you. I can tell you straight away, the Army is here because of certain traces of explosive that have already been found, both your life assurance assessor and your building and contents loss adjuster are far from convinced that the explosion was an accident and my colleague here, who's from the Fraud Squad, is extremely keen to talk to you. Long before you may talk to your neighbour, perhaps you would like to think seriously about appropriate legal representation. At this moment, you are not being formally charged with anything, but I wouldn't count on needing to find somewhere to sleep tonight."

I'm glad that I'm already sitting down, because my knees have gone weak and, despite whatever I've had to drink, I'm stunned into stone, cold sobriety. What the hell is this? I can't believe what I'm hearing. I need the world to stop and let me off. I get the feeling that I'm in deep shit and have been set up very cleverly. Whatever's happening to me sounds to be unreal and I'm the victim, in more ways than one.

Chapter 3

Around me, I can hear frantic activity. People are running about, calling out orders and other indistinguishable shouts that sound full of panic. It makes me think of the television coverage I saw about the 7/7 London bombings and it's beginning to sound scary, both because I'm getting scared but, far worse, so are some of the voices I can hear outside the mobile office in which I'm seated.

What am I thinking about? Why should I be worried? If I was guilty of anything, it was being guilty of enjoying a beer too many and of outgrowing my marriage. It wasn't as if I was a serial philanderer – well not by some peoples' standards, anyway. Sure there has been the odd moment, but nothing serious. Christine and I have merely outgrown each other. I haven't betrayed her – much – or killed her. Hell, she's the one who's left me! I have witnesses to that. Come to think of it, the only real witness is Jason Horton and where the hell's he?

My mind has become easily confused and I try to remember all the things that the policeman mentioned just a few minutes ago but my mind has gone blank. The insurance issues are particularly worrying because my wife's the insurance expert, being a broker in a well-known City broking company and she handles all of the policies. I have no idea of any recent changes because I leave all that sort of thing to her. She's the expert. I know nothing.

"Excuse me," suddenly flows unannounced from my mouth. "You have an unfair advantage over me and I think we need to sort that out before we go any further." All five faces turn towards me and change. If there has been any empathy at all, it's vanished instantly. Perhaps whatever's about to flow from my mouth is out of control and wrong, but what the hell? It seems to me that I've absolutely nothing left to lose. "You all know who I am. Who are you? Nobody has introduced us and I find that somewhat offensive and unfair!" Hush my mouth! Where did that come from?

"OK," says the only one who'd spoken so far. "As far as we are concerned," and he is struggling to pull an ID holder out of his pocket, "This is Sergeant Ian James from the Fraud Squad and I am Inspector Jonathan Thorburn from Southend CID. I pass you over to my learned colleagues from the Army to introduce themselves." The two policemen offer me their IDs and allow me to read them, not that I'm focusing terribly well or know what I am looking at. I nod acknowledgement and then turn to the three flat-hatted soldiers, who look at each other briefly before one of them says,

"It doesn't matter who we are until we have completed our initial examinations. Let it be said that we have suspicion that there is an explosive involvement here and until we rule that out, we shall just quietly investigate. For your sake, it is better that you don't know who we are, because if you do then things aren't going so well for you."

Fine. That puts me in my place.

The three soldiers then stand to leave, at which point the door bursts open, without any prior announcement or knock.

"Ben. We have a bit of an issue – a quiet word, please." The newcomer is a uniformed police officer who looks to me rather high-powered, like an Assistant-Chief Constable, but what do I know, apart from watching episodes of Frost?

The Inspector whose name I thought was Jonathan, not Ben, stands and walks out accompanied by the soldiers, leaving me with just Sergeant James.

"Can I ask you a question?" I start. He looks at me as though I'm a deaf mute who's uttered his first words. This shakes me somewhat but I don't stop.

"Try me," he says.

"If you're from the Fraud Squad and this fire was started only this evening, you obviously don't have much work on. I've always assumed that you guys appear after loads of in-depth investigations. Help me here."

"Let me just say that we've been looking into things for a couple of days at the suggestion of an insurance company who've been concerned about one of their brokers. They have asked that we check some odd recent changes and your cover level was very much one of those. So tell me about your sudden decision to up, so substantially, you and your wife's life cover." Nothing like being blunt.

"I'm sorry to disappoint but I know absolutely nothing about that," I say. "My wife is, or was, the insurance expert and she always deals with all of that, apart from paying the premiums, which I always did by direct debit. Are you telling me that I am paying a higher premium?"

"From last month, your life premium increased from £25 per month to £200. Didn't you know?"

"Not a bloody clue, Jesus. How am I supposed to pay that?" I'm stunned. "Was there a change in the house and contents cover too, then?"

"I'm not really interested in that but the simple answer is yes. I believe that may have come down. One of my colleagues is looking into it."

"Come down?" I ask. "I doubt it. We discussed that a few months ago and my wife was going to increase the level of cover because it hadn't changed for years and I thought we might be under-insured. I do know something about average clauses."

"Well, like I said, it's not my area but I can get the officer concerned to talk to you tomorrow," comes his reply.

"One more question," I ask. "Who's Ben? I thought the Inspector's name was Jonathan?"

Before he can answer, the door opens again and the Inspector re-appears.

"Mr Johnson. I need you to think very carefully before you answer. Your house's dustbin. Where is it normally stored?" The Inspector is nothing if not direct.

"Stored? Down by the back door. I keep a black bin with a black plastic liner and a steel bin with pink, recyclable liners inside. They're both there. Why?"

"Why would my officers find traces of explosives in the recyclable bin, sir?"

"Shit. I have absolutely no bloody idea. I don't have any connection with weapons, explosives or anything like that at all. I don't have a clue. What have you found?" Now I'm getting scared. Something is very wrong here and I don't have any clue what this is all about.

"Edward Keith Johnson. Under the Prevention of Terrorism Act, 2005, I am advising you that you are being detained for questioning. I can hold you for up to 28 days without charging you and I would advise that those days started two hours ago. Unfortunately the mobile facilities here do not comply with the minimum requirements for such a detention so I am therefore obliged to transfer you to Southend Central Police Station, where you can be held for up to a further 27 days and a lot more hours, unless I seek to extend that period. In the event that I seek to do so, you will be advised appropriately and any formal charges can be deferred until then."

Christ. Now I'm in trouble and I haven't got any inkling of why or how. Set up? Stitched up? And how!

Chapter 4

At this point, the handcuffs do appear. I have no idea whether this is legal or not. Unfortunately, I've nobody to turn to, well certainly not at this time of night, whatever it is.

"Empty your pockets, Edward." Oh yes. The personal touch. That'll help. If you think that calling me by my first name is going to sweet-talk me, forget it. I have never liked Edward anyway.

"Mr Johnson is my title, Inspector, and I would prefer that, at least until we have slept together, we stick to that more formal relationship. When this is resolved and you need to apologise to me, maybe then I might consider something far more laid-back." Yes, that certainly hacks him off.

So I empty my pockets, which reveal that I have a wallet, my useless front door keys and a mobile telephone. No guns, no knives, no chains and no knuckle-dusters.

The handcuffs are instantly clipped around my wrists and I'm helped to my feet, fairly roughly, I reckon, but I suppose I am suspected of being something nasty, so if I'd been in Inspector Jonathan's shoes, I might have been even rougher. The Sergeant looks at me, and I feel sure I notice a slight smile on his lips. That I do not understand but, come to think of it, I don't understand any of this at all.

"Am I allowed to talk to my neighbour, who *is* expecting me?" I ask.

"Christ knows," comes the Inspector's reply, "but I doubt it."

Oh! That fills me with warmth and confidence.

"I'll ask Sergeant James here to contact her. Give me her details. We'll make up a message for you."

His experience of man management and dealing with security and terrorists is obviously very low but I can't think of anything controversial enough to pass across as a message, other than "Help me – I appear to be in deepest shit!"

I don't think he views it as a coded security weakness message as he writes it down verbatim and hands it to Sergeant James, who this time really does smile, although I fail to see the funny side of anything. I tell them her address and assume that Carole and Tony will both still be up because of all of the excitement. I'm not excited but a change of underwear will be needed soon.

"Is there a chance I could go to the toilet, please?" I ask and could see Sergeant James's face twist as he tries his hardest not to burst out laughing. The Inspector launches his eyes upwards and snarls.

"Take your shoes off, your belt off, and go through that door there," he points, which is much easier for him than me because my hands are cuffed in front of me. I do both with immense difficulty and am immediately hindered by my trousers, which fall to the ground. This time the Sergeant does laugh out loud and Inspector Thorburn growls at both of us. I step out of my trousers, leaving them in an ugly heap on the floor and walk across to the door. The Sergeant beats me there and opens the door for me and lets me through, giving me a wink as I pass him. I get the distinct feeling that he doesn't like the Inspector and I was making his day for him by being today's awkward customer.

After a few minutes I re-appear smiling myself, although I can't really think of a good reason to do so, other than relief. As I shuffle back into my trousers, which are exactly where I left them,

I notice that one of the soldiers has re-appeared and is talking quietly to Sergeant James, whose tentative smile is now an enormous beam. James laughs out loud for the second time and slaps the soldier on the shoulder. Inspector Thorburn is on a telephone call and looks puzzled. So I hoist up my trousers and tuck them in as best I can to stop a repeat performance of the descent to my ankles. I stand there and wait.

Thorburn comes off the phone and points to me to sit again. He then comes and stands next to me, deep in thought.

"How come you have just driven onto a Eurotunnel train whilst you are sitting here?" he asks. "I am confused."

"That's easy," I say. "My wife and I have a house in France and travel across the Channel often by shuttle, and we book crossings in advance. We share the same credit card number at Sainsbury's Bank but book a carnet of ten crossings in each name but using the same car. She has obviously booked a crossing using my name and the car has just passed through an ID check which assumes that I am driving since the crossing is booked in my name. I bet they haven't checked her passport at English Customs on the way out – they rarely do. If she comes back, you'll pick it up on a scan in Calais – if she comes back!" Well I understood, but I could see that he didn't. His eyes had glazed over and he needed to ask another question but didn't know what.

"Look," I explain more patronisingly, "she books a crossing in my name using our car. When she gets to the automatic check in, the ID reader sees my car, EK59WWT, and, because of the date, assumes I have turned up to travel. It greets me as Mr Johnson and she presses yes and inserts her Sainsbury's card, which carries the same number as mine, which the machine checks, and her name, which it doesn't. Therefore Eurotunnel thinks I'm boarding its train, but HMRC don't bother to check a departing British passport, because they rarely do. Easy? When was this? It's too late to do anything at the other end because there is no further passport control now – they pass through the French one at Folkestone too but they check it even less than the British control. Anyway, the crossing takes only 35 minutes, so they are probably already on their way through France. Now do you understand?" I can tell by the way he's shaking his head and saying yes at the same time that it has gone totally over his head.

Sergeant James leaves the room, clutching his sides. The soldier with him follows, looking very confused.

"Stay there," says Inspector Thorburn and follows James, who is standing outside howling with laughter. Inspector Thorburn grabs the soldier and hauls him back inside, sitting him down next to me.

"What's your problem?" he asks the soldier, who turns to us both.

"Mr Johnson," he asks me. "Have you any children?"

"No"

"Any child relatives living round here?"

"No."

"Where were you going to tonight?"

"Nowhere. We'd been to the rugby club and were coming home for dinner, or so I thought. I know my wife's cooking's bad, but it's not bad enough to blow up the whole bloody house. Perhaps she was trying to blow only the bloody doors off!"

The soldier has seen The Italian Job, Inspector Thorburn hasn't.

"Mr Johnson," retorts the soldier. "Have you at any time recently bought any explosives of any description?"

"I most certainly haven't," I reply instantly.

"Not even fireworks?"

"Shit!"

"Precisely. Now think again before you answer."

"I haven't but my wife was going to get a few boxes to take over to my nephews and nieces for Guy Fawkes Night next week."

"Did she?"

"I don't know – but she usually gets them early so it is possible. You don't think........."

"I'm not paid to think. That gets left to your friend here, Inspector Thorburn. We just glean the facts.

"Stay there, both of you, while I see if the bins have got any traces too." The soldier strides out of the door triumphantly.

About ten minutes later, by which time the Inspector has still not been able to leave, the soldier re-appears with his two colleagues, two pink plastic sacks and an agitated dog. The dog is tethered but fighting to get free and snarling at the pink bags.

"I always wash any pet food containers before I put them in there – I can't answer for my wife," I say.

"I don't think Benedict is interested in pet food," says the soldier, "he's an explosives specialist. He also does drugs but, unless either of you guys is carrying, I think we have a hit here in the sacks." The dog's snarls are getting more and more aggressive and the soldier is having difficulty holding him back.

"Separate the bags," he orders the Inspector, who does as he is told. The dog totally ignores one of them and lunged straight at the other. Before he can rip it apart, the soldier puts his hand into his pocket and pulls out a couple of biscuits, at which the dog yelps and sits down instantly. The soldier immediately feeds him the biscuits and the dog flops and calms down in one swift movement.

The two guys start to undo the suspect bag, which contains stacks of read newspapers and flattened cardboard cartons.

"Geronimo!" says the soldier and appears with six or seven flattened empty cartons each smothered in bright flashes of fireworks. "These are interesting. When did you say the fireworks were being used?" he asks looking at me.

"Next week – Guy Fawkes Night. We are supposed to be going over to a party at my sister's house in Southchurch, but as far as I'm aware nothing has happened yet." I can feel my head swimming with confusion.

"Name, address, telephone number?" asks the soldier.

I give him the details and he is gone. In less than thirty five seconds, he is back. Presumably she is out.

"No – nothing has been delivered yet but we are sending a team round to check. They are taking dogs with them." Thorburn is still trying to work out what question he should be asking.

The door opens again and Sergeant James strides back in, his hysterics now under control.

Sergeant James turns to the Inspector and says, "Sorry, Ben, I need to ask a few questions of Mr Johnson here. Mr Johnson. I am hearing some disturbing things which I need to run past you.

"First, why on earth would you want to store fireworks in an oven? To keep them dry? What on earth was your wife cooking tonight?"

I say nothing.

"On a far more serious note, do you, or have you ever had, a numbered Swiss bank account?"

"No, never."

"Do you, or have you ever had, a property in France?"

"Yes, I've already told you that."

"Have you recently sold it?"

"No – it is probably going to be our retirement home."

"So you still own it?"

"Yes."

"You haven't recently sold it to a Monsieur and Madame Serge Rouvrais of Rue Hippodrome in Arras for 150,000 euros?"

"Not that I am aware of – shit! Are you saying I have?" I can feel something draining out of me. "Hey, what's going on here? I get the distinct feeling I have been tucked up."

"Oh, I think this is just the tip of the iceberg, Mr Johnson. My colleagues in Europe tell me that your property was sold about a month ago to Monsieur and Madame Rouvrais, who are already resident. The process was done through an English estate agent in Hesdin and the proceeds paid immediately into a numbered Swiss bank account, which is now empty and closed.

"Your English property insurance expired two weeks ago and was not renewed with the same insurer. It's possible that it has been transferred to another insurer but our recent examination of your bank account shows that no new insurance policy appears to have been paid for. Your mortgage provider asked that very question a week ago and is still awaiting your reply, because the property appears not to be insured.

"However, I can advise you that your increased life insurance cover is not being considered a potential fraudulent activity any longer because you appear to have cancelled the direct debit instruction to your bank immediately after the payment of the first increased monthly premium of £200 and your policy has now been cancelled.

"We are withdrawing investigations into any fraud and are closing our books.

"There is, however, one more point. Your mobile telephone wasn't off when you were arrested and you received a text message which we read whilst we were checking the call logs.

"Apparently somebody called "Whore-ters" says "Cheers.""

"All yours, Ben. I'm nearly out of here."

I feel everything drain out of me. Christine has screwed me completely. I'm now penniless, homeless, wifeless and even Horton-less but that's not too much of a loss.

I have nothing.

Bitch.

Thorburn leans over and says, "I am going to take off your handcuffs and you are free to go. Thanks for your help."

The Sergeant hovers in the background and tries to draw my attention. It isn't difficult because the only option left open to me now is to descend on Carole and Tony and hope they can put up with me for a day or two before I decide where my life is going. At least I still have a job – no clothes to wear to it and not even a season ticket on the train to get there.

Inspector Thorburn takes less than five minutes to be gone and the Army is backing up a tractor unit to remove the mobile office as I climb out of it.

Sergeant James comes across to me and puts his arm round my shoulder.

"Looks like you're in a spot of bother, Old Chap. I am going to take you back to your neighbours' via a beer at the police club, but I think you need just a little laugh. Inspector Jonathan Thorburn is not the most brilliant man on the force and can be a complete, but well spoken, pain in the arse most of the time. But I think I should answer the question you tried to ask.

"Ben. – Inspector Jonathan Thorburn. – Jon Thor – John Thaw – played Inspector Morse – Endeavour. There the similarity ends but you know boys. Thus the posh tosser gets called Ben as in Ben Deavour.

"Let's go and have that beer," he adds.

I manage to raise a smile. Well, I have absolutely nothing else to offer. Any legacy I might have had left from my life is obviously toxic.

Journey into Darkness

By Colin Butler

Mama, why did we have to leave our house,
And travel on this terrible train?
To start a new life, my little mouse.
But the train's so crowded, smelly and dark.

Mama, the train has stopped, where are we?
Why are the soldiers shouting so loudly,
And pointing their guns at me?
It's all part of the adventure, my dear.

Mama, What does the sign say,
Arbeit macht frei, – does it mean we're free?
But I am so frightened, shall I pray?
I am so hungry, thirsty and very cold.

Why is everyone undressed here?
Even nanna and granddad.
We all need to take a shower, my dear,
To make us all clean and pure.

Mama my hands are shaking with fear,

The water tastes and smells so bad.
Have courage, God is with us and very near,
But Mama, – I just do not understand………

The Suburban Weekend that Wasn't

By Simon Woodward

Chapter 1

It was a suburban life and as such, mundane. Days passed like irrelevant seconds during the week; work all encompassing; and the weekend – nothing more than time to recover ready for Monday's re-entrenchment.

Occasionally, when Saturday dawned, I took the mower to the small grass patch at the back of my house and gave my usual neighbourly wave to Old Mrs Midfich who, peculiarly, was always in her garden tending to her patch of herbs; tilling it, sowing it and weeding it, whenever I decided to cut my lawn to size.

It seemed the herb patch was the only part of her garden that needed constant care; the rest was spick and span and I assumed, during the times I was not mowing, she tended to the rest of her garden, or had someone in to do it for her. But I'd never seen anyone.

If I was to take a guess she must have been in her mid-eighties and although she walked with a stoop and a cane to support her, she scuttled about quickly enough, always hugging a black knitted shawl during the winter, and, come to think of it, during the summer, for that matter.

Friday had come around again and the suburban and mundane dissipated as I pulled into my driveway. Old Mrs Midfich was being guided, by two police officers, to a waiting car.

The old woman didn't seem too concerned. In fact she was smiling as she was led from her house; as if she knew something more than the police assumed they knew.

The scene being played out I settled back into my usual weekend ritual, or at least attempted to. Though exhausted by my week's trial my head would not stop replaying the incident as I lay in bed waiting for sleep to overtake my wakefulness.

It must have been 2 am before I fell asleep, only to be awoken, what felt like a few seconds later, when the letterbox clunked and the local paper dropped to the floor. Giving up my regular rest regime I got up and lifted the usually useless paper from the carpet.

I rubbed the sleep from my eyes not sure that I'd read the headline correctly;

"83 year old woman in custody – On Friday an eighty-three year old woman was taken into custody after witnesses came forward claiming they'd seen the woman with missing teenager Sophie Chadwick, the third such teenager to go missing in as many weeks. Not an unusual circumstance for cities like London, but for Trelevern, on the outskirts of Bodmin, certainly very unusual...."

Although I agreed with the article's sentiment, Old Mrs Midfich a suspect? This couldn't be right.

I have to admit I don't really know my neighbour that well but I couldn't associate the old dear with everything that was being claimed in the paper. However, the police had taken her away and, I suspect, it had more to do with their failure to uncover any truths about the two other missing teenagers.

As I was up earlier than expected I convinced myself it was time to get rid of the old and dead pot plants that festooned my kitchen windowsill and take them to my miniscule garden shed, with the good intention of recycling them at some stage.

Still in my dressing gown I yanked at the kitchen door – something else that needed to be done; I can't for the life of me remember when the damned door had actually worked without major force, but damp autumns always brought the issue to the fore.

It was a sodden blustery morning with leaden skies and the red-golden leaves of the last few weeks now nothing more than black slimy patches to step and slip on.

Committed as I was I pulled the dressing gown's belt tighter and made my way down the short path. As was habit I glanced over the fence at Old Mrs Midfich's herb garden ready to wave, but, of course, she was not there.

I almost turned back without a second's thought but something jarred in my mind. I came to a dead stop. Though the old woman hadn't been gone for much more than sixteen hours, the garden – all of it – was in utter disarray. Foregoing the dead autumnal leaves that littered it, late weeds were scrambling across the raised borders; grass had miraculously grown in between the paving stones of the path that snaked the length of her garden. Even moss had suddenly appeared in places – but that wasn't the weirdest thing, the entire garden was strewn, hither and tither, with apples suffering varying degrees of decomposition; from pristine to completely decayed – no apple tree in sight, not in her garden, mine, nor other neighbours'.

I shook my head trying to fathom what could have possibly occurred during the night – as far as I was aware there hadn't been any major storms – then all thought of the weather left me as my eyes lighted upon the herb patch.

No longer were her different herbs in their soldierly rows, they were fallen, higgledy-piggledy, uprooted from ground level, with random furrows breaking the previously flat black-brown earth of the herb's parade ground.

Before I could consider the peculiarities of Old Mrs Midfich's garden further, measly icy-cold raindrops began to fall from the sky and I rushed the final yards to my garden shed, pulling open its door and slinging the old plants onto the workbench within, noting that sometime in the past I had done the exact same thing, and if I were to do this again, I really would need to consider some serious recycling beforehand.

I shuddered, brought out of my mental soliloquy by a myriad of raindrops hitting home between my neck and the collar of my dressing gown. I closed the shed door, and with my head bowed, I started towards the warmth of my kitchen.

Habit is a beautiful and poisonous thing in equal measure and as such I glanced over the fence, ready to wave, before I knew what I was doing, particularly because it caused me to pause my retreat from the ever increasing downpour.

Through the vertical lines of sheet rain a pale shape, bordering on the mottled colour of the top of a large edible mushroom, could be seen, filling the crevasse made by one of the larger furrows in Old Mrs Midfich's herb garden. And I lingered; hypnotised by the slow reveal the rain created through its dissolving action upon the furrow.

Water was now cascading down my face and every few seconds I cleared each eye with my forefingers so I could watch the birth of the huge mushroom, as it happened in real time.

Anyone looking out over their neighbours' gardens from an upper storey window must have come to the conclusion I'd totally lost it. I was soaked through, but couldn't tear myself away from the scene, even when a cold dread, that had nothing to do with the rain, began to seep into me.

The top of the mushroom was becoming corrupted, no longer circular in shape because the edge closest to me was crenelated in a fashion, with three or four slender protrusions pointing in my direction.

"Holy shit!" The words slipped from my mouth before I could do anything about it as my brain pattern-matched the shape before me.

I moved towards the wooden split between my garden and Old Mrs Midfich's, in order to confirm what my eyes were telling me.

Without thought I covered my mouth with the palm of one hand, my subconscious already reacting, and leant closer to the fence, grasping its top with the other, morbid fascination taking hold.

I stretched my eyes wide in an attempt to compensate for the rain and what my brain was telling me the shape was, sincerely hoping I'd been mistaken.

But there was no getting away from it; the silver ring on the second protrusion told the story: This was not a large mushroom; it was a hand, and a feminine one, if there is such a thing.

I pushed the fence away, its rotten top breaking and falling into Mrs Midfich's garden as I recoiled, not only from the shape, but also from the realisation; all mental constructions I'd made about my next door neighbour crumbled into nothingness, like a carbonised sheaf of paper plucked from the remnants of a recently extinguished fire.

I pulled the kitchen door closed, then twisted the key in its lock, and stared, gazing at nothing, through one of the many small panes of steamed up glass that constituted my back door, creating a puddle where I stood.

My face became slack as I fumbled with the thoughts in my head; had it really been a hand? Each time the thought came to me I reached for the key in the kitchen door, to unlock it, ready to go and check. And each time I reached something within forestalled my action and I dropped my hand to my side.

The entire weekend was turning out to be something less than the recuperative I expected my weekends to be. The time was coming up to a quarter to ten in the morning and I was feeling as stressed, possibly even more so, than I did during the week.

I was certain no one had seen me, standing in the pouring rain, gazing over my fence into Old Mrs Midfich's garden. And for a fact she hadn't been there. Not my problem, I tried to console myself.

But what if she finds out? a thought came from elsewhere; underlining the fact that part of the fence had fallen into her garden.

I took a deep breath and put the kettle on for some coffee; I certainly needed it, being up as early as I was on this Saturday morning. And as I focused on making my coffee the rigours of the previous hours began to dissipate, allowing me to slip into my usual regime of doing extra things I fancied and nothing else besides.

Chapter 2

By late afternoon the early morning's shock had been consigned to the misty – just one of those things – memory pile: An experience that one could either take or leave without consequence.

Saturdays are a day for something light to eat in the evening, washed down with a beer or two. With nothing interesting on the telly I turned it off, wrenched myself from the sofa and made my way into the kitchen wondering what delight I could rustle up. With my culinary expertise being what it was I decided on two poached eggs on toast, flavour enhanced with a lick of Marmite.

As I took the poacher from the cupboard I glanced briefly at my kitchen door, with its steamed up panes of glass, and a shudder crucified the warmth in my body, the vision, a vision I thought I'd forgotten, flashed through my mind's eye; the pale, almost bleached hand that had nestled in the furrow of Old Mrs Midfich's herb garden blazed in the non-Technicolor cinematography of film noir.

I knew then that I needed to distract myself if I wasn't going to cock-up the simplest of dishes, so I turned on the radio and the light and informative banter of BBC Cornwall began its easy listening.

I lifted the lid of the poacher and saw that the eggs were on the cusp of being ready – the majority of the egg white, white, and the translucent film that covered the yoke now opaque.

The radio squawked the pips for six o'clock and the news began by announcing terrible flooding and mudslides around St Austell. I felt sorry for my fellow Cornishmen but was glad that we, on the north coast, had missed such a downpour this time: It was only a few years ago that floods had almost entirely demolished the small seaside village of Boscastle on our coast.

The toaster ejected the toast and I struggled to stop the caramelised bread falling to the kitchen floor – I had the same problem every time I used sliced bread – the toaster was really designed to toast doorsteps perfectly and nothing else.

I buttered the toast thickly then spread lashings of Marmite onto the butter, mixing both with the tip of my knife. Lifting the lid of the poacher I began the highly skilled task of removing the eggs from the poacher's cups without leaving half of the newly poached egg behind. No matter what anyone says, there is no such thing as a non-stick cup and unless you use the right butter, in the right quantities, the egg will always stick; though there are secret ways, known only to a few, to get around the problem of the ripped poached egg and it is my belief that those who never discover the skill become the most stalwart advocates of the scrambled egg.

As I lifted one of the cups from the poacher BBC Cornwall carried on with its announcements; "In other news today police released the eighty-three year old pensioner, Mrs Midfich. A police spokesperson stating they were happy with what they'd been told and had eliminated Mrs Midfich from their enquiries."

The poacher's cup dropped from my hand and, as I tried to catch it, I knocked the edge of my plate flipping the toast into the air, everything landing face down on the kitchen floor; one piece of toast taking a more circuitous route via the top of my foot.

All my appetite dissolved there and then. The news of my neighbour's release transmuting hunger into fear; I had seen part of what obviously laid beneath the herb garden, and knowing three teenage girls had gone missing I suspected that there were another five similar hands somewhere under that soil.

I looked at the remaining egg sitting in the poacher; it was perfect, but no matter how so, all urge to eat had been crushed out of me.

I turned the radio off, interrupting the weather forecast, and before I knew what I was doing I'd tested the kitchen door to check that it was still locked, and it was.

Chapter 3

I sat in my almost completely dark lounge, only a few table lamps providing light, seeking comfort from the beer I'd intended to have with my tea. I would have laughed at the situation if things had been different; the fact that, although not hungry, time for beer can always be found, but I was not of good humour.

After the announcement on the radio I'd gone about my house switching off the lights in the vain hope that the news had been breaking news and Old Mrs Midfich was on her way home, as opposed to already being there.

I hoped to make out I was away, ensuring the old woman, once she'd gone into her garden and seen what had been revealed, could not come to the conclusion that, somehow or another, her neighbour, i.e. me, had discovered her secret. I prayed she wouldn't notice the rotten part of the fence that was now sitting in her herbaceous border.

I sat in silence listening for the tell-tale clunks, clicks and thumps that would tell me she was home, my house being part of the same semi-detached house, but I heard none.

By the time I'd finished my fifth can of beer, and not hearing any sign of occupancy from next door, I was settled enough to go to bed, my fears about possible retribution being sated.

In an instant my mind was active and my eyes were gazing at the back of their lids. Something, I didn't know what, had roused me. I opened my eyes.

All was dark and I rolled my head to glance at the clock – its red digits told me it was only one forty-three in the morning. *Bloody hell*, I thought as I studied my bedroom's ceiling, knowing that this weekend was really not going to be the recuperative I'd hoped for.

The ceiling was a dark grey plane only interrupted by the lighting fixture. Barring that I couldn't make out any detail because my bedroom was at the back of my house, its windows opening onto my small garden, with little light pollution.

Fully awake and with all chance of regaining the bliss of sleepful nothingness gone, I attempted one of the three tricks I'd discovered, over time, that always resulted in a return to that state; I started my two to the power of two times table – two to the power of one is two, two to the power of two is four, two to the power of three is eight, two to the power of four is sixteen.

Most times I'd reach a result that was five digits long then wake up in the morning to the alarm, but this time no such thing happened. As I was telling myself four thousand and ninety-six, I was brought to a sudden stop and held my breath. There was a noise. I wasn't sure where from, but it sounded like some furniture protesting as it scraped across the floor downstairs. It was all I could do to stop myself from pulling the duvet over my head.

What the hell was that noise? I held my breath as I listened for other noises.

A gasping inhale escaped me as my body burnt through the last vestiges of air my lungs could hold. My heart skipped a beat then thumped twice in succession telling me I ought to start breathing again if I wanted to remain conscious and aware. I acquiesced, fearing whatever fates unconsciousness may bring, and took a long deep breath. Then I exhaled, but before I could finish, my mouth clamped shut as one of the floorboards on the landing outside my bedroom door creaked and a chill swept through my body; hair prickling on my forearms and the nape of my neck. The skin of my forehead tightened as a cold papery sensation crossed it. Blackness encroached upon my vision and my lungs gave out; I took another breath, and another. And as I exhaled for the third time I was sure that, even in the near complete darkness of my room, I could see the result of my breathing form vapour in front of my face.

Then the darkness of my room turned down another notch or two towards a deeper and more impenetrable blackness, one that seemed to have tangible substance.

I looked at my clock; its red digits were dimmer than before, a thin frost covered the clear plastic of its display. The vestigial warmth of my duvet vanished as if pulled by a conjurer whose party piece was to remove a tablecloth from beneath the cutlery and crockery sat upon it. Every part of me started to shiver and my teeth chattered.

I recalled nightmares from my childhood when, in the darkness, in my bedroom, unknowable sounds wrenched at my sanity and I would pull the duvet over my head and pillow, and clamp my head under the pillow, holding it tight, availing some kind of false protection from the dark creator of the unknown sounds.

But this was worse; I couldn't move and my eyes refused to shut. I was being forced to face fears beyond those of my childhood.

The clock stopped; its vague light slowly extinguished as the electricity drained from the capacitors within.

Chapter 4

I don't know how long it was before I dared to move but if I was to guess my estimate would be about an hour. Whatever amount of time it was, I needed to straighten my arms. All sensation in my hands had been lost, the terror of my predicament fixing them clasped to the top of the duvet as I held it under my chin.

I unfurled my grip and lowered my arms to my side; a numb but warm tingling sensation filled my forearms indicating the onset of pins and needles. I opened and closed both hands to get my circulation going once again.

With no further sounds emanating from the other side of my bedroom door the little man inside me, the one with some semblance of courage, decided to make an appearance, and I decided to investigate the source of the noises.

However, I'd been fooled. The hour's lull in events had been nothing more than a deception. As I pulled the bed covers back and dropped my legs over the side of my bed, my feet seeking the slippers that should have been there, a strange movement in the shadows, cast by the little external light making it past the top of my curtains, froze me to the spot.

I stared at the blackness in the corner of my room made by the meeting of walls and ceiling. I was sure I'd seen the ceiling bow, just for a moment, like a huge hand had pushed it down; the ceiling somehow becoming nothing more than a rubberised skin.

I sat on the edge of my bed as still as I could, though my feet, as was habit, still sought my slippers. It was a few seconds before I realised I'd been holding my breath again. Slowly I exhaled and once more vapour formed before me – but something was different this time; I couldn't hear the passage of my breath. Something had stolen the sound. It seemed like time itself had fled.

Before I could test any other movement to confirm what I was sensing the ceiling bowed again and the bulbous dip glided towards the wall opposite me. Instead of stopping there the wall started to bulge as the shape made its way to the floor, disappearing behind my tallboy, making it judder then move towards me; not a single sound breaking the intense silence that encapsulated me.

Then, as if the invisible soundproof glass that had made my noiseless cell had been smashed, I was immersed in full Dolby 5.1 surround sound; my breathing echoed around the room and a *clickering, clattering* noise came at me from behind the tallboy. It sounded like a multitude of Bic biro lids tapping staccato on the wooden floorboards of my bedroom. But it wasn't a random clattering; it had rhythm and purpose.

Although my eyes had adjusted to the dark in my room there was nothing more that I could see than blobs of blackness beneath the line of my bedroom's windowsill. It was at this time my feet gave up searching for my slippers; it was obvious they were no longer where they should be.

I wanted to get out of the room, slippered or otherwise, but the marching *click-clack* rendered any option to move, impotent.

A flash of negative inspiration hit me; what if it's a mutant spider, grotesquely large, coming at me with its shiny, pointed black fangs, beating like a jackhammer, getting ready to sink into my shins?

I continued to stare at the corner of my room, the source of the noise, and the spot where the black bulge from the ceiling had stopped its journey. My eyes blinked furiously in the continuing attempt to resolve the blackness before me into a shape my mind could comprehend. But it didn't work.

I felt naked; without weapon or protection; Jimjams being nothing more than the Emperor's new clothes.

Suddenly my worst fear was crystallised; an amorphous, clattering, black blob started towards me and I could make out its shape.

Whatever entity that had possessed my room had delved into my subconscious and plucked out my greatest fear. Coming at me, in the near total darkness, was the largest deformed form of a spider I could have ever imagined. It didn't have eight legs. It didn't have eight eyes; though it did have only two glistening, shiny fangs.

I couldn't count the number of legs it had; the darkness and their staccato movement stopped that. But I could count the eyes – two; each with lashed lids and the horizontal oblong pupils of gleaming goat's eyes.

Its spikey back pointing fur, on its swollen abdomen, bristled as the points of its legs hit the floorboards. And some kind of glutinous fluid dripped from between its fangs.

The child in me told me to withdraw my legs and pull the duvet over my head, and I wished I could comply. But even before the grotesque before me could sink its fangs into me and fill me with paralysing venom, I was already paralysed by the fear the monstrous shape conveyed. And I knew that no matter what I tried, neither hand would relinquish its grip on the mattress.

My number was up and I wished I'd never set eyes on Old Mrs Midfich's herb garden with its secret revealed.

A blinding flash stung my eyes, followed by a wrenching crack that threatened to split my house from roof to foundation as an errant thunder storm let lose its pent up energy. And in the after-image that had rendered my eyes temporarily useless in the dark of my room, the reality of the grotesque, revealed by the clarity of light that only lightning could conjure, was the crumpled form of my Parka, fallen from the back of the chair, lumped like an overly large rugby ball with its fur edged hood pointing in my direction; each tooth of its silver zip reflecting light. I shook my head. But before I could finish admonishing myself for my folly, cold fingers wrapped around my ankles like glassy handcuffs, and the certain knowledge as to why my feet couldn't find their slippers, came to me in a sudden blast of icy terror.

My feet were ripped from under me, pulled back beneath the bed; my hands, frozen as they were, refused to release the mattress and my face was flung to the floor. In a split second I managed to turn my head to stop my nose from being crushed, but I knew my head would pay, one way or another, for the force at which it was being thrown at the floor.

I heard a bang and felt shockwaves through my jawbone.

Chapter 5

I don't know what woke me; whether it was the pulsing thump of pain in my head or the violent rattling of my bedroom door, or both. But, as I opened my good eye, the other swollen shut; I was relieved to glimpse daylight.

As I pushed myself up, press-up style, the back of my head quickly made contact with something, and for a short moment the thought that I was in some kind of coffin dominated reason and a cloying panic gripped me.

But there's light, a small voice inside my head told me. I realised I was under my bed. Then I realised *I was under the bed*, memories of the previous night flooded back. I scrambled out, my head's pulsing pain set to one side.

I turned around, sitting on the floor, gazing at the gap; there was nothing there.

I jumped as the door vibrated in its frame once more; my bedroom curtains came at me as a low *whomping* sound filled the room in fits and spurts. And I recognised the sound. It was a sound from the past, one reminiscent of the great storm of '87 and its damaging winds.

I breathed a sigh of relief. My bedroom door rattled again but it didn't bother me — it was just this draughty old house being draughty.

I picked myself up from the floor and cradled my left eye as the pulsating thud behind the damaged skin re-emerged from the thin membrane of panic that had briefly concealed it.

I needed some Paracetamol, which I knew I had in my bathroom cabinet and momentarily considered whether the beef stew for one, ping food, I had in the freezer, would be just as good as a steak at taking down my eye's swelling. Perhaps I would try it; but first a couple of Paracetamol.

In the mirrored doors of my bathroom cabinet I stared at my bruised and swollen eye and wondered whether last night's experience had been nothing more than an intense and violent nightmare, brought about by too much booze and an overactive imagination.

I gulped down the painkillers with a glass of water and brushed my teeth.

Shaken by last night's excursion into an evil version of a Disney Land attraction, more likely than not hosted by my brain, I had no appetite for breakfast but needed a coffee.

I left the bathroom and descended the stairs only to be brought to an abrupt stop five steps from the bottom; my wooden coffee table was not where it should have been. Rather than being somewhere at the centre of my lounge, it was now next to the final banister at the bottom of the stairs: the rucked up rug around its stubby feet spoke volumes.

Then I noticed the dangly thing above it, hanging from some twine that had been pinned to the ceiling. Though crudely shaped, the form was recognisable; it was the effigy of a person, no more than five inches in height, made from dirty wax with ragged squares of material barely dressing it. I looked closer. I recognised the material. I frowned. It had to be from the old plum coloured work shirt I'd chucked out some weeks ago.

Being a Cornishman I knew the myths and what this was; it was a poppet – a vehicle for hexes and curses to do ill-will against those who wished harm to the poppet's creator or for whom the poppet had been created.

I remembered the dragging sound that had interrupted my quest for sleep.

Then, without any conscious thought, my eyes focused on the poppet's shiny, brass coloured, left eye – it was made from a drawing pin, and the stories I'd heard as a child, about how the poppets were used, came back to me with a terrifying force.

My hand went to my half-closed eye. I was beginning to feel that the previous night's nightmare had at least one foot in reality – though the reality, in the cold light of day, was still hard for me to accept, even with my penchant for excessive imagination.

I leant over the coffee table ready to push it back to its place, putting a hand on either side – it was oak and very heavy, but before I could start heaving it across the floor I noticed four or five, probably five, one not being that well-formed, muddy concentric rings, no larger than an old penny piece. They reminded me of the rubberised end of a cane or walking stick. I let go of the table and studied the muddy marks.

Come off it, Dan, I berated myself. *It's myth, fantasy. Not real.* But the marks were there on the table, and Old Mrs Midfich did use a cane.

As soon as the thought came to me my mind was swiftly filled by one word and one word alone – witch.

Chapter 6

It was a few hours before I could hold a cup of coffee without spilling it; the shakes becoming greater as I'd checked the front and back doors, plus all the windows, to see if I could find any signs they'd been forced or even opened without force. But I'd found none.

I sat on my sofa hugging my cup to my chest as I tried to think whether I'd ever been told of ways to stop witches entering one's home.

Garlic garlands sprang to mind. Should I wear one or hang it above my door? The thought was dismissed. Nope, that's vampires – I was fairly certain it was vampires and nothing else.

Silver bullets popped into my head. Possibly right, but an entirely useless idea; I didn't have any bullets, silver or otherwise. And if I did, I didn't have a gun, and the thought of shooting something or someone was completely abhorrent.

What about removing the head? My thoughts continued and again I had to dismiss the notion. All I had was a crappy hedge-trimmer or a pair of secateurs. And I knew a plan based on the hedge-trimmer would surely fail. How would I know where I had to plug it in? What if its lead reached its maximum extension and I was still not close enough?

I wished my mum, bless her heart, had not put me off reading the horror fiction comics I liked as a child. She'd had good reason – my nightmares and overactive imagination.

And now? I was well-read, but purely non-fiction. Biographies, histories, programming languages, and maps, filled my bookcases.

Although only mid-morning I had to put the lights on. The storm was getting worse; the wind more furious and the leaden sky was even more leaded. My front door rattled in its frame as if to underline the fact the storm had plenty more to give.

"Oh God," I sighed, though not a follower of any faith. But in my breathing of the words another idea struck me; Prayer! For a millisecond I felt relief – then the questions came; who would I pray to? Should it be God (if there was one)? But witches surely didn't follow any god of a monotheistic faith. Who was the god of witches?

I had no clue, so it was time to turn on the computer and search the Interwebs.

An hour of clicking and pointing, typing and reading, revealed nothing more than; hanging, burning, drowning, pouring water on them (I got that from the Wizard of Oz), getting a divorce or plain old; asking them to leave. I knew now that I had to figure out something for myself, as the options I'd discovered were mainly impractical or down right impossible or just would not work.

I turned the computer off and returned to the kitchen for another cup of coffee.

As I supped the hot drink, again attempting to gaze out through the steamed up panes of the kitchen door, a new tactic crystallised in my mind.

For a fact I couldn't get rid of her. But I could impede her mobility, and hopefully stop her getting into my property; at least for a short while.

I wiped the condensation from a couple of panes in the kitchen door with a tea towel and looked out. The rain had stopped and over the fence I could see Old Mrs Midfich tending the herb patch; then my cup slipped from my hand as I tried to comprehend what I was seeing – the whole garden was pristine once again; no apples, no weeds and no moss.

All there was was the old lady, wrapped in her black shawl, tending to her herb garden, her cane leaning up against the rods that would support her pea plants when they grew again.

My eyes focused on her cane – this was it. This was my goal. Get her cane and destroy it. And at least for a while, until she was able to get another, she would be incapacitated and I would have the breathing space to concoct another more permanent plan.

I looked at the kitchen clock; it was mid-afternoon. If I was going to do anything it would have to be soon.

Chapter 7

I made my way upstairs to change into a pair of black jeans and a navy top – something more practical and weather resistant than my dressing gown, and as I changed I began to formulate my plan to relieve the old woman of her cane.

For sure, I couldn't use my kitchen door to enter the garden; it was quite likely not to open on the first attempt due to the moisture it had absorbed. The last thing I wanted was to signal Mrs Midfich that I was on my way out; it might prompt her to get up, take her cane, and approach me for a chat or something – no, to get the upper hand I needed a plan that was as covert as it could possibly be. I would go out my front door and then go through my garage whose rear door opened onto my garden and had never had any swelling problems.

I walked back downstairs deep in thought. There were two remaining parts of the plan to devise: one – securing the cane and, two – destroying the cane. Whilst I pondered these final elements I decided to check that all was well with the first part of the plan and left the warmth of my home for my garage.

The garage door opened without issue; I was glad I'd been distracted from parking my car inside that strange Friday afternoon, a day that seemed much more than just the two days ago it had been.

Inside, the solution to part three of my plan glowed in front of me; it didn't actually glow, but in my mind's eye it did. Under a plastic cover, at the back of my garage, was my gas barbeque. I nodded to myself. I knew this was the tool I could use to destroy the cane. Obviously it had some downsides; namely, where I could set it up. The garage would have been ideal, but the old pots of paint, bottles of methylated spirit made it somewhat dangerous. Reluctantly I decided my lounge was the only place – it was large enough to be a little safer than the garage, and I was sure, because it was a gas barbeque, the smoke wouldn't be that bad. I'd bought it on a deal but so far, never had the chance to use it. But now was its time.

I looked at my watch; twenty minutes had passed. I knew time was against me. Everything I had to do, had to be done before another downpour, sending the w... Old Mrs Midfich (I was having trouble using the word, as contemplations of the fact muddled my thoughts; fear usurping any clarity) back indoors.

I dragged the barbeque set out from the garage and into my lounge, shutting the front door behind me.

I moved all my furniture from the middle of the room, to the sides, and replaced it with the barbeque. As fast as I could I got the thing burning, then made my way back into the garage.

I peered out of the garage window over my garden, but it afforded me no view of the old woman's garden and I wondered how, from my side of the fence, I could reach her cane without her noticing. I knew I needed a piece of equipment that had a long

reach and had something at the end that could grab. It sounded like a fictitious piece of equipment; a long reach, cane grabber.

I glanced at my watch again; another ten minutes had passed. I needed a solution, and quick. I looked around the garage. There was a long pole, couldn't remember why I had it, but what could I attach to it?

My secateurs came to mind, but they were in my shed, and I'd have to figure out a way to attach them to the pole with a mechanism to close them around the cane. I was good with my hands in as much as I found turning pages in a book pretty straightforward, but making something that wouldn't fall to pieces; that was for other people.

MY SECATEURS. Yes! I thought. Not my secateurs though, that had just been the prompt I needed. In my shed I had a pole tree pruner. A thing I occasionally used to cut the upper branches of the fir trees at the end of my garden. The snipping curved blades at its end would be just the thing to capture and trap the cane. But that tool was also in my shed and left me with only one option; I had to sneak down my garden, get into my shed and retrieve the gangly piece of garden equipment, all without being noticed.

Time was running out and I had no other choice.

Chapter 8

As quiet as I could I opened the rear door of my garage, stepped through and closed it behind me. Now came the difficult bit.

I really didn't want to crawl down the garden on my stomach SAS style. The ground was wet and muddy and the last thing I wanted was to stymy any grip I had on my cane grabbing tool, though the thought of getting mucky played a part. I decided to risk a crouched run. If I kept my head down there was no way she would notice me.

Half way down the garden I thought it prudent to take a look through one of the many holes in the garden fence to check whether my quarry was still there leaning against the upright struts of the pea plant guide, although on second thoughts the struts might have had something to do with tomatoes; I couldn't be sure.

I took a deep breath and left the path and slowly made my way across the grass towards the fence. I looked through one of the many empty knots in the fencing and nearly choked. Yes, she was still there, her cane against the poles, but the hand I'd seen the other day was a hand no longer; it had an arm attached to it and I could hear the old woman muttering in a language unknown to me as she poured a strange effervescent fluid over it; then I saw one of the fingers twitch.

I reversed direction and again started towards my shed, only taking a breath once I'd reached its door. What the hell was going on? What the hell was she growing?

No time for those thoughts though. I had to get my tree pruner and put my plan into action.

On my knees I reached up and opened the latch that kept the shed's door closed. The door opened without a sound and I entered.

The storm reasserted itself and the wind picked up, catching the door. I swivelled on point just in time to put my hand on the door jamb. The door wobbled as it smashed into my knuckles. I covered my mouth with my other hand and hissed through my fingers in response to the sudden pain. But it was enough; my hand had muted the door's slam.

I stepped backwards one pace and placed a foot on the ground outside the shed to block any further efforts the wind made to shut the door. I reached for the tree pruner, which was hanging on hooks attached to the wall of my shed.

With tree pruner in hand I backed out of the shed, but there was a problem; the pole was long and to control it I need both my hands, and my legs weren't long enough to stop the wavering door from slamming again. I placed the pruner's end on the sill of the door jamb, grasped the door, and eased the pole out of the shed, then closed the latch.

The obstacle dealt with, I made my way back up the garden, still crouched, wobbling tree pruner held out in front of me, to the point in the fence where I could slip the pruner through.

I peered through the hole. Mrs Midfich was turned away from me; if she had not her shawl I would surely be able to see the back of her left ear, and, partially, the hole that led into her head.

To her left, just behind her, but within reach of her left arm was the cane and the pea stands. She had moved a bit since I last looked and I could no longer see that mushroom-white hand and arm. But I could still hear her mumblings and they were more rhythmic now. I suppose I ought to be calling them incantations.

Now it was time for the really difficult bit.

I knelt on my left leg and placed my right sole firmly on the sticky mud that was my border, lifted the cutting end of my tree pruner, and started to slide it through the hole. Inch by inch my end of the pole shortened. Inch by inch, my long reach cane grabber sought its prey.

I placed my right elbow on my right knee aiming to retain control over the extension that was now reaching out over Mrs Midfich's garden towards her cane.

I prayed the wind would keep its lull at least until I had my hands on Mrs Midfich's mobility. Then my right elbow slipped and

I knew that I should not have dismissed wearing my best black corduroys when choosing the clothes for this mission.

The end of the pole flicked to the right as my face crashed into the fence, and the pole struck something hard. I peeked through another empty knot in the fence; fortunately it was next to my right eye which, in my awkward position, was now pressed to the fence. I saw her attempt to raise her hand to her temple, but she collapsed to the floor without succeeding.

"Sorry," I hissed through the fence, before I realised what I was doing; habit being a poisonous and beautiful thing in equal measure.

I re-focused on the job at hand, pulled the lever on my end of the pole, opened the metal beak at the other end, moved the pole to the left and sunk my cane grabber's two blades into the cane.

As fast as I could I pulled the cane back to the fence then placed my end of the pole on the ground and stood on it. The hole through which it was poked acted as a pivot and I grabbed the cane over the top of the fence.

"Yesss! I've got it," I said to myself. But my feelings of victory dissipated in an instant as my gaze lighted upon the recumbent body of the old woman.

Chapter 9

I stood transfixed. Although the old woman was lying on the ground, as still as a still thing, her arm wasn't. It dipped beneath her shawl and pulled out, what looked like a twig.

I like to think I'm a quick learner and when the end of the twig began to glow a putrescent green, I knew exactly what it wasn't, and that was a twig.

The air crackled and the small ball of green light leapt into the furrow in the herb patch. As soon as it had disappeared another hand and arm drove itself from beneath the soil; each hand placed itself palm down on either side of the furrow. Then the arms heaved and a head pushed itself from beneath.

I felt my breath had been snatched from my lungs. Before me was a cadaverous white mottled oval, outlined by long lank hair, caked with mud, two oil-slick black eyes, all pupil, and a silent screaming black-hole of a mouth, surrounded by small serrated teeth.

Luck smiled upon me and I fell to the ground as my legs gave out, fear getting the better of them – this broke the evil spell of transfixion that had kept me there, staring at the unknowable.

Schlupping noises came from the other side of the fence and I willed my legs to work. It sounded like the wet mud of the herb patch protesting at its loss of grip on something it wished to retain.

I got up and was half way to the kitchen when my fence caved in. I glanced back over my shoulder and hunched on its ruins was the lithe body of a teenage girl, the colour of a freshly picked mushroom. My stomach rumbled as I realised I hadn't had any breakfast, thoughts of a full English crossing my mind. Then the teen-creature started towards me, teeth snapping shut every now and again, and in between times an impossibly long rotten-green tongue licking its lips. It raised its arms in my direction and it was all I could do to stop myself dry-heaving there and then; the ravages of its sub-soil incarceration being more than apparent as black slimy creatures slithered in and out of tears in its throat and breasts.

I re-doubled my efforts and ran for the kitchen door at full pace. I reached out with my free hand slamming the door handle down and broke my nose on the unmoving entrance. The bloody door was locked.

The she-thing stumbled on, gaining ground. I think it had forgotten how to walk and I realised luck was still with me.

I darted around the back of my house, then through the garage into my front garden. I was almost home and dry.

I yanked open my front door and was greeted by a wall of thick and pleasantly smelling nothingness. It reminded me of the summer and times when my father, bless his heart, had cooked burgers on an open fire.

"Oh shit!"

I clawed at the smoke, trying to create a path to the gas barbeque, which hadn't been as smokeless as I'd been led to believe by the salesman. My eyes stung, but I knew I had to find it and destroy this cane. I stepped inside and locked my heavy front door.

With one outstretched hand I tried to detect the heat of the barbeque, and found it. Through scrunched up eyes I located the burger machine, snapped the cane across my shin. Cursed more than a few times as the cane failed to break, but won in the end, and dumped the damned pieces into the searing heat of the charcoal.

Through the burger-fog I could hear incessant thuds against my door. I looked at the barbeque, praying that something would happen and it did. The cane started to smoulder, but not as normal wood would; green and purple vapour eased itself from the cane and dissolved in the heat of the barbeque. It was only then that I noticed the intricately carved handle, reminiscent of the head and forelegs of a rat, but soon those details disappeared as the defining edges began to glow and reduce in the barbeque's heat.

Not being able to stand the smog any longer I felt my way to the kitchen, opened the door and stepped into a space more conducive to sustaining human life.

I shut the door behind me and pressed kitchen towel into the gaps around the door, then opened the kitchen's fan-light windows to let in some less polluted air. With the remnants of the kitchen towel I dabbed my sore and bleeding nose.

Chapter 10

Now I had some time to think, forgoing the thumps at my front door, and I wondered whether my plan had been effective in its goal to stymie the old woman's mobility.

The only way to ascertain this was to see whether Mrs Midfich had recovered from the accidental brain bashing; I needed to open the kitchen door.

I must admit I was reluctant, but as I knew she was dependent on her cane for movement, and the fact the strange, naked, mushroom coloured teenager, with muddy hair, was still thumping my front door, it wasn't beyond the bounds of reality that I could open my kitchen door, and check the situation, without incurring any further trouble.

I slid the key into the door, pulled at it sharply a couple of times, and opened it.

Near the bottom of my garden I spied the shawled woman standing in the gap the weird teenager had made. Mrs Midfich was waving a clenched fist at me and in her crackled voice, was screaming.

"My staff, you idiot, give me back my staff. I'll turn you into…"

A gust of wind took her last words away. "Pardon," I said, cupping an ear. "Can you say that again? I didn't quite hear."

Suffice it to say she didn't repeat whatever it was she was saying. Instead she pointed the twig/wand at me and another flash of light formed at its end. She raised her arm and flicked it in a motion similar to a person cracking a whip; the yucky-green orb headed in my direction.

Though dazed from my nose incident, I managed to close the kitchen door in time for orb to smash against it. It fractured, many pieces glittering peculiar colours as they *twinked* out of existence, falling to the ground.

Hah, hah, I thought, *can't beat Dan the Man. I'm better than you.*

I wiped the condensation from the glass pane level with my eyes, and cupping my hands to my head I peered out into my garden. Then I frowned; Mrs Midfich had gone.

I needed to consider my next steps – obviously I'd annoyed my next door neighbour somewhat – but I knew I was perfectly within my rights; a Cornishman's castle was his home, etc., and I had every...

I turned to my kitchen door – the muffled sounds of the thumping from my front door seemed clearer. It was then I noticed my kitchen door rattling in its frame in time with the thumps.

I looked around my kitchen, knowing I needed protection from the mushroom-woman with breasts and slimy creatures. But what could I use? My thoughts were drawn to the drawer next to me. I pulled it open whilst keeping an eye on the door. I plunged my hand in and my fingers felt for a long steel blade – I couldn't look, and I trusted my hand to grab the most appropriate tool. If I was to turn away from the door I knew, whatever creature it was, that was trying to reach me, it would get the upper-hand, should my concentration be diverted.

I lifted the implement from the drawer and held the palette knife out in front of me. I stared at the long, blunt, and nicely curved steel tool. But before I could berate my hand for selecting the most useless weapon for defence it could have possibly chosen, the door to the kitchen fell from its hinges and crashed to the floor.

It was a kind of unidirectional Mexican standoff; I waved the palette knife in the creature's direction. The creature staggered towards me, arms outstretched – the palette knife having no deterrent effect.

I needed to act quickly before the burger-fog from my lounge eased its way into the kitchen, completely filling it. Still holding the cake-tool in front of me, I moved sideways around my breakfast table at the centre of my kitchen; my plan "B" being to get back into the lounge and leg it out of my front door.

As the creature hissed at me and licked its lips with its strange tongue, I manoeuvred around the table, towards the door to my lounge, and a way out.

Time seemed to go in slo-mo.

Then I reached the door, and in triumph I decided to see what this eight inch long tool could do. I held the blade in my hand and threw it. The palette knife flicked through the air, end over end, and embedded itself in the creature's forehead.

Dan does it again, I thought, but only for a second.

The mushroom-woman staggered back, and frowned! Moving its uncoordinated hands it reached for the steel icing manipulator that was sticking out of its head, and removed it, throwing it to the floor.

I turned and ran into my lounge, aiming to get through the smoke and out into the road. But as I came level with the gas barbeque I had to stop; Mrs Midfich was standing in my doorway.

Chapter 11

Things were getting desperate; I had Mrs Midfich in front of me, and sooner than later mushroom-woman, with her big tongue, pert but creature infested breasts, would figure a way out of the kitchen.

You know, if I could have worked out a way to die on the spot, I would have done – but nothing came to mind.

Through the smoke I could see Mrs Midfich's cane, something she'd called her staff, still sitting in the charcoals, smouldering, but not destroyed.

Even though the old woman was at my front door, obviously more mobile than I'd realised, I'd only one other plan, one option, and I had to follow through, though the likelihood of it working was moot. But being a man of his word, I went ahead anyway.

I grabbed a bottle of liquid firelighter, from the base of the barbeque, opened the lid, and sprayed the contents on the remains of Mrs Midfich's staff, as she'd called it.

The old woman screamed at me, uttering more strange words and I knew I had to accelerate the combustion of the old woman's staff – her demeanour indicating this was probably the best tack.

What could I use? I looked around my room, then I saw it; Ordinance Survey map, sheet 431, Glen Urquhart & Strathglass – I was certain it was a place I was unlikely to visit in the near future, but was there another of my maps I could use? Was this really the least used one?

I heard something bump into my kitchen table and knew I had to make the decision.

I pulled map 431 from my bookcase and started to fan the flames of the barbeque; with each flap the charcoals glowed and the staff became bright.

I looked at Mrs Midfich, for some reason she hadn't come any further than the threshold, but she was reaching for her twig/wand once again.

I fanned harder than I'd fanned any fire in my life and Mrs Midfich pointed the wand in my direction — its end beginning to glow the putrid green once more. Then, as the staff began to burn more thoroughly, she staggered and the glow at the end of her wand vanished as she collapsed to the ground.

Icy hands grabbed at my neck, sharp finger nails strived to break the skin. I let go of the map with one hand so I could turn to see the thing that would ultimately be the architect of my demise.

The teen-mushroom was right behind me, but seemed weaker. As I stared I felt a burning sensation in my hand that still had hold of the map. Was this another dark power it had? I wondered. I turned back to the barbeque and knew luck was on my side once more. The map was alight and the flames licked my fingertips. I twisted as fast as I could and thrust the flame engorged map into the wretched face of the living mushroom. It didn't scream but its pale skin sizzled; whisps of steam produced where the flames touched, melding with my smog filled room.

I shoved the flaming map into its mouth and pushed it back towards the kitchen. There was no resistance. The she-creature fell back and crashed to the floor.

I turned back to face Old Mrs Midfich, hoping beyond hope, that she'd been incapacitated somehow. But there was nothing to be seen of her, barring her shawl that was now on the ground just outside my front door.

The barbeque crackled and the staff puffed its strange colours, then vanished. The shawl vanished. I looked into the kitchen but there was no sign to be seen of the teen-creature, except the smouldering remnants of OS map 431.

Then the street was filled with a wailing sound and I recognised it. I was something I'd heard before. It was the fire brigade.

Chapter 12

"Mr Rogers," the fire officer started. "What on earth possessed you to use you barbeque in your lounge?"

I was having great difficulty explaining the events of the past few days and the last thing I wanted to mention was the attack on my property by an eighty-three year old woman and her deceased victim.

"I've never used it before," I said, by way of an explanation.

"And this is why you decided to try it in your living room?"

"To be quite honest, sir, the garage was too dangerous. There were pots of paint and methylated spirits in there."

The officer rolled his eyes. "Sir, barbeques are meant for the garden and you're damned lucky your house wasn't burnt down."

I tried to offer a reason. "You must admit, at this time of year, the weather isn't conducive to having a barbeque in the garden. Surely you can see this. And there was a storm."

I got the impression that the fire officer wasn't too pleased with my answer, he said; "If I have any advice I can give to you, it is this; never have a barbeque in your house unless you use your oven. Is this clear Mr Rogers?"

"But…"

"No buts, Mr Rogers."

I conceded his point and after he'd checked the house to make sure there were no secondary fires he left, along with his fire crew.

Suffice it to say, my weekends have now become, once again, the recuperative I expect from them. I've never seen Old Mrs Midfich again and her garden has become completely overgrown.

I quite like my new open plan lounge-dinner, though I still have to knock down the wall to match its doorless entry. And to save future problems I have decided to sell my gas barbeque on eBay.

Life is suburban and mundane once more and I know, now, this is the way I like it. And because the house still stinks, I will continue to do my best to erase this toxic legacy from the carpets, the walls and my memory.

Where did it all go wrong?

By Sandra Maynard

A toxic legacy or... poison left behind.
Debilitating the soul, frying the mind.
Blisters, scabs, ulcers too.
A burning throat. Whatcha gonna do?

All around the smell of death permeates the air.
Unnecessary loss of life. So unfair.
Blindness, disease, a loved one gone.
Gotta try and carry on.

Aliens clothed all in white.
Sniff around the barren site.
Smelling the blood, the guts, the gore.
It's just too much. Can't go on anymore.

Forward to the Past

By Nicolette Coleman

Chapter 1

I measured out 25 grams of bran flakes and poured them into the bowl, adding a small amount of skimmed milk. Sitting at the table I took my time, trying to make this seem like a larger meal than it really was. I was used to being constantly hungry, but never managed to accept it, although I really knew no other way. Sometimes I thought there was something wrong with me. Why did I always feel the need to eat more? To eat things that would get me into trouble?

I washed my bowl and spoon then got myself ready for work. The ultra-tube stopped almost outside the door of my pod so there was no real need to rush. I found myself longing for a day without work, a day when I could sit around and not do very much. A day without exercise in the gym. I sighed. Really, there must be something wrong with me.

Once I arrived at the factory, I was too busy to think too much, which was a good thing. My job was putting together the components for hand held computers. A fiddly, exacting job, but it kept me busy and stopped me from thinking too much. After working on a few I looked up and smiled at Jenna who worked opposite me. We often went to the gym or canteen together, and today we would eat lunch together. The factory canteen is large, clean and busy. We are given vouchers for one meal for each seven hours that we work, and the food isn't bad. Each meal has its calorie and fat content advertised, which does make life slightly simpler. Today I chose a salad with a hummus dip, followed by a fruit salad. That way I would have enough left to enjoy a pasta dish for dinner in the evening.

Jenna was in a chatty mood. She had been to the picture show the previous evening with Brent, a guy she'd met in the multi-gym. It was hard to have dates these days as the government were trying to encourage us to opt for what were basically arranged marriages. If you went to the marriage bureau and went for the bureau's choice of spouse you were given a larger pod and a higher income; whereas, if you chose your own partner, you got no extra help. I was in two minds about the whole thing. I was still quite romantic and liked the idea of falling in love, but on the other hand it would be nice to have a larger pod and bigger income. So far I'd managed to avoid the issue by avoiding the bureau and having no dates, but I didn't think I could put it off forever. I was twenty five years old and getting to the stage where I really needed to think about the future.

It was nice to see Jenna so happy. She had had a difficult previous few months, when she had managed to find out who her birth mother was, but had been rejected by her. I had chosen not to go down that route. The government discouraged such things, and I didn't think I could bear the pain of rejection. In fact I was beginning to think I was good at avoiding a lot of things.

After work I went to the factory gym for a while and spent some time on the running machine, watching a music video whilst I jogged. Usually I went to the free gym nearer my pod, but I fancied a change today. There was a man on the machine next to me who kept smiling at me, and although I tried to ignore him, I found I couldn't help smiling back after a while. He had a very engaging grin, and really it was nice to meet someone who didn't seem too serious. After a while he began chatting to me, and he seemed harmless, so I talked to him. When we had both finished our runs, he invited me to join him for a drink. I hesitated for a while, unsure about going for a drink with a stranger, but he talked me into it by asking; "What harm can it do?"

We went to a bar near the factory – the Come On Inn. The man, who had by now introduced himself as Mark, ordered us each a beer. I sat at a table near the window as I felt safer there. When Mark came back from the bar he had a plate of bar snacks with him.

"I can't eat those!" I exclaimed, although my mouth watered at the sight of the cheese and pickles. Mark laughed and said "Well if you can't, I certainly can!" and started to tuck in. I watched him enviously. Tomorrow was my weigh-in and I didn't dare eat too much.

"How do you manage it?" I asked.

"Manage what?"

"To eat things like that, and drink beer, yet stay in shape?"

Mark grinned. "Lucky genes perhaps? But I go to the gym regularly and I like walking, rather than riding the ultra-tube. It just balances itself out I guess. Here, have an olive," and he popped a green olive into my mouth before I knew what was happening. The flavour burst in my mouth and I chewed happily.

We talked for hours, and I was surprised to find how much Mark and I had in common. At the end of the evening he insisted on walking me back to my pod, and we laughed and giggled all the way there. I couldn't believe that I'd allowed myself to drink three beers and eat cheese and olives. I tried not to spoil the evening by worrying about it now.

When we reached my pod we said goodnight, and Mark bent down and kissed my cheek, filling me with joy.

"Can we meet again, Nina?" he asked. "I'm free on Saturday if you're not working."

"I'm free. It would be nice to see you again," I said.

"Great. Shall we go hiking for the day?"

"Hiking? What's that?" I asked.

Mark laughed. "It's walking in the woods. Outside the Centre, not in the gym. In the fresh air, under trees. It's great and the fresh air does you a world of good."

I hesitated. Although it wasn't forbidden, going outside the Centre wasn't encouraged, but it did sound like fun. Surely it could do no harm? So I agreed, and we arranged to meet Saturday morning.

Chapter 2

The following morning I went nervously to the clinic for my weigh-in. I couldn't get the previous evening's food and drink out of my mind. I had to wait in line for quite a while. A woman three ahead of me in the queue looked overweight to me. There was a roll of fat around her middle, the like of which I hadn't seen for a while. She was sweating as she waited and I imagined she was nervous. She was a long time in the weighing room, and when she emerged she had obviously been crying. I waited my turn with some trepidation. If I had gained weight I didn't know what I would do. Eventually my name and number were called and I entered the room, lifting my arm to have my tag read as I reached the nurse. I took off my shoes and stepped on the scales, last night's beer and cheese feeling like a rock in my stomach.

"Hmm," the nurse said, "you've gained a kilo." My stomach lurched as she read the printout. "Your BMI is now 24.4. You're doing OK, but keep an eye on things, you don't want to keep gaining." I nodded numbly as I headed for the door. 24.4 was still within limits. I was just about OK, but had to keep myself in check. I decided to skip lunch, just having an apple to keep me going.

I found myself nervously getting ready very early on Saturday. I was unused to leaving the Centre so had no idea what to wear. Hiking probably meant a lot of walking, so I wore my jumpsuit and most comfortable shoes. I was ready long before Mark knocked on my door, although I hesitated before opening the door so he wouldn't think me too eager. Mark was wearing comfortable clothes, heavy boots and had a bag on his back. "I've brought supplies" he grinned, noticing my look.

We walked along the gangway for a while before Mark hailed an ultratube. We went far further on it that I had ever done before, and I was beginning to feel a little out of my depth when Mark said "This is our stop" and stood up. We were in a deserted part of the Centre which was completely unknown to me. I looked around as I followed Mark towards a tunnel which had a few doorways leading off it. He took the third door, which led into another tunnel, at the end of which were elevator doors. Mark pressed the button and we waited in silence for its arrival.

In the lift Mark pressed the top button and stood back, leaning against the wall as if he was totally at ease. I was becoming more nervous by the minute as I was taken further and further away from all that I recognised.

When the lift reached its destination, Mark stood back to let me out. Ahead of us were huge electronic doors, flanked by two security guards. They made me nervous, standing there with their arms folded, watching as we approached them. The larger held out his scanner and I automatically raised my left arm for him to read my tag, watching as Mark did the same to the other guard.

"Off somewhere nice?" my guard asked. I opened my mouth to answer, but Mark grabbed my hand, smiled at the guards and headed for the doors, which opened as we reached them.

"You don't need to explain where we are going, Nina. We're doing nothing wrong," Mark said, his smile softening his words.

"But they're Centre guards!" I replied.

"True. But that doesn't mean they have the right to know where we're going, does it?" Mark asked. I was stumped and said nothing. I had always answered whenever a guard asked me a question – it was just conditioning. But I supposed Mark might have a point. Why did they need to know where we were going? My heart lifted a little at this thought and I turned and smiled at Mark.

By this time we had walked a few metres from the door and I looked to where we were going. Ahead of us were trees, grass, flowers. Mark marched happily up the nearest slope as I hurried to keep up with him. There was a warm wind blowing, and, unused to it, I struggled as it whipped at my hair and clothing. Mark turned around and laughed as he saw me fighting the wind as it tore at my hair.

"Don't worry about the wind. It's only natural and there's nothing so sweet as a girl with wind-swept hair." I laughed and stopped trying to tame my hair. After a while I settled into the rhythm of Mark's walk and began to enjoy the feel of the air on my skin and the sun on my face. The wind lifted the small hairs on my arms, tickling its way over me. As we reached the top of the hill, I turned to look back and gasped as I saw the outside of the Centre.

"It looks so small doesn't it?" I asked, "When you think how many people live and work in there."

"Well, most of it is underground," Mark explained. "What's really amazing though is how big the world is out here and how seldom so many of you get to see it." He looked sad.

"Do you often come out here?"

"As often as I can," he replied. "Once I got the taste for the outdoors, I couldn't bear the feeling of breathing that reproduced air inside the Centre. I try to get out here at least once a week or I feel I'll go mad."

I looked at him in surprise. I had never heard anybody talk like this before. When I was in school we had been taken on 'nature walks' in the summer, but I don't remember anybody particularly wanting to go. But then again, we had been super-tagged before leaving the Centre, which meant that if we went more than 5 metres from the group an alarm sounded and we received a small shock. Therefore the walks were an unpleasant affair where all the children hurried to keep up with the teachers.

This, however, was something different. Mark strolled along, touching trees and plants, smiling up at the sun and chatting about all sorts of things. I found myself relaxing and starting to take in my surroundings. I began to realise what Mark meant about the air – it felt very different to breathe in this sweet-scented warm air and I felt I could soon get a taste for it.

After an hour or so Mark stopped in what he called a glade – a clearing under some trees. From his bag he took a cover which he spread on the ground, asking me to sit on it. As I sat, he took out a bottle of orange juice and a plastic box, which turned out to hold cheese sandwiches. I was amazed, having never eaten other than at a table.

"This is what people used to call a picnic," Mark explained. "Apparently hundreds of years ago people would regularly go out and have picnics when the weather was nice."

Once we had finished our sandwiches, Mark took out two apples, rubbing one on his shirt-sleeve to make it shine before passing it to me. I had no idea why, but I found my eyes filling with tears, and I looked away so he wouldn't notice.

After lunch we lay down on the cover. Mark closed his eyes, but I lay and looked up at the canopy of trees above us. I had never seen anything so peaceful as the way the leaves swayed in the wind, and the sound they made was almost hypnotic. I looked over at Mark, to find him propped up on one elbow, watching me.

"Happy?" he asked, and I nodded, once again feeling overwhelmed and emotional. Mark reached for me, and gently pulled me towards him. He kissed me on the mouth, so gently that the tears fell from my eyes and landed on his cheek. He opened his eyes and looked at me for a moment, before pulling me down so that my head rested on his shoulder. We lay like that for some time and I allowed myself to feel the happiness that filled me.

Eventually Mark stood up.

"Come on, I want to show you something before we have to go back." Reluctantly I allowed him to pull me to my feet, although I wanted nothing more than to rest on his shoulder all day. We walked a little way further, and the ground began to change. There were fewer plants and more rocks under our feet. I began to see large square stones, some on the ground, some looking like the walls of buildings. We reached a stone building, or what was left of it, and Mark led me towards it, although at the last minute he veered to the left and went behind the building. There, the grass was high, but we could see lozenge-shaped stones sticking up from the ground. Some were leaning at angles, while others stood straight. I walked towards the nearest one. Reaching out, I moved some greenery away from the stone. There was writing on it.

"Hilda Coggles. 18th May 1924 to 24th June 1998" I read out. "What does it mean?" I asked Mark.

"These are grave stones," he said. "In the past when people died their families used to bury them in the ground and put these stones above so they knew where they were buried."

"How barbaric," I said.

"I don't think so. Come see this one." and Mark led me a few metres over, to a stone which read 'Emma Gould, 21st March 1960 to 3rd August 2021. Loving wife, mother, Nana. Sadly missed.'

"Don't you find that moving?" Mark asked. "People would bury their loved ones and then visit the stone, or grave as it was known."

"Loved ones?" I asked, "Where did you get that expression from?"

"History. I am very interested in the past and I spend a lot of time looking into our history and trying to find out how the world used to be. Doesn't it interest you?"

"I never really thought about it to be honest," I replied. "I just kind of got on with doing what I was supposed to do."

Mark smiled. "Well, I want to do what's right for me, rather than what the government say I should do."

"Don't you believe they have our best interests at heart? That's what we've always been told."

"No, Nina, I'm not that naïve any more. I believe the government tell us what they think we want to hear so that we will do what's best for them. What is best for us would be to live out here in the fresh air, with people we loved, rather than stuck inside the Centre for the rest of our lives." He sounded upset, and I didn't really know what to say.

When we returned to the Centre later that day, I had a lot to think about. I had enjoyed my day out with Mark, more than I could remember enjoying anything for a very long time. But I also felt confused. I had been taught to believe that the government wanted what was best for us, and had never before considered that this might not be the case.

Chapter 3

The next few days passed in much their usual way, apart from the fact that Mark kept in constant contact by instant messenger and I quickly became used to the quiet vibration of the handheld in my pocket. We met up twice at the gym and both times went to the bar for drinks and snacks afterwards. I tried not to worry too much about the food Mark encouraged me to eat, but it was hard as I knew what could happen if I gained too much weight.

The following weekend we went for another hike. We headed in the same direction as before, but at the top of the hill Mark led me to the left rather than the right. I had been looking forward to seeing the graveyard again and felt slightly disappointed. But Mark smiled and took my hand before leading me down a small pathway between some bushes. As we cleared the greenery I stopped, stunned by the sight that met me. Further down the hill were small buildings. Some were in a state of disarray, with broken roofs, but others looked smart.

"What is this?" I asked.

"It's the edge of a village our ancestors used to live in," Mark replied. "Come on, let's go closer," and he led me down the hill. As we got closer I could see that the buildings were larger than I had previously realised, and when we reached the front of the nearest intact building, I could see that it had a large door and broken glass windows. Mark walked up to the door and pushed it open, beckoning me inside. I followed slowly, wondering what I was so afraid of. Inside I found myself in a small hallway with stairs leading upwards. Mark had disappeared through a door on my right, so I followed him to find a large room with what looked like the remains of chairs and a table. I stood still, looking around in wonder. I ran my fingers over the table which was thick with dirt. Had people really lived here once? Outside the Centre? I raised my eyes to Mark in query.

"This would once have been a family house. Probably a father and mother and some children would have lived here. This would have been the 'living room' and through there is the kitchen." I followed him through to the next room where we could see a dirty sink and what I assumed had once been work surfaces and cupboards.

"What happened?" I asked.

"What do you mean?"

"To the people? Why do we all live in the Centre now? Why would people have left and gone there?" I felt shaken, as though the floor was being pulled from under me.

Mark moved over and put his arm around my shoulder. "It was the government. Don't you know the history?"

I shook my head. I had never looked into history that much. Having been taught in school that the government were our loving parents I hadn't bothered to challenge the fact. All I wanted was to be loved and looked after.

Mark moved me back to the living room and sat me down on the least broken chair. He pulled another over and sat by me, his arm around my shoulders.

"People lived like this for centuries," he began. "This was the usual way of things. Families lived together – usually mother, father and children, in one house. I think it was a more natural way, and it worked for centuries with no real problems.

"But back in the early twenty-first century the government started to try to take charge of people's health. It started, I believe, as a genuine desire to help families who struggled to stop themselves from being unhealthy. Apparently people had started to gain too much weight and do too little exercise and they became fatter and fatter, and of course it caused enormous health problems. People began to have surgery to help them to lose weight, but things didn't really improve at the rate the government wanted it to. They really started to worry when children started getting too fat, and they put nurses into schools to encourage families to eat healthily.

"But when children were still gaining weight the government started having them taken away from their families, saying it was child abuse. The children were put into Centres and kept on a healthy diet.

"Then, bit by bit, they started bringing adults in to Centres to encourage them to lose weight. I think it was originally quite a gradual process, but that was how we ended up having no choice but to live in the Centres and to keep our BMI under twenty seven.

"They also decided that children were better brought up in nurseries than with their parents, so we now have children taken away at birth and brought up in nurseries."

Mark finished talking and I sat for a while, absorbing this shocking information. Was the way we lived now so very unnatural? A question was buzzing round in my head, but I was afraid to voice it. Eventually though, it had to be asked.

"What happens to people who don't keep their BMI low enough? They just disappear – are they sent out of the Centre?"

Mark squeezed my shoulder. "I think you know really, don't you? They are put to death."

I gasped, not wanting to believe something so terrible. All those poor people who struggled more than I did. It was hard to believe, but I recognised the truth of what Mark had said. I remained quiet for some minutes after this revelation. My mind was in a whirl as I was confronted with truths I had until then managed to ignore.

At last Mark stood up. "Come on. Probably time for us to head back." He pulled me to my feet and we left the house and began our walk back to the Centre. We walked in silence for a long time as I continued to digest all I had heard. Mark appeared to understand and did no more than squeeze my hand from time to time.

As we neared the Centre I stopped. I couldn't go back in there with my mind in this kind of state. I pulled Mark behind a tree, holding on to his hands.

"What am I supposed to do now?" I asked. "How do I go on now that I know this? How do you manage?"

Mark stroked my hand, not looking at me at first. "It's hard, Nina. I've known about this for a few years, so it's something I've learned to live with. I don't know what to say to make it all right for you. In a way I wish I hadn't told you, but I care enough about you to want you to know the truth." He paused, looking into my eyes. "I can't take back what I've told you, and, although I hate hurting you, I want you to know the truth. This is hard for me to say as I haven't known you long, but, Nina, I feel very strongly for you and wonder if we might have a future together? And if we do, I want it to be an honest future where we both know what's what."

I was stunned. I had very strong feelings for Mark too, although I hadn't allowed myself to think too far ahead. I leant forwards and kissed Mark, allowing him to pull me close, and we stayed that way for some time, locked together.

Chapter 4

The next few months passed in much the same way, with meetings, drinks and weekend walks outside of the Centre. I was aware that our comings and goings had been noticed, but, as I was sure we were doing nothing wrong, I didn't worry too much. Each week Mark showed me something else new in what I had begun to think of as 'the old world'. We found houses, shops and a number of old household items such as rusting old baby prams and aged cookers.

The weather began to get a lot colder and our walks weren't as much fun as we shivered in the cold air. One Saturday in November we walked back to the graveyard, where we had a cold picnic seated on the side of an old grave. As we finished our meal Mark knelt down in front of me.

"Will you make me very happy and agree to marry me, Nina?" he asked, completely taking me by surprise.

It didn't take very long for me to know that my answer had to be "Yes, please!" I knew by now that life without Mark wasn't a life I wanted.

The following week Mark put things in motion so that we would be allowed to marry in January. "A new start in a new year," he said happily. We agreed that we would live in my pod as I had room for a double bed, whereas he shared with a workmate. Nothing was put in our way as we made our plans, so in early January we met at the government offices on the top level with

Jenna, and Mark's pod-mate, Luke, as our witnesses, and made our vows. After a celebratory drink and dinner at the bar where we had had our first date, we went back to our pod, where we found ourselves alone indoors for the first time ever. Mark pulled me into his arms, kissing me before starting to undress me.

Life was good. We would have liked a bigger pod, but there was no possibility of that unless one of us found a job working directly for the government, and that wasn't going to happen. Mark's rebelliousness had rubbed off on me, and I found myself horribly aware of how much our lives were manipulated by the powers that be. Neither of us could have borne to work for such an organisation.

But we were happy. Our weekend walks continued when the weather was nice enough, and we enjoyed being out in the open, away from the constant scrutiny in the Centre. We spent little time with other people, except for Luke, who it turned out, shared Mark's views on the government and their ways. We would occasionally go for walks with Luke, as we never felt confident of our privacy when talking inside the Centre.

Luke knew a lot about past history of families, and he had very strong feelings about the issue. "Families should live together," he told me one day. "Children should be brought up by their mothers and fathers. It's barbaric to take them away to live in nurseries where they are brought up by nurses; nurses who are under the pay of the government and so will do as they are told."

It certainly made me think. Children living with their parents sounded odd to me, but strangely right. I had never liked the idea of having babies by insemination and then giving them away at birth. Although I had been taught all my life that this was the right way to do things, it had never sat happily in my mind.

I soon discovered that Luke and Jenna had been spending time together, and it made me happy as they were our closest friends and seemed to have a lot in common. I also knew that Jenna had been searching for love for a very long time. I was glad for her as I saw them getting on so well, and when Luke invited Jenna along on one of our walks I knew he was serious about her.

We had a lovely day in the country. The sun shone although it was early April, and we had taken along a picnic to enjoy. We walked to the houses that Mark and I had previously visited and ate our lunch in a garden there. After we had eaten, we sat for a while, enjoying the warmth of the sun on our skins, and I listened sleepily as Luke explained our feelings to Jenna. I could almost feel her disbelief as he talked, so I sat up and told her all I had learned in recent months.

"I guess that explains the changes in you," Jenna said thoughtfully. "I thought it was just being in love with Mark, but this does explain a lot." She looked upset, so I went and sat next to her and put my arm round her shoulders. I remembered well how shocked I had been when Mark had explained things to me such a short time ago.

It was a strange afternoon. Jenna was visibly upset, but trying to be strong for us. I felt that she was afraid of losing our friendship if she showed disbelief, so I stayed close to her, trying to pre-empt her questions and fears. When we were in sight of the Centre late in the afternoon I pulled Jenna into a hug. "Don't be afraid, my friend," I whispered to her. "We will always be friends. There's a lot to learn about all this, and I feel I barely know anything yet. But we'll be ok if we stick together." Jenna hugged me back and we went on our way in silence.

For the next few days I felt troubled, wondering if Jenna would be too distressed by what she'd heard, and would feel she had to tell someone what we'd told her. I didn't see her at the factory, other than in the distance, so there was no opportunity to talk to her, which was probably for the best as we wouldn't want to be overheard.

Chapter 5

By the following weekend we were fairly desperate to get away from the Centre so that we could talk. Mark had asked Luke to join us, bringing Jenna if she was agreeable. To our delight they both joined us as we met by the hill, and we walked on towards the graveyard where I had received my first lesson in the realities of life. We led Jenna on a tour of the graves, explaining as we went, and she quietly listened to all we had to say.

After lunch I found myself alone with Jenna when the men went to relieve themselves behind the bushes.

"Are you OK?" I asked.

"Yes," Jenna replied. "It's been a funny old week. I've had a lot to think about and process, but having dug a little in the library I've come to the conclusion that you are all right, not completely mad as I'd feared. What Luke said makes sense, doesn't it?"

"Yes," I replied. "Rather horrible sense, but it does fit. I now find myself realising that bringing up children in a family, rather than a government nursery is probably the kindest, most natural way. It's what we do from here that bothers me. Now that we have all this knowledge, what can we do with it?"

"I know," Jenna said. "That's what's been bothering me the last couple of days. Once I realised that you are right, I found myself wondering where we go from here. Of course, I have no answers yet, but I'm working on it." And we both laughed as the men joined us again.

The following weekend I was feeling off colour, so Mark and Luke went for a walk by themselves. I found that I missed the feeling of fresh air which I had begun to get used to. I wondered then how I had lived without it all my life. Mark came back very late, but in a very good mood. It seemed he and Luke had had a good time on their walk, although Mark declined to tell me just what they had got up to.

Two weeks later Jenna and Luke came to tell us that they had decided to marry and wanted us to be witnesses. I was very happy, even though I was still feeling unwell. The following day Mark insisted that I visit the doctor in order to find out what was wrong, and hopefully put it right before the wedding.

I sat for some time in the doctor's waiting room, surrounded by people who coughed and sniffled. I was sure that I would walk out of there feeling far worse than I did now. One man, very thin and grey, coughed horribly into a handkerchief, which came away from his mouth stained with blood. He worried me, and I found myself wondering just what was wrong with him. The thought took my mind off my own worries for a while, and when the doctor called me in, I was feeling slightly better.

I explained my nausea, lack of energy, tearfulness and the doctor asked if I was married and when I had last seen my monthly period. Thinking back I was surprised to realise it had been more than two months. The doctor smiled and asked me for a urine sample, which he tested, and rather too quickly gave me the news that I was pregnant. For some reason I felt stunned. Although not naive, I had given no thought to pregnancy, and it wasn't something Mark and I had discussed.

Considering the conversations we had had over recent months I felt scared. Could I really give a baby that Mark and I had made to the government? I was desperate to see Mark and discuss it with him. But first there were the tests and trials to go through. I was weighed and measured. My blood pressure was taken and then I was quickly despatched to see a nurse, who congratulated me on doing my duty in providing for the future of our Centre. Plans were made, and I was given a date for a planned caesarean section, and told where my baby would be delivered afterwards.

I chose not to go back to work for the rest of the day, and called in sick. I sat at home, waiting for Mark, almost wishing I had gone to work as my mind whirled. When Mark did arrive home – ten minutes late, wouldn't you know – I practically fell on him as he came through the door.

He asked how I had got on at the doctor's, so I told him the news. Mark sat down on the bed, pulling me down beside him.

"This changes things rather," he said very quietly into my hair. "We need to go for a walk at the weekend. We need to talk." This was all said so quietly that even I had trouble hearing. I was more frightened now, not less. What did he mean by 'this changes things'?

"What do you mean, Mark?" I asked, trying to keep the fear out of my voice. "What does it change? Please don't tell me you're going to leave me?" I could feel tears in my eyes, so I kept them wide open to stop the tears falling.

Mark looked at me, pure shock on his face. "Leave you?" he asked, "Leave you? Why on earth would I do that? You're the best thing that ever happened to me. I have no intention of leaving you, Nina," and he pulled me into his arms, where I allowed the tears to fall.

Chapter 6

On the Saturday I was slightly surprised to find that Luke and Jenna were coming on our walk with us, but I was sure Mark had a good reason for inviting them. We set off early, as the sun was rising over the hills. It looked as though it would be a beautiful day, and I felt happy to be with the three people I cared about most as we climbed slowly up the hill. Nobody spoke much until we reached the graveyard. Mark and Luke settled our things on patch of grass and sat down. Jenna and I joined them, waiting to see what they would say.

Mark told our friends about my pregnancy. Jenna squeezed my hand and I found that my eyes misted with tears. There was a silence, until Mark broke it.

"Now, this changes things a little, and we need to make plans. I really do not intend to see my child sent to the government nursery. I want to be able to bring the child up in a family, with me as father and Nina as mother. And I'm sure she will make an excellent mother." Mark smiled at me and my heart melted.

"Now, what you girls don't know is that Luke and I have been in touch with a breakaway group who live away from the Centre. They have rebuilt some houses a few miles away from here and they live in the old way. They bring up their children in families, they grow their own food and keep chickens for their eggs. It's hard work but we think it's worth it. What do you think? We were planning to get more information and get more supplies together before making a break, but Nina's pregnancy changes things. What I think now is that we need to make a move in the next five or six months.

"The group are willing for us to go and live with them and are allocating a house for us to start off in. It will need some work doing to it but I think we can manage that. What do you think?

"Are you up for the challenge of a new, happier, more natural way of life?" He looked at me and Jenna, waiting for our answers. I was excited at the prospect of a new way of life, but terrified too. I had never lived anywhere other than the Centre, and had no idea how to give birth, let alone how to rear a child. My heart thudded painfully in my chest as I tried to find an answer. Looking at Jenna, I thought she was probably feeling similar thoughts.

"It sounds exciting," Jenna started, "but I'm very scared. So many 'what ifs' are whizzing through my mind. Won't the cops come after us and force us to come back? And then punish us?"

"We asked the group about that," Luke replied. "They said it was unlikely. The first settlers who left were pursued, but they refused to leave their new homes and after some time they were left alone. Apparently the ones who've come after have more or less been left to get on with it. They think the cops think they are not managing out there and probably think they've all died by now."

"How would we take all we need to our new home?" I asked.

"Luke and I would go for weekend walks over a few weeks and we'd take things with us each time we went. That way it won't seem so suspicious," Mark answered. He moved closer to me and put his arm round my shoulders. "It would be so great if we could do this, Nina," he said. "A new way of life, you and me and our children, living together without fear. Think how lovely that would be." And I could see how good it would be, despite my fears.

Chapter 7

By the time we reluctantly returned to the Centre that evening, we had reached an agreement that we would move to the settlement by the end of August, two months before the baby was due. I was very excited, but also very scared.

The next few weeks were a thrilling time. Each weekend we went out, but Luke and Mark would leave us in the evening and travel on to the settlement, taking food, clothes and medicines with them.

Jenna and I would return to the Centre, chattering all the way about our new lives. In between times I was surprised to find that Mark took a great interest in my pregnancy. When I questioned him, he explained that I was carrying a baby that we had made through our love: a baby who was half Mark and half me. My eyes filled with tears as I thought about this. I had never before considered this pregnancy to be much more than an inconvenience, but Mark was forcing me to look at it in a totally new way. This baby would not be handed over to the government nursery at birth. He or she would live with me and Mark, in a little home where we would learn to be good parents. The more I considered the idea, the more I realised the rightness of it.

In June, Jenna and Luke were married. We celebrated in much the same way as we had when Mark and I married, other than that the following day we went to the graveyard where we toasted our new lives with glasses of orange juice.

Chapter 8

By mid-July I was noticeably pregnant and was required to go for weekly check-ups with the nurse. Each time I was weighed and had my blood pressure taken.

"Your blood pressure is fine, very good," the nurse said. "It must be all those outdoor walks you take." I felt a tremor run through me. How did she know about our walks?

"What do you mean?" I asked.

"The walks you take each weekend with your husband and friends. It's all documented here," and she indicated my notes on her computer. Although we had to show our identification each time we left and returned, I was still stunned. How much more did they know about us? Did they listen to our conversations?

"We like the fresh air," I said feebly. "I expect it's good for the baby."

"Indeed," the nurse replied, smiling, "but you must take care not to overdo it. By the end of August I think it is best if you stop walking so much and start to rest." I nodded dumbly. Would they try to stop me? I wondered. But hopefully we would be long gone before then.

I couldn't wait to tell Mark what had happened. Afraid of being overheard, even in our pod, I simply told him the nurse thought it was good that we went for so many walks, that it must be good for the baby. When he hugged me I knew that he'd understood.

"Never mind," he said. "We'll stop going for so many walks before the end of August. We must make sure that you and the baby stay well." And I loved him more than ever for his understanding.

I was allowed to have extra time off work as a result of my blossoming pregnancy. The government wanted 'their' babies to be as healthy as possible, so expectant mothers were well looked after. We were given coupons for extra milk and vegetables and encouraged to rest each afternoon. We were also invited to free ante-natal exercise classes, which I was happy to attend.

August approached and with it my happiness and excitement bloomed. I was also sorely afraid that something would happen to prevent our going. We had settled on the second weekend in August as this was just before the date when I had been advised to stop going for long walks. I was aware that the advice would most probably be enforced, if I didn't do as I was advised.

The week before departure was hard for me. I found that I wanted to say goodbye to all my colleagues and friends, but of course I must not give any intimation of what we were planning. I also wanted to pack anything I might need in our new home, but was aware that we were probably being watched, so I contented myself with slipping the odd small item into my rucksack when I felt safe. I wanted desperately to talk to Jenna about what was happening, so I found that I avoided her at work to stay safe. Jenna also seemed to be avoiding me, so she must have been feeling the same.

Chapter 9

On the Friday afternoon, Jenna approached my work bench. "Are you on for a walk tomorrow, Nina?" she asked. "Luke and I thought it would be nice to get out while the weather's still warm."

I admired her bravery. "Good idea, Jenna," I managed to reply, "I think the fresh air would do me and the baby some good."

The following morning the baby woke me very early by performing somersaults on my bladder. When I returned to bed I was unable to sleep. I snuggled up to Mark, who put a sleepy arm around my shoulders. "Too early to get up," he murmured, kissing my head.

I lay as still as possible, knowing I had a long walk ahead of me, but I couldn't force sleep to return. At last I got up and made coffee, bringing a cup back to Mark. I sat on the edge of the bed. How wonderful it would be to feel free to talk about whatever we wanted in our own home! There was so much I longed to say, but it would have to wait. As I showered I surreptitiously packed soaps and shampoo into my bag, hoping I would be able to get it out of the Centre without raising suspicion.

As agreed, we met Luke and Jenna at the lift at 9:30 am. They were both holding rucksacks, which, to my mind, bulged suspiciously. We smiled at each other, suddenly shy, but Mark took charge and led us into the lift and up to the exit doors. The security guard on duty that day seemed ridiculously uninterested in us and where we were going. Can't you see? I felt like shouting. We're leaving! Never to return! But I kept quiet and merely smiled at him as we passed through the doors.

Outside we walked sedately up the hill. "I feel like running and shouting!" Jenna whispered to me and I grinned back at her, rubbing my bump where the baby squirmed inside me. We were headed towards the old houses we'd seen before, but Mark had explained that we were not stopping there, but going much further and would probably not make our destination before nightfall.

I was extremely nervous about being followed, even though we had never before been followed on our walks. From time to time I thought I heard rustling and cracking in the undergrowth beside us. When I told Mark of my fears, he laughed and said it was most probably wildlife.

We walked for what seemed like days, stopping only to eat at midday and then a few hours later. As the light began to fade Mark and Luke led us to some nearby houses, where we were to set up camp for the night. We made ourselves as comfortable as possible in an upstairs room, all sleeping in the same room for safety and warmth. When we awoke in the morning, the sun was shining and it looked like a glorious day. As Jenna and I were getting breakfast ready, we realised that Mark and Luke were whispering outside the room. We opened the door and went to them.

"What's happening?" Jenna asked. They hummed and hahed for a while but eventually Luke admitted that they had heard noises and were afraid someone was watching the house. Cold fingers of fear ran through me as they ushered us back into the room.

"We're going to look around and see what we can see. You girls stay indoors and try not to worry too much." Try not to worry! I was so scared I could barely think.

Jenna led me back indoors and tried to keep me calm. It seemed a very long time until the boys came back again, although Jenna's watched showed it had only been just over an hour.

"We found evidence that someone has walked around these houses recently," Mark said. "But there is absolutely no sign that they are still around. My feeling is that we should go on our way, but be more careful and aware."

We breakfasted on some bread rolls we had brought, although I felt too wound up to eat well. Eventually we continued our journey. I was feeling sore and achey from the long walk the day before, and it was a struggle to keep going. The baby rolled around inside me, making me nauseous.

After a short while Mark turned to watch me. "Are you feeling OK?" he asked, coming to my side.

"Tired," I mumbled, "and feel a bit sick."

Immediately Mark took charge. He made me sit on a nearby wall and told Luke and Jenna we needed to rest. We all sat down, and I could see Mark was thinking.

"We need to think about what to do," he said at last. "Nina can't keep up this level of walking. But we are not really that far from the settlement. How about if Luke and Jenna go ahead, and Nina and I come behind at a slower pace?" Everybody thought about this for a while. Just as I was about to speak up and say that I would rather feel ill than split up, Luke spoke;

"No. We will all go at Nina's pace. I'm not splitting the group up." And he patted my knee. I felt quite teary, but very grateful.

From there on we went at a much slower pace, resting every few miles. Along the way we had a few more scares when we saw things out of the corners of our eyes, or heard sounds nearby, but somehow we stayed safe.

Chapter 10

It seemed we were never going to reach the settlement, but I began to notice Mark and Luke smiling to each other, and then we rounded a corner, to find high walls ahead of us, with a large gate set into them. There were metal spikes set along the top of the walls. Mark marched up and rapped on the gates and after a short time they swung open to reveal a small bearded man who beamed at us.

"Here you are!" he said, delight written on his face. "Come on in!" and he swung his arm to indicate we were to enter.

I was stunned at the sight that greeted me. Houses that were not ramshackle stood side by side. Plants grew in neat rows around the houses, and there was a smiling group of men, women and children moving towards us.

We were led towards a small house attached to four others. "I hope you won't mind sharing a house until we can get another ready for you?" a woman asked. Mark laughed, and I knew why. We had had no more than a room per couple at the Centre, so a whole house for the four of us was an unbelievable luxury. We were shown into the downstairs part of the house. There was a large room plus a kitchen, and upstairs were two bedrooms. Each bedroom contained a large bed, covered in a patchwork cover, which I later learned had been hand-sewn by some of the women on the settlement. Out the back of the house was a toilet in a small wooden house. "We don't have access to the sewerage systems the Centres use," one of the men explained, "so we've set up a septic tank system." I had no real idea what he was talking about, but was grateful that we had the use of some kind of toilet, as, on our journey here, we'd had to make do with using bushes and it had made me wonder what we would have to deal with when we arrived.

We were introduced to a number of people who lived on the settlement. There were all kinds amongst them: - children of all ages, young and old, men and women. A lot of the men had beards — something which was almost unheard of in the Centre, and the women nearly all had long hair which they wore tied back or on top of their heads. Their clothes were very different to those I was used to. The women wore long skirts which were patched with all kinds of materials, and the men wore tattered and patched trousers. It was all so different, but I sensed a calmness and happiness amongst the people, which was not usual in the Centre.

Left to our own devices for a while, we made ourselves at home in our new house. Jenna and I were interested in the kitchen, which naturally lacked the hi-tech elements of the kitchens we were used to. The cooker had no electric supply, and appeared to be run by burning wood. We had been left a couple of battered looking saucepans and some plates and cups. I was so thankful to these people for their help, which allowed us so much freedom.

I was tired and aching, so took myself off to bed. The bed was comfortable and warm, and tears of tiredness and relief filled my eyes as I pulled the covers up over my shoulders. I was beginning to allow myself to believe that we might be safe. So many thoughts and images filled my head as I drifted off to sleep.

I awoke later when Mark sat on the edge of the bed. He looked happier than I had seen him for some time. There were muddy patches on the knees of his trousers and a black smudge above his right eye.

"Did you have a nice rest?" he asked, and kissed me when I nodded. "Nina, this place is amazing! They are busy building new houses for others who might join us. They keep sheep for their wool and cows for milk, plus chickens for eggs. They are growing all kinds of vegetables and fruit. We can be safe and happy here, if we're prepared to work as hard as they do!"

I smiled and squeezed his hand. I was happy to be here, especially as we had Luke and Jenna with us, but there was something worrying me.

"What will happen when I have this baby, Mark?" I asked.

"We'll bring it up by ourselves and you will be a wonderful mother," he replied happily.

"No, not that," I said, "What about actually having the baby? I don't know how. In the Centre I would have had an operation to remove it easily, but what will happen to me here? What if I need a doctor? I'm really scared." Mark lay down next to me on the bed, pulling me close and stroking my hair.

"Look around you, Nina," he said, "there are a lot of babies and children here. So that means there are a lot of women here who have given birth. I am sure that, before you are due to give birth, you will have met some of them and can ask how they managed. They all seem kind and keen to help us. Try not to worry." and he kissed me, then kissed me again, which helped to take my mind off things.

Over the next few weeks, we were kept very busy. We had to more or less re-learn how to live our lives. Food had to be grown and harvested, then chopped and cooked before it resembled anything edible. Jenna and I had a lot of fun learning, and, despite a few disasters along the way, we found a great sense of satisfaction in making meals which our husbands enjoyed. Mark and Luke were kept busy learning building skills and also working with the animals and in the gardens.

We were too busy to worry about anything. Jenna and I were soon part of the group of women who met up each day. They sat together drinking tea and making clothes and household items. Some had learned to spin wool which would be knitted into warm clothes for winter. I had never seen a knitting needle before, but soon became fascinated at how a string of wool could become a wearable item. The first thing I made was a scarf for Mark, of which I was ridiculously proud, and he wore it round his neck every day that winter. Once I had mastered that, I was encouraged to knit small items for my baby; tiny jackets and mittens, little trousers and hats. I asked the women how they had learned such crafts, and was told that some of the earliest settlers had found books in an old library, and had collected those that would be most useful. The books remained in one of the houses, and I enjoyed reading them. I learned how to make cakes using carrots instead of sugar, and dinners without meat.

At last I plucked up the courage to ask about giving birth. Lisa, one of the eldest women, smiled and said she had wondered when I would ask. "So many of us have had babies over the years we are quite adept at it now. Mary and I call ourselves the midwives as we have had so much experience. So when you are sure you are in labour, get Mark to come and get us and we'll help you." I smiled, slightly reassured, but I had other questions.

"How will I know when I'm in labour?" I asked, and Lisa laughed.

"Sorry! We forget how these things are kept from you in the Centres. Here," she reached behind her for a book, "read this book. It explains everything you need to know. I think that in the past you would have been given this information as soon as you got pregnant. And try not to worry. Remember that giving birth is very natural. Your body knows what to do and we will help you."

For the next week I read the book over and over. I looked at pictures of how big and developed my baby was at each stage of pregnancy, and read the fairly scary parts about labour. I felt better for being informed, although still frightened.

Chapter 11

Six weeks after our arrival Jenna and Luke told us they were pretty sure that they were also expecting a baby. I was happy for them. We had begun to see how children enhanced life in the settlement, and we were all getting used to seeing small children sitting on their parents' laps and running around playing in the gardens. Children were no longer the alien, alarming things they had once seemed and, behind my fears, was a little bit of excitement.

By this time my stomach was huge, and it was getting harder to do my chores. I was grateful to Jenna for her help around the house, and wasn't looking forward to the day when she and Luke would move into their own home. We all got along really well and it was nice to have the support and friendship they supplied.

One dark, cold day, I felt the first twinges of labour. Fear and excitement filled me. Mark was out with some other men, building a kitchen, so I found Jenna and told her. She hugged me and put the kettle on.

"Let's have a drink while we wait and see what happens," she said. It turned out to be a wise move, as to my surprise it was a very long time before anything much happened. The pains eventually became stronger and closer together, and when they were coming every five minutes Jenna left to find Mark and Lisa. By the time they returned I was kneeling on the floor, breathing hard through a contraction. Lisa was pleased with how things were going, so, after examining me, she went to find Mary, as they preferred to work together. Mark was acting like an excited child, dashing from one room to another until I snapped at him to sit down. He laughed. "I'm so excited, but there's nothing useful for me to do." I suggested he talk to me, so he sat down and talked, soothing me with his stories of how our lives were going to be once this baby came along. He told me about the school that had been started in a house down by the stream, and how our child would go there with his or her friends and learn all they needed for the future. By the time he had aged our child to an age where they would be working in the fields with Mark, I was in too much pain to listen. Lisa had returned with Mary some time before, and they decided it was time to go to the bedroom as it wouldn't be long now.

It took some time for me to get up the stairs as I was having contractions every minute or so, but at last we arrived in the bedroom, where I saw that Lisa had rearranged things so that it was easier for me. I couldn't sit down, although I was tired by now, so knelt on the floor as the baby made his entrance.

After a time when I forgot everything apart from my body which felt as though it was being turned inside out, I heard Lisa say "It's a boy! Congratulations!"

I looked at Mark who was grinning from ear to ear, tears in his eyes. He bent down and kissed me very gently, as though I might break.

"Here you go, Mummy," Mary said, and a warm, wiggly bundle was placed in my arms. Mark sat on the bed and put his arms around both of us. "My family," he said, pride swelling in his voice.

I must have slept for a while as I awoke to the sound of the baby crying, and opened my eyes to see Mark bouncing the baby in his arms. When he saw that I was awake, he passed him to me for feeding. As we sat quietly, Mark asked if I had thought of a name for 'the little dude'. I shook my head. I had been too busy being frightened of the birth to give much thought to what came after.

"I was thinking of Ben," he said. "What do you think?"

I considered it for a few minutes before smiling and nodding. "Ben it is," I said.

Two weeks later, I left the house for the first time. I had been afraid to go out before as the weather was so cold that I was afraid that Ben would freeze. But today the sun was shining in that hard, glinting way it does in midwinter. Jenna joined me as I walked along the path towards the buildings where Mark was working. Jenna's stomach had already started to grow and I was flooded with happiness at thoughts of the future we could now all face.

I spied Mark ahead, working with Luke and two other men. They were fixing brickwork on a house ('pointing', Mark had told me it was called). Mark was dressed against the cold, the scarf I had knitted wrapped snuggly around his throat.

Ben stirred and mewled, and Mark looked up. He grinned and starting walking towards us. "That's your Daddy," I told Ben. "He's building a new future for us all." And I swear Ben smiled at me.

The Door

By Colin Butler

At the end of the country path
Overgrown with weeds and brambles,
I came upon an ancient door
Half-hidden by leafy branches.

I turned the rusty handle with difficulty,
As it creaked like a complaining patient.
And there before me spread a garden
Untended, neglected and unloved.

In its wildness was a strange haunting beauty,
As my eye followed the overgrown path
Meandering to a once elegant manor-house,
Now shuttered, sinister and slowly decaying

I was overcome with a strange feeling
Full of dread and awful foreboding.
Who had lived there and why had they left?
What tragedy had overcome them?

I felt myself curiously drawn to the house,
As if a magnet drew me ever nearer.

Toxic Legacy

The sense of dread grew stronger,
As I slowly pushed open a side door.

The sight that greeted me
Turned my blood to ice,
Such horror was indescribable
And would change my life forever.

Invisible Friend

By Paul Bunn

Prologue

My world is like your world, it's important to know that. They are separated by an incredibly thin barrier, so thin they often cross boundaries and merge like conflicting signals on a TV screen. That's when people see ghosts.

I sit firmly on the ghost side of the fence having died a number of years ago, but it's not a bad existence. I don't wander around scaring people by moaning and rattling chains in the middle of the night. That simply doesn't happen; it's been cooked up by storytellers and filmmakers just to make a fast buck.

Let's just say that the place I inhabit is not a whole lot different from the "living" person's space. We have our problems, although not with normal human frailties like death and disease; we've done that and got the t-shirt! However, ghosts do have personalities, which are carried like fingerprints from our time in the living world. Therefore clashes with other spirits do occur, just as much as in any normal Homo Sapien's society.

Each of us has a role, allocated to us when we pass over and I am no different. No one comes up to you and says you must do this or you must do that; it is planted like a seed, which should be nurtured and grown. How do I know this? Well, I just know, it's that simple.

Not all spirits take up their allocated niche; these are the ones the living normally see, wandering with seemingly no purpose.

Before I tell you more about what I do it's important to understand how and why I died so let's start there.

Sudden Death

My name is Gavin and I was just a normal man leading an average existence. Well, that's what I used to tell myself, except it wasn't true.

You see I was lonely, living in a one bedroom flat on a housing estate, surrounded by properties full of families. Some of these people were happy and some weren't but I was jealous nonetheless. My mother and father had died within a few years of each other when I was a child. The big "C" was the culprit in each case, although neither of them had smoked. Just one of those unhappy coincidences, I suppose.

I'd had a string of girlfriends, none of whom lasted long. I didn't think my looks were the problem; at just under six feet and weighing in at thirteen stone I didn't think I was that bad. Still, perhaps it was my thinning hair, missing front tooth or slightly bulbous nose. Whatever the reason, I never found out why; they just dumped me and ran.

The fact that I lived alone shouldn't necessarily have meant I had no friends but, alas, that was the case. Again, I could never figure this out. I tried but perhaps I just didn't have the necessary skills to form long lasting relationships of any kind. My view on this was just to shrug my shoulders and get on with my life, which is what I did.

Anyway, I digress from telling you the most exciting thing that ever happened to me in life – my death.

I was relaxing in my bath one evening thinking of nothing in particular (me all over I'm afraid) and realised that I had no soap to wash with. Annoyed with myself I knew that there was a bar on the sink just a few feet away. Lifting myself up, I realised I had to get out to retrieve it as it was beyond my reach. Having forgotten to put a floor towel down I stepped onto the tiles with my wet feet and, well you can guess what happened. I fell back slamming my head hard onto the side of the bath. This would normally have just made me see stars and shout a few expletives but my head hit at such an angle that it broke my neck "snap" and that was the end for me.

New Beginning

I can remember watching myself from above, not quite understanding what had happened to me. (This is quite normal for ghosts I can assure you.) I wasn't sure how long I waited for, time is very warped in the spirit world, but I know my body had decomposed quite badly before anyone found me - a consequence of not having anyone who missed me. Only after my remains had been taken away did I feel compelled to leave.

You may have heard stories about people with near death experiences being drawn to a light at the end of a tunnel. This, in fact, is rubbish caused by a hallucination in the brain when it lacks oxygen. Both worlds inhabit the same space, just different dimensions. There is some science behind it that is beyond modern man at the moment, which I won't go into, so let's just leave it at that.

For me it was just a case of "it's time to go" although I didn't know exactly which direction I was heading. There was a feeling of drifting along but with a purpose. Just like switching channels on your remote.

I saw snippets of humanity, as walls were no longer barriers and I saw into other people's lives. People arguing, eating at the dinner table, making love, crying: in essence all of the things that you do in everyday life.

I was so transfixed at this sudden insight into human activity, it took me a few moments to realise I was no longer alone in this new ghostly world (I hadn't seen any other spirits up to that point). In many respects I was quite shocked at his unexpected appearance, and how real he looked. Let me explain; you see "living" people appear as spectral images to the spirit world whereas us as the "dead" appear solid, a transposition, you might say, of the way the living perceive us.

"Hello, Gavin." He smiled, stretching his arm out to shake my hand. Initially I was taken aback at the "normalness" this new situation seemed. Ghosts shaking hands! Whatever next?

He saw my puzzlement and nodded almost imperceptibly, his smile broadening into a grin. "There are many things you need to understand about us which may seem odd, especially as you've only recently come from the other world." He jerked his thumb in the direction of the scene I had just been witnessing (a couple arguing about some financial matter). "But it will all become clear in time."

His hand was still proffered and I took it, still in a state of confusion.

"I'm Alistair, by the way, Ali for short." He had a strong grip, his hand almost engulfing mine.

"Hi," was all I could manage in response, as tears suddenly filled my eyes. Ali seemed not to notice but I'm sure he did and probably understood. I had a yearning to be back in my boring, eventless life doing all the mundane things that I used to do. I didn't want to be here.

"Come, we have much to discuss." He moved off silently and I was reluctant to follow, as if this final step would mean there was no going back to what I knew, and was comfortable with. I could see Ali wasn't going to stop though, and fear struck me like a thunderbolt. I didn't want to be left on my own, just aimlessly wandering about.

"A little like your life really," a cold voice spoke in my head.

That spurred me into making my decision and I quickly followed Ali to this new stage in my existence, because that truthfully is what it was.

Ali

We travelled for quite some time. I would have said, "walked" but it wasn't like that. I had the feeling of putting one foot in front of the other but looking down at my feet they were perfectly motionless, as if just willing myself to move caused my advancement. I couldn't detect where we were going, as the scene around me was one of greyness, like a mist or fog.

My patience was wearing thin and I was just about to call out to Ali when he stopped abruptly and turned to look at me.

"We are here," he announced, that broad smile crossing his face once again.

I saw nothing to show we had arrived anywhere whatsoever, no buildings, streets or others waiting, just this swirling blanket of nothingness we had been in for God knows how long.

Ali indicated for me to approach. "Come," he said. Taking my hand, he closed his eyes.

I had the feeling of dropping, like descending in a lift at great speed. To be honest, if ghosts could feel sick I felt sure I would be, but before long we came to a jolting halt.

"We've arrived," Ali reported cheerfully. "Time to meet the top brass."

The Three

As we stood there the swirling mists parted and three elderly looking gentlemen materialised in billowing white robes; all had beards and long hair.

"They look like Gandalf from Lord of the Rings," was my first thought at which point I had to stifle a snigger. I turned to Ali who must have noticed something because I saw a warning flash in his eyes; needless to say, I heeded it and kept my thoughts to myself. The three gentlemen appeared to be appraising me with studied expressions as they approached, making me feel like a naughty schoolboy. If I could have shuffled my feet, I probably would have done, but they were motionless.

"Ah, young Gavin." The one to my right spoke first, in a gentle, kindly voice, "Welcome to your new home."

He spread his arms wide in preacher fashion and the other two bowed their heads, as if in prayer.

"Who are you?" I said trying to comprehend what this was all about.

The one in the middle arched his eyebrows questioningly, casting his gaze to Ali. "Alistair, have you not told Gavin about us?" Ali bowed in response to the question. "I have not yet had the time to explain, sir." Ali straightened before adding, "I wanted to ensure we got here at the appointed time."

The one in the middle nodded and turned back to me. "We are The Three," he said, with some gravitas. "We are a collective and our responsibility is for those who dwell in this place." His thin lips on his ancient face cracked into a smile as he leant forward fixing me with his gaze. "And that now includes you, young man."

My thoughts were confused with a jumble of questions I wanted to ask, but I didn't know where to start. I thought dying would be a whole lot simpler than this. Why did we need looking after by three old men? What the hell was going on here?

Ali touched my shoulder and squeezed it lightly in reassurance. "The next few moments are important, Gavin. Listen well and take note of what they say."

The third of The Three who had not spoken as yet came forward and took my hands in his. He closed his eyes as he did so. There was a frisson of electricity as we touched. It sent a shudder down my spine. How could that be, when I was dead?

"We know how you lived your life," the third of The Three said in hushed tones. "Now we must see how you perform in death."

I felt a wave of tiredness roll over me like a warm blanket.

"There is a task we will ask of you," he continued.

"Task…," I mumbled, consciousness drifting away from me in an instant.

"There is someone in the living world who needs our help." I felt my hands being squeezed tighter.

"He is alone, so alone."

If my eyes had been open, I would have noticed a tear falling gently down his cheek.

"Alone…" My voice seemed distant, detached from my body.

The contact was broken and my thoughts snapped back into place.

Joe

Joe McStay gazed out of the window onto the quiet street below, trying to forget the phone call he'd just had.

"Stupid bitch," he shouted, his breath creating a small mist patch on the glass.

The bitch he had in mind was his wife, Helen, who'd recently left him for good old Brad, once his best friend. The hurt he felt smouldered within him, ready to ignite at any time.

And then there was his daughter Poppy, just five years old, living with Helen and Brad, cutting Joe off completely from seeing her. Well, that was how it now seemed after the phone call where Helen had said he wasn't to see Poppy anymore. All because he'd brought her back home from a day out half hour late!

"She's fucking poison," he cursed, wishing he'd never met Helen in the first place. Part of his rage was down to a feeling of helplessness, wondering what to do next. He loved Poppy with all his heart and couldn't bear to lose her for good. She was the only decent thing to come out of their marriage. Even now he could picture her long blonde hair tied into two ponytails bobbling up and down as she ran towards the park, Joe just behind her, pretending to be the bogeyman. He felt a lump in his throat as he remembered her infectious giggle and those bright blue eyes that were filled with such happiness.

Joe sighed and sat down on the settee, as a dull headache started to press against his temples in throbbing waves.

He needed time to think about what to do next but due to Helen's unpredictability, he never knew how to plan for the best. One thing was for certain though; there was no way she was going to stop him from seeing Poppy.

Unable to settle and with his headache getting worse, he made his way to the kitchen to find some Paracetamol.

Expectations

I'd never taken drugs in my life (or death) but could imagine how it felt after my meeting with "The Three." My emotions were a mixture of elation whilst still feeling as if I could sleep for a hundred years. Ali stood nearby with a knowing smile on his face, his eyes dancing with merriment.

"It's quite an experience isn't it," he quipped. "I know, I fed off it for ages."

At that moment, I didn't feel I could respond, as my mind was in no fit state to formulate any words. I couldn't even think about trying to work out what had just happened – even whether it was a good or bad thing. Suffice to say, I wasn't feeling my normal self.

"You need to rest and then we can talk," Ali said. "There is much I need to tell you."

"I didn't think ghosts needed sleep," I responded dreamily. "What is the point?"

My eyes closed anyway and I fell into a deep slumber.

....

When I awoke, all I could see was whiteness. Confusion filled my thoughts as I tried to remember where I was and what had happened. Then Ali's face filled my vision with a gently mocking look.

"You sleep like a baby," he said with a mischievous grin. "I was going to sing you a lullaby to help you nod off but there was no need."

I ignored his comments, as I felt light headed, thinking I might faint at any moment. "How long have I been out for?"

"Time works differently here," he said, "but, in living world terms, probably about ten minutes."

"Ten minutes! It felt like hours." I held my head in my hands.

"As I said, time…"

"Works differently," I finished, with just a hint of sarcasm in my voice.

Ali gave me a disapproving look and I immediately regretted my rude interruption.

For a few moments, I couldn't look at Ali, my embarrassment too intense. When I had been alive I couldn't remember a time when I'd bitten back at someone quite like that, although I suppose there hadn't been that many people around me during my lifetime.

Miserable git. That unfeeling voice was in my mind again trying to make me feel worse than I already did. The last thing I wanted was to alienate the only ghost I had met whilst trying to understand my current predicament. Ali was the one who was going to get me through; of this I was sure.

"Sorry Ali, that was uncalled for." I peered over to him, an expression of regret on my face. "My head feels like mush at the moment."

Ali turned to me, his eyes ablaze. "The decision you have to make is critical, probably the most important one you will ever have had to make."

He approached me slowly, his outburst forgotten almost as soon as it was spoken. Resting his hand on my shoulder, he added gently: "Come on, let's talk further."

The Visit

Joe sat in his parked car, drumming his fingers nervously on the steering wheel. He looked in the rear view mirror at his reflection noticing, not for the first time, his dark brown-cropped hair greying at the edges. Even his deep blue eyes looked puffy due to his lack of sleep.

He was outside his old house in which Helen, Poppy and the boyfriend, Brad, now lived. The thing that annoyed him most was that this was the house he'd paid for. The only reason he tolerated it was because he didn't want to wrench Poppy from the home she had been brought up in. There was nothing worse than uncertainty in a child's life and he wanted to ensure that, with everything else going on with her mummy and daddy, she at least had the familiar surroundings of her home.

This was the first time he'd been able to visit Poppy since the argument about her arriving home late. That had been a week ago but it had seemed like forever. Helen had allowed him to come and see Poppy after much pleading and grovelling, which he hated. He was only here for a visit and there would be no arguments, just some "quality time" with his daughter. He would make sure of that. Taking a deep breath to steady his nerves, he climbed out of the car and made his way up the garden path.

He sensed trouble as soon as she opened the door.

"Oh, it's you," she said, turning and letting Joe in. There was an edge to her voice as if she was trying to control her temper, which flared constantly.

"Where's Poppy?" he asked tentatively, aware that any wrong move or word out of place may set Helen off.

"Daddy!"

Joe's little bundle of joy came bounding along the hallway in her favourite pink, flowery dress. Joe bent down and took her in his arms lifting her into the air.

"Hello, Sweet Pea."

He gently kissed her on the forehead, smelling the soapy odour of shampoo in her hair.

"Daddy, I'm Poppy not See'Pea," she said in mock sternness before grabbing his nose and tweaking it. She always had trouble saying that word and it made Joe smile.

"Mummy's been shouting," Poppy said, a small frown wrinkling her forehead.

Joe turned to Helen, a questioning look on his face.

"It was nothing," she said defensively. "Me and Brad just had a disagreement that's all." Without waiting for any response she walked away towards the kitchen.

Joe felt anger welling up inside him but held it in check, not wanting to upset Poppy. He hoped this wasn't a regular occurrence with Poppy being around; she'd had enough trauma as it was.

"Daddy, Daddy," Poppy said tugging at his shirt impatiently. He saw her beaming smile and his ire evaporated in a moment. "Come and see my new dolly." She took his hand and led him to the lounge.

The next two hours were bliss as he watched his daughter playing; everything else didn't seem to matter anymore. He remembered how uncomplicated life used to be before the separation; just the three of them in what he felt at the time was an unbreakable bond. How stupid that seemed now!

He quelled the bitterness that suddenly hit him as he saw the happiness on Poppy's face.

She was pushing Barbie along in her pink car with Ken joining her in the passenger seat.

"Where's Barbie going, Sweet Pea?"

Before Poppy could respond Helen breezed in, her demeanour unchanged from earlier.

"Ok, time's up," she said curtly, bending down and picking Poppy up in her arms.

Poppy was momentarily startled by Helen's sudden appearance. "Daddy?"

"Don't worry, love, I'll be back again soon." Joe glanced at Helen who averted her gaze. He could feel the coldness from her and wanted to shout and scream but again held back. Poppy rested her head on Helen's shoulder and started sucking her thumb, a sure sign of tiredness.

"Are you sure everything is ok?" Joe fixed Helen with a stare, trying to see whether there was anything she was hiding. "No, we're fine, can you please go as I've got to fix the dinner and put Poppy to bed," Helen's weary voice had softened. "I'm just tired."

Joe thought there was something more, but couldn't put a finger on it. Gently, he leaned across and kissed Poppy, before stepping out into the cold, evening air.

"I'll call to arrange another visit."

His answer was the front door being closed in his face.

Getting back into his car, he sat there for a few moments. He felt as if a light had been switched off; one minute he had been with his family, the next cut adrift and alone. Poppy was his light and he didn't get enough of it. As he stared into the night outside, it mirrored his mood.

"Snap out of it; you'll see her again soon." His voice sounded flat and lifeless in the confines of the car.

The Garden

We walked for some time in a land of nothingness, in no specific direction.

"What did The Three ask of you?" Ali asked.

I was surprised by the question as I thought he had known from the start. "You really don't know?"

Ali glanced at me and shook his head. "Only the person told knows; unless he divulges it to someone else." A smile crossed his face at this final comment.

I didn't immediately respond as I had noticed our surroundings were changing. In place of the bland whiteness I saw shadows of trees, which quickly became visible.

The ground we were walking on was now grass and a few metres in front of me was a small lake.

Looking up, the sky was a perfect cobalt blue with not a cloud in sight. Each tree swayed in a gentle breeze although I felt nothing against my face. Flowers of many varieties and colours were laid out in patches around the perimeter of the lake.

"Wow," was all I could say in wide-eyed amazement. There were many other ghosts here too, walking serenely around, they seemed in no hurry to go anywhere.

"Where the hell are we?"

Ali chuckled to himself. "It's definitely not hell," he said. "This place is simply called The Garden. It's where spirits come to relax and unwind."

I'd never seen anything like it in my life (or death). I had walked through many parks and gardens in my time, generally finding them great places to go for some peace and quiet away from the hectic world we inhabited. This place was different but somehow the same, I couldn't quite put my finger on it.

"Quite beautiful, isn't it?"

I said nothing in response, just drinking in the wonder of the place, and the sweet aromas of the flowers that hung thickly in the air. The birds were of not of a variety I'd ever seen before, many with deep and bright colours, like birds of paradise in the living world.

"Let's sit down over here." Ali directed me to a tree by the lake, which was shaded under a huge canopy of branches with leaves in full bloom.

I had been thinking of little else but the task set for me by "The Three". How was I supposed to complete such a thing?

Perhaps sensing my difficulties Ali interrupted my thoughts. "I am not just your guide here but have been specifically asked to help you in any way I can, if you want it, of course." His words were genuine and heartfelt and I appreciated them greatly.

"But how can you help me? I don't know where to start myself." I clasped my hands in front of me and began kneading my knuckles.

Ali reached across and gripped my hands tightly. "I do not know what it is you have to do but it involves helping someone, am I right?"

I gave him a surprised look and he held his hand up before I could speak. "Every task has that element; it's just the details that differ."

The burden I had been feeling lifted slightly; knowing someone else had an understanding of what I had to do.

Gazing around the garden once more, I knew I could turn down this task if I wished, but there was one thing that nagged at me. Throughout my life I had never felt fulfilled; something had always been missing. Like the proverbial itch that you couldn't scratch, it had been with me always. The worst of it was, I never did anything about it, just moving from day to day never thinking why. Why am I doing this job I hate? Why can't I seem to have a long-term relationship? Why is my life so uninteresting?

I made my mind up there and then. "He's called Joe, Joe McStay." Speaking his name loosened my tongue and I unburdened myself to Ali. "He's currently going through a difficult time with his wife and daughter, but I don't know how to help." I looked over at Ali, uncertainty clouding my mind as I recalled the words from "The Three" which were emblazoned into my psyche.

Ali smiled at me, a twinkle back in his eye. "If you wish, I can help you."

Life of Hard Knocks

Sitting in the café, Joe held his cappuccino to his lips and took a sip through the froth. He had needed to get out of the office for half an hour just to try and clear his head.

From his vantage point near the window he had a clear view of the High Street, and watched other office workers striding purposely with their coffees or sandwiches in hand. Life seemed normal for them.

Joe was concerned about Poppy; something didn't seem right. Looking back at how bumpy his early years were made him more sensitive to the effect his broken relationship was having on his daughter.

He had been taken away from his own family when still a baby; from what he was led to believe, his father had been a drunk and his mother just negligent. Never had he tried to contact either of them, if indeed they were still alive. There didn't seem much point in contacting someone who had never loved you. He had never felt resentful towards them; they had played only a tiny part in his life story and had nothing to do with his upbringing. His adoptive parents had been the rock he had used to build upon.

Joe had wanted his daughter's life to be normal without any worries or cares. Was it too much to ask?

Again the anger towards Helen flared within him and he forced himself to control it. Even so, he noticed his hands shaking and placed his coffee gently on the table so as not to spill it.

Glancing at his watch, he saw the half hour of his lunch break had already passed, so quickly finished his drink. Grabbing his jacket from the back of the chair, he made his way back to the office.

He couldn't focus on the spreadsheet he had in front of him, the numbers just a meaningless jumble. His boss was eyeing him from his desk at the other end of the office, eyebrows arched, questioning. Shutting down his laptop he made his way over to his boss and made his excuses.

"Sorry, John; not feeling too good. I'm going to get an early night and start sharp tomorrow."

He didn't wait for a response, just slipped through the door and made his escape.

Teacher and Pupil

"You cannot make the living do anything," Ali advised. "It's a case of trying to manipulate their thought patterns when they are asleep."

I gave him an expressionless look. I didn't have a clue what he was going on about. Ali looked at me with some exasperation; "It's probably best if I show you what I mean."

For some time now I'd been sitting in the garden with Ali whilst he'd tried to explain to me how I could help Joe. From all my time in the living and breathing world I could never remember being advised by a ghost. The idea seemed, no was, laughable.

Ali led me from the garden, which simply melted into the background as we travelled, until we came across a small building surrounded by a low trimmed hedgerow. It was a brick built, one storey, and square shaped structure but with no other real defining features. We entered silently through the wrought iron gate and made our way up the cobble path to the front door. It struck me how similar this place was to many other buildings in the living world. Did they have ghost builders?

Before I could ask the question, Ali had knocked on the front door and we waited.

Within moments, the door was opened and we were ushered in and taken quickly through to some form of reception area. There were a number of chairs arranged in neat little rows, all facing one way.

"What is this place?"

Ali saw the perplexed look on my face and laughed, slapping me on the back. "All will be revealed," he said, once his mirth had subsided. "Come this way."

We walked through one of the many side doors off the reception area and found ourselves inside a tiny room. Three of the walls were simply whitewashed and non-descript. It was the furthest wall that drew my attention and I gasped in sheer amazement. My first impression was that it was like a television, but it was much more than that. A kaleidoscope of coloured images came into focus and then blinked out again within a few seconds. There were people going about their daily lives: walking a dog in the park, going to work, drinking in the pub, having a meal — all the humdrum things that everyone does. Other images caught my eye though, strange things I had never seen before. Things I could only describe as pink monsters with green scaly backs, chased children through dark woods; crab like creatures, with black beady eyes and razor sharp teeth, ran amok in someone's bedroom; a headless chicken strutted around in circles before falling onto its back with legs still kicking.

"The human imagination is wonderful, isn't it?"

I managed to tear my gaze away from the screen for a few moments, giving Ali a questioning look.

"This is our window into the world of the living, how we try and communicate if you like." Ali stood right in front of the screen, his eyes reflecting the images he saw. Turning towards me he continued; "Over the course of human history, the spirit world has tried many ways of contacting the living." He clasped his hands together and put them to his lips, as if in prayer. "Mediums have been our best bet but their service is erratic with many charlatans in their midst." His voice rose in anger as he finished the sentence, obviously annoyed at the fact. "This method is proving a little more reliable." He pointed to the screen for emphasis, "By joining with them through their dreams."

To me, the concept was mind-boggling. It sounded like something out of Star Trek where Mr Spock would mind-meld with other people to share their thoughts and experiences.

"How on earth does it work?" I finally managed to say, trying to take it all in.

"I honestly don't know. I had no input to its development. Some of our more intelligent ghosts put this together." Ali approached me, his eyes searching mine, "But this is what you need to use if you are to be successful."

I already knew my decision was to proceed. "Let's do it," I said.

Stuff hits the fan

Having got home from work early, Joe's first instinct was to phone Helen and confirm arrangements for his next visit and also try to speak to Poppy. Picking his phone up, he paused, finger just above the buttons of his mobile. He'd just remembered her saying she was going out for the day and wouldn't be in until around six o'clock. That was another four hours away.

Dropping heavily onto the settee he picked up the TV remote control and began scanning through the channels trying to find something interesting to keep his mind occupied. Away from work he had tried many hobbies over the years, including painting, learning a language (French) and various sports including badminton and squash. None of them lasted for long, Joe's interest diminishing almost as quickly as it had begun. He could never understand why his focus on his hobbies seemed to fade; perhaps it was a matter of just finding the right interest. At this moment, it didn't concern him too much as he was mostly worried about Poppy.

Joe's mobile rang, taking him away from his thoughts. He saw it was Helen and immediately answered.

"Hello, Helen?"

The line went dead.

He tried calling back instantly, but his call went straight through to voicemail. Leaving a quick message, he picked up his car keys and dashed from his flat, a worm of fear coiling around in his stomach. He kept telling himself it was nothing but with the way things had been lately he didn't want to wait to find out. Knowing she wouldn't be home yet meant he'd have to wait outside until she appeared later. He preferred to do that, rather than wait around at home.

Joe tried not to drive too fast on his way to Helen's, telling himself she wouldn't be there, so there was no point. It seemed strange calling his family home Helen's; he'd spent a few precious and wonderful years there but now it had been severed from him like a detached limb. Calling it 'his wife's house' he felt was more appropriate and less painful for him.

Arriving outside he parked up, knocking on the front door just to check if she was in. As he expected there was no answer so went back to his car to wait. He tried the phone again a few times over the next hour but still there was no response. Each time his dread increased a notch.

Her phone was always on – even if left on charge. Perhaps her battery had died while she was out. That was a possibility, but she was always careful about it. Like most people today, her phone was her lifeline, stuck to the palm of her hand like glue. He tried to calm himself; there was no need to panic. She wasn't due home for a little while, so he tried to sooth his frayed nerves with that knowledge. He fell into a fitful sleep.

Contact

I sat in front of the huge screen at a small desk which had a set of headphones placed upon it. Ali picked these up and gave them to me. "This is simple to use, you just need to focus."

I looked at him questioningly, a sliver of doubt clouding my thoughts.

"Just put these on and I will tell you what to do." Without waiting he placed them over my ears. "Now, you know the person whom you are to help – think of him and nothing else. Clear your mind."

At first, this proved difficult. So many shapes and images came into my head that I just couldn't think straight, feeling overwhelmed by millions of individual thought patterns. "I can't do it."

I was surprised at the desperation in my voice; so keen was I to make contact. "Relax, Gavin." Ali rested his hand on my shoulder. "It will come."

This time I closed my eyes so as to avoid viewing the screen in front of me. I pushed everything from my mind except the thought of Joe McStay. I had never met him, so tried to create my own image of what he might be like. The earphones became warm and began to release a not unpleasant tingling sensation, which flowed through my head and sank into the rest of my body. I felt calm and relaxed as a picture appeared in my mind's eye, a man sleeping in the driver's seat of a car. I knew instantly it was Joe and was overjoyed. Then the scene dematerialised before I could get a good look at him, I was disappointed and almost broke the link, reaching up for the earphones.

"Wait!" Ali said sharply. "Be patient, not everything will be revealed immediately, tell me what you see."

A new image suddenly appeared, "I can see a car hurtling along a motorway, driving too fast, I'd say." A shiver ran down my spine as I watched, something was wrong with this scene.

"Will yourself into the car so you can see what is going on." Ali's voice had a sense of urgency to it.

It was easier than I thought, I just imagined myself inside the car and I was there. I sensed the tension as soon as I entered the vehicle. A man was driving with a female passenger in the front. In the back, in a child's chair, sat a little girl, who looked frightened out of her wits. My heart went out to her.

I relayed this information to Ali.

"I am sure there is a connection between these people and Joe, my feeling is we don't have time to work out what it is."

My attention turned to the girl and I attempted to find out what was going on, not really certain what I was doing...

...Blind panic; her mind was a maelstrom of conflicting images making me want to draw back from her. Angry voices were interspersed by screams in what appeared to be a nightmare for the girl, something she was finding difficult to understand or cope with. I needed to delve further, so gently probed into her deepest thoughts and was confronted by the image of Joe. I knew it was he even though I had not seen his face properly before. He was looking down on this girl with a look only a father could give; Poppy was her name.

"When will we see Daddy?"

The girl's voice snapped me back into the reality of the moving car in an instant. She was sobbing now, her tiny hands trembling as she rubbed tears from her eyes.

The woman (her mother?) turned around in her seat, reaching across to stroke the girls' face. There was a hint of sadness as she spoke, "soon love, soon." She tried to smile encouragingly but it came out as more of a grimace. "We're just going away for a while, Daddy will understand."

"But I want to see Daddy now."

Before I could hear a reply I suddenly lost contact with the car, moving away at great speed until I felt myself back in the "dream" room with Ali.

For the first time I could remember in a long time I felt a real connection with other people, wanting to know more about them and in my own way caring what was happening in their lives. I sensed with this family some real tension that threatened to tear them apart.

My main thoughts were with Joe. They were taking Poppy away from him, how was I going to stop this?

"I lost the connection, I need to get back."

Ali's voice soothed my anxiety, as he tried to re-assure me. "This sometimes happens. You just need to get 'into the zone' again."

I re-doubled my efforts and within seconds was back with Poppy and was instantly aghast at what I saw. A red mark had appeared on her cheek and she was now bawling her eyes out; it was in the shape of a handprint with the finger marks almost up to the temple. The woman and the man were arguing but I wasn't listening to them, a feeling of rage and powerlessness overcoming me.

Ali must have sensed a change in my demeanour as I heard his somehow distant voice asking me what was going on.

"They've hit her," I heard myself whisper, still not quite believing what I was seeing. "Bastards."

I heard the voice of "The Three" going through my mind again, urging me to help Joe but this was beyond me. How could a ghost interfere with or change something in the living world? Sure, you could see what was going on but that was it.

"There's nothing I can do." I sounded like a whining child who couldn't get their way. "Nothing."

My hands reaching up for the earphones, I didn't want to see any more of this cruelty.

"Wait." Ali's commanding voice broke through my repulsion. "You must take note of everything you see and relay it to Joe while he is still asleep. There is a chance he may recognise where they are going and give chase."

A cynical part of me almost laughed at this. Who took any notice of anything in a dream?

"It is the only thing you can do," Ali stated. "You must try."

Part of me wanted no more to do with this; it was too painful. As in life, I wanted to bury my head in the sand and keep myself to myself. Other people's problems were nothing to do with me.

Same old Gavin, even death hasn't changed you.

Those stinging words from my conscience finally drove me into action. Ignoring the bickering couple, I gave all my attention to the route they were taking, memorising where they were. It was the most difficult thing I'd ever done, trying to ignore Poppy's agonizing sobs in the back. As soon as I felt confident of the location, I willed myself back to Joe.

Nightmare

Joe was running from something or someone; he didn't know what, as he couldn't see it. He was terrified. It was getting closer and his running was becoming slower, as if going through treacle. He turned; there was darkness in the distance, something that encompassed his innermost fears. It was almost upon him when he heard a voice, a child's voice.

"Daddy."

He was confused, what was a child doing in this place? A niggling thought told him he should listen. It was important. And then there was a blinding light and he saw...

Joe woke up, his heart leaping into his mouth stifling a scream. "What the f...?" He rubbed the side of his neck, which was sore from sleeping with his chin on his chest.

"Poppy...," he whispered as the vividness of the dream he'd just had came back to him. Instinctively, he glanced at his watch and realised they should be home by now. Looking up at the house, it didn't look like there was anyone in as there were no lights and it was starting to get dark. He had to be sure.

Running up to the front door, he slowed, his mind confused as the dream replayed to him again, burning itself into his memory. He saw Helen and Brad in the front of Brad's car driving along the motorway and then there was Poppy in the back seat...

"Oh my God."

An inner part of him knew this was happening now, defying all logical explanation, but still he held back.

This was ridiculous; he had got himself wound up over the relationship break up with Helen and was now having vivid dreams about them; that was all. He was overcome with indecision. He realised his index finger was hovering over the front door bell and without any more thought, he pushed it.

No one came to the door, as deep down he knew nothing was going to happen. The silence from within mocked him, making him feel a fool.

"Where the hell are they?" He banged his fist on the front door in frustration.

Closing his eyes, the dream came back to him again but not strongly enough to give him any clues. With a despondent air he made his way back to the car.

"Joe?"

Startled he looked up to see his old next door neighbour Daphne, standing at her front gate. She looked exactly as he remembered her from his time living at the house. A small woman in her mid-sixties he guessed. She always seemed to wear her cooking apron with a flowered pattern, in stark contrast to her pale chubby face and blue rinsed hair. She greeted Joe with a warm smile.

"How are you?" she continued in her unwaveringly cheerful voice.

"Fine," he said, not really in the mood for a chat.

"Are you looking for Helen and Poppy?"

That caught his attention; he walked over to her, hoping she would have some information.

"Do you know where they went?"

Daphne shrunk back and her smile wavered slightly as he grabbed her arm in his keenness to know where they were. "Sorry," he said letting go apologetically. "It's just I was hoping to see Poppy."

Daphne recovered her composure, patting Joe's hand sympathetically. "Well, Helen did say something about Brad's parents but I have no idea…"

Joe raced back to his car as the pieces fell into place, now understanding where the car in his dream was going. "Thanks Daphne," Joe shouted from the window as he sped off.

End of the Road

Poppy was hurt and confused. Why did Mummy hit her? She only wanted to know where Daddy was so he could take her to the park. Her tears had slowed to a trickle as she rubbed her cheek, which still stung a lot. She wanted to cover her ears as Mummy was arguing with Uncle Brad, who wasn't being very nice to her. Some of the words he was using were the sort she had once heard some older boys saying in the street when she had been shopping with Mummy.

She was really scared; Mummy had never hit her before. She had only started shouting since Daddy had gone and Uncle Brad had come to stay. Well, she had been told off once when Daddy was at home, after she dropped a glass of milk but Mummy had said sorry and had given her a big kiss later on.

She wished Daddy was back home all the time; it was a long time to wait after he came to visit before he came back again. Sometimes when she knew he was coming she'd get her best dress out especially. She picked her favourite teddy up from the seat next to her and gave it a big hug. "Daddy," she whispered.

....

"I need something to eat," Brad brought the car to a halt in the service station. He was a big man, over six feet tall with a muscular stature. His short-cropped scalp hair reflected the sunlight from his head like a beacon. "Bring Pops with you."

Helen lifted Poppy out of the car seat and held her hand as they walked across the car park. She felt as guilty as hell for slapping Poppy but with her whining and Brad shouting at her she had just snapped. She'd make it up to her later when they got to Brad's mum.

Her main worry was this trip. Brad had suggested it so that the three of them could have some time together, without Joe "getting in the way" as he called it. She didn't like just upping sticks without planning for a trip first. Brad had been on at her for weeks about it but it wasn't something she was comfortable with. As usual though, she had given in and here they were.

Brad and Joe had been the best of friends since their early school days but the affair had killed it stone dead. Helen blamed herself for this and she still didn't understand fully why she had embarked on this relationship. She had loved Joe deeply but after a few years had become bored and restless, developing what she now recognised as an infatuation with Brad. He was always around with Joe, they socialised quite regularly so meeting up was commonplace. Helen knew that Brad liked her as well, so there was no need for her to try too hard when she pushed him.

Helen looked down at Poppy who was clearly still upset, staring fixedly in front of her, not looking at her or Brad. Looking at Poppy's face, she hoped the red mark, which was now fading wouldn't bruise.

"Well I'm having a bacon sandwich, what about you, Pops?"

Helen cringed at the word, knowing Poppy hated it. She said nothing and Brad tussled her hair. "Let's see what they've got."

The Waiting Game

I sat at the "dream" house now back in the reception area. There were quite a number of other ghosts going in and out of the rooms, some with what I guessed were guides, others just on their own. Most of them looked apprehensive and I felt for them. The experience had drained me and I still didn't know whether what I had done was going to make any difference.

"What happens now?" Ali was sitting next to me his brow furrowed in deep thought.

He raised his eyes to me seemingly troubled. "We wait to see if your intervention has changed their destiny."

I waited for more but there was no more wisdom from him. Finding it difficult to wait, I stood, "I'm just going outside for a bit."

He didn't respond, his head down and eyes closed.

I didn't want to wait for whatever destiny had in store for the people I was trying to help. When I had visited Joe earlier I had realised that there was more to my connection with him than just the dream patterns I was weaving for him in his head. He was kin – my brother. It wasn't something I could prove; I just knew. Once inside his head I sensed we had shared memories, some from before birth, in the womb. We touched and saw each other. This was a fact.

Determination gripped me, if there was something, anything more I could do, I was going to be there. Hurriedly I made my way to the scene of a forthcoming death.

From The Jaws of Death

Joe was breaking the speed limit but he didn't notice, alarm bells were telling him to hurry and that was what he was going to do. The dream's image replayed in his mind again and again. He estimated it would take half an hour to get to where the image was taking him; he had recognised the service station about fifty miles south of Brad's parents' home.

How this dream had come to him he didn't understand, probably never would. Perhaps there was an invisible bond between Poppy and him, something which traversed the physical plane. He did have a passing interest in the supernatural, but had never delved into it too deeply.

....

I stood nervously at the site. It was a place of wilderness with very few cars on the small, snaking road. The range of hills surrounding the area were extensive, in the middle of which was the large, silent lake, its surface as calm as a millpond. Not really knowing what I was going to do I waited (or should I say floated) by the side of the road on the hairpin bend. The appointed time was drawing near.

....

Mummy and Uncle Brad were arguing again and this time Poppy really did cover her ears. Mummy never did this with Daddy.

Looking out of the window, she wished that he was here now, giving her one of his special big cuddles.

Suddenly she heard Mummy scream and the car lurched to one side. Poppy had one clear thought about why she was upside down before a large crashing sound made her cry out for Daddy in utter terror.

....

I saw the car coming and knew it was the one, even in the semi-darkness that was dusk. I wondered again why I was here; there was nothing I could do to change this course of events. Then I remembered Joe and his daughter Poppy and chastised myself for such thoughts.

The car was going too fast and would never make the bend unless it slowed considerably in the next few seconds. It wasn't until the car was virtually on top of the hairpin that a sudden screech of the brakes indicated the driver had realised his error, but too late. Hitting a kerb, it spun upside down, making a complete rotation before hitting the water with a whoosh. There it sat, slowly sinking; the only sound being a small child's pleas for help.

Acting on impulse I glided to where the car bobbled and immediately entered. The driver sat with his head covered in blood, clearly unconscious and breathing shallowly. The mother, Helen was pale but conscious, her eyes wide open and panic stricken, frozen with fear. As I turned to Poppy, I could see that she, too, was awake but crying. My relief was tempered almost immediately by the fact the car was filling up fast with cold lake water. Without realising my disadvantage, I tried to unclick Poppy's seatbelt but my hand went straight through the strap. I roared as my frustration overcame me, holding my head in my hands. This was a useless idea, what could I do? Nothing except watch these people die.

"Poppy!" I heard the voice and recognised instantly it was Joe. Feeling hope rise within me I left the car to see where he was. Joe stood by the side of the lake where tyre marks on the ground indicated where the car had taken off.

"Daddy, Daddy, help me."

The plea forced Joe out of his moment of hesitation and, throwing his jacket aside, he dived straight in to the lake. The car was about ten metres from the shore but the lake was deep, even at this short distance. Gasping against the coldness he reached the passenger door. The handle was already under water and he pulled as hard as he could, but the door wouldn't budge. He tried harder, his dread building with every second that passed.

"Joe." Helen had heard his attempts at getting the door open and now stared at him with pleading eyes.

"Helen, hold on." Moving to the front passenger side he tried the same thing with her door, again to no avail.

"Try the window," Joe shouted. Helen looked back at him with uncomprehending eyes. "The fucking window, open it!" She scrambled around and wasted precious more seconds finding the handle before winding it down. Releasing her seat belt she flopped out of the window into the water.

"Hold on," Joe shouted. "I'm going to climb in here and release Poppy using the same route to get back." Helen nodded, her teeth now chattering against the chill as she clung to the body of the car.

"C..c..can't s..swim," she said.

"Just hold on, I'll be back in a minute." Without waiting for a response Joe dived back into the open window and climbed over to the back.

"Daddy I'm scared." Poppy gripped Joe around the neck as soon as he was within reach. For a split second Joe let her, despite their predicament, relieved at being with her again.

Unclamping her arms he released the seat belt mechanism and grabbed her in his arms. "Let's go."

At that moment the car lurched forward forcing Joe's head against the roof and knocking him unconscious. Poppy screamed.

....

I was not far away when Poppy let out that anguished cry, just hoping that Joe would save the day. It was clear then however that this wasn't going to be the case. Seeing the situation, I had to act fast, but felt only torment after my previous attempt to help.

"He is your brother, you have to try something." Ali appeared next to me with urgency in his voice.

"But how…"

"We knew all along, just go to him," Ali indicated towards the car and within moments I was by Joe's side.

There was one desperate throw of the dice I thought I could try. Something I had remembered in jest when first entering the "dream" room; Mr Spock's mind meld. This was much deeper than science fiction claptrap though; in my case it was a direct link with my brother. Without further thought I entered his thought patterns again…and saw through his eyes.

Toxic Legacy

"The Three" stood before me their smiles of satisfaction clear and also a sense of pride I guessed. Well, maybe that was my own imagination.

For myself, the contentment came from saving my brother's and niece's life. Joe was none the wiser as to what had happened but Poppy kept saying he had looked "strange," as if he were someone else. "It wasn't you, Daddy," she had said, to much amusement.

I had changed the destiny of a family. Joe would have lost them all but for my interference; even the "dream" wouldn't have saved them. He would have ended up like me. His legacy would have been the same as mine. Still, the toll was high with both "Uncle" Brad and Helen perishing. I see them occasionally in my world, but I haven't spoken to them. I know she watches out for Poppy though.

Epilogue

So now you know folks...

I keep thinking to myself, if only I'd known about Joe, my life could have been so much better. They say when you die, you should have no regrets but I can't help thinking if only, even now.

I feel a tear sliding down my cheek (yes ghosts do cry) as I watch Joe begin his new life with Poppy by his side. For a moment, I see him hesitate and look directly at me. I don't think I am visible to him but a smile crosses his face and he winks. Everything seems to stand still as our eyes lock, just for a split second.

Then he plunges his hands into his pockets and continues on his way.

Murder in Mind

By Colin Butler

I'll explain why I have murder in mind,
When I opened the door, what did I find?
My beloved was in bed with my best friend,
Our relationship was obviously at an end.
So I considered murder of every kind.

But how should I do the deed,
To expedite it with all possible speed,
So I would not get caught
And end up in the criminal court,
And ensure I would succeed.

Strangulation has a certain appeal
To hear her give a blood-curdling squeal,
To wrap my fingers around her throat
That would certainly get my vote,
But of course it could be hard to conceal.

I also considered stabbing with a knife,
A just punishment for a cheating wife.
The satisfaction of plunging it into her chest
To send her to her eternal rest,

It would be the end of all the strife.

I thought electrocution would hit the mark
She always was a really bright spark.
The obvious favourite was a gun
To ensure that the deed was done,
But shooting is so chancy in the dark.

So the time has come to decide
The best method of homicide.
I could ensure her brakes would fail,
But sadly that could lead to jail,
As she went careering down the hillside.

An accident would take just a jiff,
To push her off the top of the cliff,
To watch her plunge to the rocks below.
That surely would be the best way to go,
As she lies there lifeless and stiff.

Revenge in the Sun

By David Shaer

Chapter 1 – At last

"Absolutely amazing, what a beautiful, beautiful house. It's exactly like the pictures."

Pam had had enough of their last mistake and this time they wouldn't rush into buying. Their original aim had been in the Lot Valley but they had sold out in desperation some five years earlier to get away from some so-called friends and moved impetuously to the Dordogne. Steve had tried to calm things down but even he had to admit that their previous move had been a knee-jerk reaction to get away from those dreadful, pushy people, who had threatened to take away their pioneering independence of those early days of living abroad.

Pam and Steve were kind, attractive people who were adventurous and ambitious. Pam was chic and petite and exceedingly pretty. Her auburn hair had been shaped to promote her big, beautiful, blue eyes and the rest of her body had followed suit. When they first decided to live in France, she had been happy and full of energy. Steve was far more down-to-earth and didn't really have a clue about how to dress. His hair was a permanently dishevelled mess and dressing up for dinner involved putting on a new pair of jeans that scratched all evening and made him want to go home early. Gradually she had trained him to wear smart-casual trousers but only by buying them herself and turning up the trouser legs to help overcome Steve's lacking altitude. Over the years living away from Old Blighty, Steve had lowered his levels of charm and finesse but he realised this and tried, on special occasions, to restore some of his old charisma, albeit not always successfully.

But now this was going to be different. They had both tried so hard to make the Dordogne work for them but, whilst it had so many good features, they couldn't get away from the fact that it had become a haven for pompous, ignorant Brits, the very people from whom they had tried to escape in the first place.

The Lot, however, was still French, green and unscathed. And this very house really appeared to be what they would have loved all those years ago; the old walls around the land – high, dry stone and impressive; the iron double gates standing 3 metres tall and 4 metres wide, with a long twisting driveway leading to a stone built old house perched on high with a spectacular view over the open valley. They knew that it was built with them in mind – acres of land all around, a secluded garden, with its own swimming pool, an enormous underground garage, a wine cellar and facilities rooms; there were even some tumble-down outhouses in the distance which could become a series of "projects" should they need them.

"Let's buy it," squealed Pam.

Steve was still conservative and needed to know more. The price had confused him – it seemed too good to be true. The fact that the house was unoccupied and appeared to have none of the usual long queue of French descendants who couldn't be traced, just didn't seem normal. Every other French house they had ever looked at had, like so many things in life, come with baggage. Even when released to the new owner, all sorts of things emerged. But this one certainly gave off good vibes. It was odd that the previous owners had emigrated so quickly and left the house fully furnished but with a price of 140 milliards (French properties and works of art are still quoted in old francs), the equivalent of about £140,000. This was not to be sniffed at. Despite his reservations about the property being empty for so long and yet in such perfect condition, Steve was seriously interested too.

A car horn sounded in the distance, shattering the peace of the perfect day; the sound of music from happy birds, the sun reaching high into the blue sky, a gentle warm breeze and the sounds of cattle and sheep tearing grass out of the ground as they dined. The horn sounded again and, on the dot, forty seven minutes late, the Berlingo van belonging to Alain Corale, the local immobilier or estate agent/notaire, rounded the corner at the end of the lane, with Corale hanging out of the window, waving.

Alain Corale was ruddy, slightly overweight, fortyish and had a reasonable command of English; but Pam's French was better. Steve was conversant in neither, mainly because his English had been corrupted by being born in Southend-on-Sea of local parents.

The details of the house, however, had looked great in picture form and the only point Pam and Steve could raise was why the house had become vacant and not sold before at that particular very affordable price. Corale could or would not give the name of the current owners but Pam and Steve assumed that they were probably British, who had fallen on hard times and had simply done a "runner" leaving the 'notaire' to obtain sufficient funds to cover any outstanding charges.

The gates were easily opened using a code number (how difficult was 1415 to remember? – Battle of Azincourt (or Agincourt in England) – quarter past two?) and they drove in two cars down the light grey gravelled driveway towards the house. By the time that they had wandered into the entrance hall, or vestibule as Corale translated, Pam was in ecstasy. The house had obviously been maintained and cleaned so well that it was as though it were already inhabited. The only thing missing was the smell of coffee brewing, or any evidence of life.

It had everything Pam needed and a lot more besides. In fact, their problem would be that the contents of their own house were not necessarily up to the standard of some of the equipment that was currently in this house. Oh, what a problem! In common with their expectations, the owners turned out to be, in fact, a Société Anonyme, an anonymous limited company that was probably a Trust. Tracing the previous owners could be a problem but everything could be signed, sealed and delivered within four weeks, due mainly to the Power of Attorney that had been granted to a notaire. So they need never meet the former owners.

Their own property had been on the market for less than only three weeks but already they had three British punters interested and one French couple. Whilst they would prefer to deal with the French couple, mainly because, unlike the Brits, they don't fanny, they were still waiting for somebody to commit. It would almost certainly be the French.

Pam and Steve were getting excited and felt that they needed to buy this house.

Corale explained how he had never actually met the current owners, who had apparently already emigrated and were dealing through an agent, the notaire. Although the house had not been lived in for many months, possibly years, it was exquisitely maintained and totally clean. It seemed odd to Pam and Steve not to be talking to the owners but often deals were completed, nowadays, without the vendor and buyer ever meeting. Further explanation from Corale implied that the owners had other income that funded the refurbishment, cleaning and other running costs from other rental incomes.

Obviously lucky people, whom nobody had actually seen for years.

Chapter 2 – Sewing the seed

Robin and Lester had worked hard in their short lives, made good money and had decided that, in their late thirties, deserting the shores of Mother England was their ideal self-pat on the back. They had watched the Channel 4 program of other people who had decided that being a bingo caller in Burnley or reading the radio newscasts in Rochdale were no longer rewarding and, besides which, it was still raining in both places. If those people could run away to Spain or France or Italy, they were equipped to do it much better.

Robin was an assertive girl who had worked hard in an Australian insurance group for twelve years and had serviced some of their major accounts with unqualified success. Not that she was unqualified but her rate of success with some of the largest European power companies was unrivalled. She had foreseen their need to head into the future sourcing of power almost before they did and was primed ready to offer insurance coverage of which some of her competitors had never even heard. Renewable energy power sources and windfarm cover, in particular, had earned her superb City bonuses and hers was an income of which even money brokers would have been envious. But, despite being not even forty, Robin felt tired.

Lester, however, was a pushy, surly lad, who had met Robin on a rugby tour when he had badly misjudged a tackle on a flying winger and ended up in an A&E ward at about the same time as

Robin had tripped over a blade of grass on a hockey pitch and broken her leg. They sat together for three hours waiting for x-rays and junior doctors, then spent the rest of the evening in a curry house laughing and drinking, despite their mutual aches and pains.

Two weeks later they moved in together in a small ground floor (because they both had broken legs) apartment in Camden and, except during the working day, had hardly been separated since. Lester was a typically boring compliance accountant, also in the insurance industry, and what he didn't know about the FSA, Lloyds London Market and MIB statistics really wasn't worth knowing. Robin questioned whether any of it was worth knowing either but only when she was trying to perform some magical underwriting deals that had never been conceived by anybody else and were, therefore, suspect, particularly to competitors or fellow specialists who felt threatened by her amazing ability.

Lester's knowledge of compliance law and indirect taxation also put him in a class of his own and he was in great demand, not only from his own employer but from many others too. Thus he also was a receiver of good bonuses and various financial handshakes to ensure that he didn't pack his toys and go to play elsewhere.

Over a relatively short period of time, they both began to earn considerable sums of money and each was so well organised that they decided that they should plan for a future life when they had burned themselves out early. Pensions, ISAs and other Government sponsored arrangements were for the masses but, although the couple had invested wisely therein, Lester and Robin had other ideas too.

Unwilling to put all their eggs in one basket, they had started two distinctly different property portfolios and had acquired several properties which they had successfully let. In the first selection they had bought a small modern block of two bedroom apartments, four in all, in Chafford Hundred, a mere thirty-five minutes from the City but close enough to the sea and countryside to attract good, young tenants.

Their second collection was a group of six, slightly cheaper but much bigger, mock-Tudor semi-detached three bedroom houses on the outskirts of Enfield. These had come from a housing trust, who had been letting to hospital staff from the Middlesex Hospital, but they needed substantial investment and overhaul. They had split the Enfield properties into two categories, the two smaller ones continuing to cater for the more affordable housing needs but four of the properties were restored to desirable housing for up and coming, young families who wanted to give an image of success but couldn't yet afford to. Renting property had become the short-term solution to that. Robin and Lester had been poised ready at the right time.

All of the properties had mortgages on them but they were being paid off rapidly, partly from rental income and also by the regular settlement through additional bonus earnings. Property management companies were looking after the maintenance and upkeep and, much to her embarrassment, Robin had never seen either collection of houses. In fact, for more than two years, neither of the couple had actually done anything in respect of the two operations other than check their bank statements, over the Internet, of course, to see the surplus income. Everything was self-activated and required absolutely no intervention whatsoever.

For themselves, Robin and Lester had gradually outgrown their Camden apartment and bought a split-level maisonette in Islington, which had bored them within six months. They moved out, letting the place to a couple of gay interior designers, who became good friends and, eventually, consultants to Robin and Lester for future property options.

Neither Robin nor Lester could be considered beautiful people to look at but both knew very well how to present themselves for maximum effect. Lester bought his suits and shirts from some of the better known houses in the City and E.T. Lewin welcomed him with open arms whenever he crossed their threshold, which was usually at least once a month. His collection of their produce centred around pinks and greys, which he thought complimented each other well. In his case, however, his blond curly hair needed cutting far more often than he bothered. His eyes were dark brown but positioned slightly too closely together, making people distrust him.

Robin, by contrast, was always immaculate in her total appearance. She was slightly taller than Lester and made no attempt to disguise it. Her hair was always neat, tight and usually up, revealing a pale but perfectly formed neck. Her fair hair exaggerated her blue eyes and she made a point of wearing shaped jackets that accentuated her tidy and attention deserving body.

For relaxing, both chose expensive, designer, casual clothes but always with smartly polished leather shoes. They fitted in well with the more exotic sections of Islington.

But there they had had their first difference of opinion. Robin wanted to live in Docklands so that she could cycle, or even jog, to work. Lester had found an old Elizabethan mansion close to Ingatestone station near Chelmsford, for easy commuting into Liverpool Street station. By the time they had nearly come to a compromise, the old mansion had gone and Docklands was becoming split into different classes of property, which again was a subject of differing views. Lester wanted somewhere quiet with a green parkland surrounding, Robin wanted a riverfront site with open views and activity.

So, by way of a further compromise, they chose a penthouse suite at the top of a converted office block opening out onto Mitre Square, a former City hunting ground of Jack the Ripper. Whilst it was incredibly convenient for both of their offices, it lacked the tranquillity of a weekend retreat. It was after a particularly demanding period around the year end of both of their employers, which lasted for nearly two months from the beginning of December until the end of January, that a couple of their work colleagues - they had few real friends – invited them away for a weekend in Northern France. Not really a booze-cruise but potentially it could have turned into one. Their friends owned an old *fermette* in a small village in the heart of Pas de Calais. Nobody in the village spoke any English and, thus, everybody was forced to speak at least a little French.

At the end of this first weekend, they seem to have relaxed totally, met some amazing French people, tasted some excellent wines and dined in two superb restaurants at about half of the prices that they were paying London, but at a much higher quality.

Afterwards, on the Monday morning, they all left the fermette at about 6.00am and caught an early train from Coquelles direct into St Pancras, arriving at their desks in the City before 09.05am. Everybody had had a really enjoyable weekend and, apart from the odd momentary garlic waft, they all felt a warm, smug glow.

Even their hosts and colleagues had commented on how laid back and relaxed Robin and Lester had become and suggested inviting them to come back again, perhaps for longer next time. The idea appealed considerably and within days they were planning the next trip.

Lester and Robin insisted on footing the whole bill for the next trip and were stunned to discover how much cheaper it turned out to be compared with a weekend in London. And they loved the amazing feeling of space. Instead of putting their watches forward an hour, it was more like putting them back twenty years. After several more trips, a love affair was taking place. Easter arrived and a whole week was planned. Since they were in the north of the country, it was only appropriate to visit some of its history and they all began to understand some of the battles fought there, the costs, the scars and the gains. They visited Agincourt, Vimy Ridge, Crécy, Thiepval, Bapaume and even the Normandy Beaches - Arromanches, (Mulberry Harbour), Omaha, Gold, Juno and, one murky evening, the enormous American Cemetery at Coleville, which made them all cry, especially when a single crack of gunfire was followed by the playing of the Last Post.

They had fallen in love with France.

Chapter 3 – Pressure

Within several months, the original hosts were beginning to feel usurped and even Robin and Lester realised that they were taking over, a trait that was not altogether uncommon in their lives. The four of them enjoyed each other's company but it was becoming difficult for the hosts to relax in their own time, in their own home.

Inevitably, the guests, Robin and Lester, had 'heavied in' and all good things had to come to a close. In fact, the hosts decided to sell up their *fermette* and head further south, especially since they were both thinking of early retirement from the City, being about fifteen years older than Robin and Lester.

This was distressing to the guests, who were used to getting their own way. In fact, they offered to buy their hosts' house to "help them on their way." Lester had used that expression without thinking and had caused instant offence.

"Don't you dare patronise us," snarled the husband. "We came here in 1987, long before the masses of Brits started their second invasion of France. We were pioneers and gained the respect and friendship of the locals. We have made many good friends over here and brought a change to their lives, which they appreciate. We brought them work, an understanding of England, a wish to try to understand and empathise with us and we brought them *entente cordiale*, (loads of whisky). So don't try to buy that – we worked very hard to gain all of that."

Three months later, the snarling husband rang Lester in his office and asked him "How much?"

"150k," came Lester's instant reply.

"Pounds?" came the response

"Yes," was the immediate answer.

"170k – pounds," pushed the husband.

"160 – final offer," said Lester.

"Done," and Robin and Lester were on their way into la belle France.

Chapter 4 – Learning Curve

As soon as they "signed," Robin and Lester found out that they knew nothing whatsoever about running such a house in France. Their hosts had done everything when they were around and now that the guests had become the owners, even fetching croissants from the boulangerie was uncharted waters.

But the new owners were determined. They had never failed at anything in their lives and this would be no exception. French classes became paramount and they even began to spend consecutive weekends in Pas de Calais to help them pick up accents, albeit corrupted deliberately by some of the more adventurous local villagers. In fact, they found the weekend break more fun than when they were guests of the couple who had spoken all of the French for them.

Sure they made a couple of silly mistakes, the worst of which was burning "green" wood which gave off an evil smelling sap and lining the chimney with a highly flammable toxin. Inevitably it caught fire and everybody in the village was present to watch the arrival of the *sapeurs pompiers* (fire brigade) who seemed to spend an awful amount of time shaking hands with people before they turned their attention to the burning chimney. Within minutes, they had brought the blaze under control and then the work started. The number of forms to fill out was unbelievable but not until everybody had consumed at least two or three Ricards. Ricard is a dark coloured drink that stinks of aniseed until you add water, when it goes grey and cloudy, and still stinks of aniseed. Then you add ice. Apart from the smell, it seems harmless enough but about thirty seven minutes after you drink it, it punches you under the chin. It clings to your teeth, your tongue, your clothes and then, when you are not looking, it punches you again.

Then they had to listen to a severe lecturing from the Chief of Police, of which they understood very little. He then consumed three large whiskies before getting Lester and Robin to sign some more papers, and then he drove off into the night.

Then a representative from the *Voix du Nord*, the local newspaper, appeared and asked some very fast questions which the *sapeurs pompiers* answered, with lots of raucous laughter. By now they had switched to whiskies as well and would probably have stayed the night, had not they got an urgent call for another domestic fire. Each firefighter finished his whisky before asking for another, then he prepared to leave. As the fire engine finally backed out recklessly into the road, the driver lent out of the window and handed Robin a piece of paper. As the truck took off with flashing blues and reds and sirens wailing, Robin looked down into his hand and found an invoice for 600 euros, payable within two days before a 10% surcharge would be added.

Unable to determine whether they could re-light the fire or not, Robin and Lester, went to bed to keep warm, even if it was only 7.17 p.m.

In the morning, the house stunk. A green gunge had trickled down the chimney and was spreading across the floor tiles in the lounge. Unsure whether to spray it with foam, WD40 or water, Lester decided to branch out on a first. He decided to go round to his builder, who spoke absolutely no English.

However, his journey was unnecessary since there was already a knocking on the front door and, standing outside, was Masson, the builder. He was skipping from foot to foot, obviously somewhat agitated. As Lester tried to open the front door without unlocking it (life in the City), Masson was giggling. Eventually succeeding, Lester opened the door and shook hands with the builder who, covered in something dirty and greasy, just offered a wrist for Lester to shake. In the other hand, however, was the source of Masson's amusement – the early edition of *la Voix du Nord*, which carried a front page picture of the burning chimney, obviously taken long before the fire had been reported, and a half page picture of Robin and Lester, both with heavily blackened faces.

To add insult to injury, there were six paragraphs of commentary, mostly from other members of the village but there was a comment attributed to Lester.

"Le bois dans la cheminée était trop mouillé et donc j'y ai versé de l'essence pour allumer le feu" ("the wood in the fireplace was too wet, so I poured some petrol over it").

"No I bloody didn't say that and I'll sue that bastard journalist."

Masson understood nothing and chuckled to himself every couple of minutes as he slowly consumed his bottle of beer. By the time that virtually everybody in the village of 257 inhabitants had been round to shake hands, Lester had had enough and had decided that they also would be leaving the village. South, West, East? He didn't care as long as it was "away from here."

Having eventually worked out how to use his home telephone without putting a 9 in front of the number, Lester contacted two English speaking Estate Agents locally and put the house on the market. Working out that the two numbers went through to the same office, because he was speaking to the same person each time, Lester also discovered that the person was actually a woman, who spoke very poor English. So Lester woke up Robin to tell her of his decision and they started to pack their bags, leaving the single Agent to lock up and clear the house.

Lester and Robin went back to their London - and waited.

Chapter 5 – Second stab

Having waited for at least twenty four hours, they got bored and started the inevitable trawl of the Internet. After a respectable period of time, like about twenty minutes, Robin decided to speak to the two gay designers to see if they knew anything about France, and then discovered that the two guys were, in fact, French and had not mentioned it for fear of losing their maisonette.

Within a further twenty minutes, all four were having dinner in Frederic's in Camden and drawing little pictures on serviettes. By midnight, they were booking shuttle crossings, overnight hotels and all sorts of meetings with contacts.

From the hilly South Western region, between Figeac and Cahors, absolutely smothered with good vines, there was an almost black wine that really was exceptional and anybody who tasted it could not fail to recognise it. This was where they had decided would be the perfect place. However, one of the problems would be finding land available, since everybody else seemed to have the same idea. The very existence of so many good vines meant that, although finding somewhere for seclusion should be easy, the ground was already being used and nobody gives up a good vine, except for money. Lots of it.

So, two days later, a grey four-wheel drive Mazda CX-7 MZR DIZI Turbo growled its way onto the perfect site for the construction of the house of their dreams, particularly with the help of designer Jean-Luc, who knew more about French house construction than all of the Barratt Housing engineers in England all put together.

Lunch would normally have been first priority but, much to the chagrin of the two Frenchmen, Lester decided to push on and visit a couple of the sites that seemed to have potential. By the time they had found both but were unable to do anything because the rest of France was at lunch, Lester finally conceded and the four of them sought a quick snack, which, equally, failed to endear him to anybody.

Chapter 6 – How to offend without really trying

Thus, the afternoon started badly. Everybody had an attitude, each caused by Lester.

The first site was to the west of Figeac, a small village called Boussac. The area was secluded in that the only properties nearby skirted the main road, D802, which was hardly the most attractive route and carried too much traffic for its size. However the land on which they had focused was high enough to look down on the River Drazou, yet sheltered by trees, which protected it from the road about a kilometre away. The only issue was a small village street called Rue Châteaubriand close-by which Lester thought was too "plebian by half." That would have been their address by the time the house had been built and he just found it annoyingly laughable. Nobody agreed with or understood him.

So they moved on to the second site, which was further up in the hills on the outskirts of a small village called Assier. Lester had almost wet himself before they even reached the place, believing it to sound too similar to a name he had been called since he was a small boy. Nobody else could see the funny side of this and they didn't even bother to go to the agreed meeting place with the local agent.

The third site had a name that tickled his fancy, Théminettes. Being a fan of Phil Spectre, this had appealed to Lester's puerile sense of humour. But, by virtue of ignorance and stubbornness, he took a wrong turning and, much to everyone's surprise, stopped suddenly and had to get out of the car as he fell about laughing. Who in their right mind could possibly call a village Les Scapvals?

Lester wanted to find somewhere here but Robin finally put her foot down and shrieked, "You've had your say now. You've screwed up everybody's day. Now grow up and listen to someone who knows what they're talking about!" and stormed off back to the car, got in the driver's seat and started up the engine. She roared over to the three men, being ultra-polite and pleasant to the two Frenchmen, and told Lester that if "you really want to come with us, get your ass into the car now and don't you dare speak again until I give you permission. In – sit – don't!"

The car took off in a cloud of dust, scattering wildlife and shrapnel. By the time they got back to the large car park in Figeac where the petanque matches were held, everybody felt car sick, including the driver.

This was not a good basis from which to start. Robin was still steaming angry with Lester and slammed the car into reverse. As she hurtled backwards to turn the car round, she failed to notice a large hole in the ground next to her and the left side front wheel dropped about a foot into it. That side of the front of the car not only followed the wheel into the hole but jolted the complete vehicle. Robin's head was thrown to one side and she bit her tongue. Now there is biting a tongue and biting a tongue.

On this occasion, Robin bit into her own tongue and almost severed it. The screams and the blood that followed were probably fully justified but Lester couldn't quite see that.

"Oh, for Christ's sake woman – it's only a little cut."

Wrong! It was terminal – not for her but for him. Even the two Frenchmen winced as she spun round towards Lester and poked her finger in his eye.

The day was not going well.

Chapter 7 – Redeeming oneself

Lester needed to win some points back and spotted on his Michelin map one of those "panoramic view" points that looked like a blue sun rise, to the east of Figeac on a small road, the D994, that appeared to have a couple of steep hills in it.

At that very view point was a spectacular house. It was old, stone, walled, gated, beautiful and in need of much tender love and care. It took everybody's breath away. They all thought it was truly magnificent and had vast potential. Best of all, it carried an old and shabby "À vendre" sign hanging off one wire, with the name and telephone number of an agent notaire on it. The potential was enormous.

Robin could see its high, secluded position would be even more breathtaking when all of the land around was tidy, green, plush and perfect for breeding ostriches.

Jean-Luc was far more oriented for turning it into an art school where people could stay for fifteen days and learn how to express themselves in paint with a true hands-on experience.

His partner, Didier, could picture its perfect restoration into a centre for teaching haute cuisine with some of the best ingredients available from the land; delicate herbs, fine wines, especially the dark wines of Cahors, ingredients perfect for some of the best sauces in France, in the world.

Lester was a dick-head. He wanted to demolish it and build a modern, efficient mansion with up to date features including a central tower that looked as though the architect had, by mistake, left his coffee cup on the plans and a round turret was built on the mark left behind.

"Merde," responded the two Frenchmen. "Shit," said Robin. Lester had instantly lost any points he may have recovered by finding the place.

In true fashion, nobody spoke for ten minutes, then Robin, Didier and Jean-Luc started talking all at once and even pulled out pieces of paper that caused them much grief in the wind that had sprung up. But they were drawing similar pictures and having almost identical ideas. Lester sulked like a small child, because nobody liked his idea. At all.

Whilst the three creative members got together, Lester sat in the car playing like a moaning seven year old and read, for the fifth time, the Times 2 supplement for Thursday 27th September 2007, which had been lying in the car for months. Suddenly his face burst into a beam and he grasped a page which read "The hotspots – and consequent cold spots – that occur in microwave ovens. It appeared that the wavelength of microwaves are the reason why ants can survive unscathed and uncooked inside a switched-on oven. They immediately scurry to the cooler areas and ride out the microwave storm." He read it three times and recalled his evil days as a child when he had often experimented on creatures less fortunate than himself – like his pet mouse, his mother's cats and even his younger sister. All had survived but certainly not due to him. Now here was another opportunity to have some more fun.

Lester finally left the car, mainly because it was beginning to become hot and sticky without the engine and climatisation running anyway, and rejoined Robin and their friends. They were slightly surprised to see him and even more surprised when he started to join in the discussions, without insisting that the place be demolished and rebuilt.

Perhaps Lester was going to be a good guy after all.

After about twenty minutes of conversation, it was Lester who finally said, "Well let's go and find this notaire chappie and see what the asking price is. I'm sure we have enough experience here amongst us to come up with an offer."

Chapter 8 – Making an offer

M. Christophe, the notaire, had a small, bedraggled office in Capdenac, which looked, from the street, as though it dealt in piles of paper with pink ribbons tied around them. At first glance, nothing had ever been filed. The receptionist was a pretty little thing with a disturbing twitch in one eye and a nervous sniff. Robin wanted to hand her a tissue but Lester tried to flirt with her in what little French he had.

Jean-Luc stepped tactfully in between and took over in French. Despite being gay, he also found her very pretty and felt sorry for what Lester was about to do to her. In his opinion, Lester was about to throw all sorts of questions in rapid succession at the poor girl, rendering her confused and probably more likely to start sniffing in earnest.

"Bonjour, ma'amoiselle, nous voyons que vous réprésentez les vendeurs d'une vielle maison, mal réparée près de la route de Sonnac."

Didier translated for the benefit of Robin and Lester, "Good day, young lady. We see that you are agent for the sale of an old, run-down house on the road from Sonnac." Nothing like making one's intentions clear – the price was going to be negotiable in their eyes.

"Nous voudrions connaître touts les détails de la maison...... même un prix â débattre pour commencer......" but he was interrupted by the door to the outer office being opened and a most unlikely looking, eccentric character striding in, hand of peace extended. His suit was expensive but creased, his shirt striped and loud, his bow tie skewed but properly tied and the silk handkerchief hanging out of his top pocket appeared to have been used to clean his brogue black leather shoes.

"Bonjour, messieurs/dame," came the confident voice, with an equally confident hand shake that made Lester's shoulder hurt before it stopped. "I am Daniel Christophe, ze biggest notaire around 'ere and I 'ave control over most of ze properties zat are for sale. The property you are interested in.............."

"Might be interested in," interrupted Lester, "we don't know the price yet."

"Ah, monsieur, ze price will not be a problème, it never eez wiz me."

Already, Lester disliked the guy but he had to stay sweet to ensure they got the property for a good price. Ironically, Christophe had exactly the same views about Lester but each knew that they could not afford to let it show, yet.

Christophe found the papers for the property instantly and they were able to ascertain that the place had belonged to an ex-mayor of the village, which seemed sort of appropriate in view of its size. It was a four bedroomed house but only one had ever been used thus. There were two reception rooms and outside facilities. There were also several outbuildings capable of conversion. A tremendous amount of work had to be done before it was habitable, let alone be able to take new owners and guests.

The house had been left to the single, maiden daughter of the ex-mayor when he died three years earlier but she was in a home for people of mental instability to where she had been condemned about a year after the death of her father but not before she had given Christophe the Power of Attorney to dispose of her assets when the time came. The property had undergone a formal valuation upon the death of the ex-mayor and the government valuer had deemed it to be worth about sixty Milliards, which seemed exciting to Robin but Jean-Luc, Didier and Lester expected to reduce it.

"Oh, we were not thinking about paying that much," said Lester instinctively, when Christophe put the figure on the table. "In view of the time it has been unoccupied and the potential damage that can cause, we were thinking more like fifty-four."

Didier coughed and Jean-Luc's eyes rolled heaven bound.

"Cinquante-neuf – fifty-nine," responded Christophe immediately.

Didier cleared his throat and Jean-Luc stood up, as though to leave. He looked at Robin and, with his eyes, implored her to intervene. Robin sat there with her mouth open and started to regain her control but not before Lester had replied "Cinquante-sept et demi – c'est ça," and stood up offering his hand to Christophe, who snatched it before anybody could interrupt.

"We know absolutely nothing about the house," she shrieked at Lester. "How can you be so stupid? Does it have power? Water? What state of repair is it in? Sometimes, for an intelligent man, you can be so bloody stupid. Who's buying this? What's the law about buying a "second" house over here? How are we going to pay for it? What would a surveyor say about it? What the hell have you done? Can we get out of this? What happens if we can't raise finance? Who do we get to represent us in this? How long does it take to complete? What other costs are involved? Sometimes you are so bloody pig-ignorant. Just what have you bloody done?"

Lester could tell that Robin was not happy. Didier and Jean-Luc were standing shaking their heads and getting ready to leave. Christophe had a silly smile on his face, was rubbing his hands and looked as pleased as punch. The ten percent deposit would cover the outstanding fees he was owed and had been owed for years. Without hesitation, he pulled a worn, bedraggled receipt book from the draw of the receptionist's desk and again rubbed his hands with glee. He had been hoping to stretch negotiations on the price to achieve an unlikely fifty milliards but, in France, a deal is a deal. He was even beginning to think of that holiday on Corsica he had been dreaming about for many years. Perhaps the silly Englishman didn't realise that the price did not yet include stamp duty, taxes, his fees and that was long before the costs involved in restoring the property to its former glory.

"We take Carte Bleu for ze deposit and I shall give you a receipt which will be binding." Christophe even patted his receptionist gently on the backside as she walked around the table to take Lester's Visa card and her sniff had gone. The twitch in her eye was now a deliberate wink, which she seemed to aim at all of the men, except Lester. She knew she was going to be paid on time this month.

Chapter 9 – I wouldn't be in your shoes

Walking out of the office of M. Christophe seemed to be easy enough for Lester but he had the distinct feeling that those following him were playing on a different team. The growling and snarling from Robin almost sounded as though she were humming in grief but the silence from Didier and Jean-Luc was painfully loud. Perhaps he should just run and leave.

When they finally reached and climbed up into the car, the atmosphere was rancid.

Lester decided that the best move was to find a reasonable bar and toast their good fortune with champagne. Didier and Jean-Luc decided that they would sooner be back in London and Robin was resolute – Lester was as good as dead. The silence lasted about twenty seconds and then Robin exploded.

"How dare you! Once again you thought only of yourself. You made a decision without thinking of anyone else, the people who knew far better than you. You made a complete idiot of me; worse than that, you embarrassed our friends here but, even more pertinent, you thought only of Mr I am. Mr.Big. Mr.Knowitfuckingall. Well let me tell you – you know nothing. You are about as worldly wise as a dead goldfish. You have committed us to something about which you understand absolutely bugger-all. I thought, for a moment, that I knew and understood you. I thought you were a man of reasonable intelligence. I even thought you were clever. For just a moment, I even thought I fancied you. But then I woke up. Now I know you to be a complete and utter imbecile. A prat. You are a useless and dangerous waste of space."

The Frenchmen jumped out of the car before the blood-letting started.

"Ha!" came the response. "Who negotiated a deal, then? Sixty thousand quid was far too much for that pile of poo and I got the price down, just like that. What did anybody else do?"

"Price down? Price down? You're off your bloody head! We could have got that place for less than fifty thousand but, no, Mr Busy knew best! Sometimes you are so stupid that it doesn't bear thinking about. Now, before you get any older, I want you to apologise to Didier and Jean-Luc, I want you to go and find us all an hotel and I want you to talk to London and arrange some finance for this deal you've got us into. Then I want you to go away out of my sight until I can stand being in the same hemisphere as you. Comprendez?" And then she leapt out of the car as well.

Lester, for all he was strong, couldn't handle this, got out and wandered round to Robin's side of the car and put his arms round her. She shook herself free and pushed him, but gently. He exaggerated her push and stumbled in the direction of the two Frenchmen. "Je suis désolé," he said, expressing his sorrow.

Neither of them believed him but at least he was talking to them. "Look, Guys," he said. "It's seems as though I may have screwed up a bit there and for that I am sorry. But now I'm begging you. The house is ours, or will be soon, and what we want to do is to implement a complete plan for the total re-design and fitting out of this, and we wonder whether you two guys might be interested in managing the project? You obviously have the talent for it, and, of course, the language. We would, of course, pay you the going rate but it could be a project for years. And it would be in your home country."

Silence reigned. The two men looked at each other and shrugged their shoulders in the way that only the French can do. "You look, Mister Beeg. We consider zis plan but we need to know much before we start leaving England. We love your England and its attitude towards us and our kind. We do not want to come back to France where zere is prejudice against les noires, les juifs et les PDs. But we like your lady and she is good wizz us. Get ze deal done and we will consider it serious. Now we eat, yes?"

"Yes," said Lester, "we eat." And with that he turned back to Robin and said, "OK. OK. I give in – I was badly wrong but can we now discuss this over dinner – all four of us. Jean-Luc and Didier will seriously consider leading the project for us, with your blessing, of course."

Robin nearly smiled – she had won, again.

Chapter 10 – Project – Phase 1

Dinner was superb. They drove south west to Les Mas des Vignes, a small town they had heard about from someone who knew the region well and found a restaurant that people came to from miles away. The town had a festive air with sports, music, dancing and competitions and everybody was outside. Hot, sunny, blue-sky happiness radiated everywhere and the setting was perfect to forgive, if not forget. By the time they had had a drink or two, a dance, a few more drinks and then a dinner prepared mostly on the restaurant's barbecue, everybody felt better and the whole idea of the house was just great. Only Jean-Luc was able to stand up and drive but he did not have a licence so his sole remaining job for the evening was to find them some accommodation.

Luck was on their side because he knew of a "Chambres d'hôte" just outside the town and they had two double rooms available. They were able to walk there, after a fashion, and when they arrived, it was still barely daylight and there was a swimming pool calling them. Being totally unprepared for such a facility was not an issue. They all ripped their clothes off and dived in naked. It was the end of an amazing day and, sitting around the pool afterwards, they were able to relax and listen to the sounds of nature all around them whilst sipping Calvados apple brandy with ice.

The next morning they all gathered round the pool, fully dressed, to discuss a plan, which started with croissants and coffee and finished with going out to buy a replacement camera for the one they had lost the night before. Heads were a little sore and it was only after they all gathered ready to pay up and leave that they realised that they had no idea where the car was. Finally it was Christian, who owned the establishment with his wife, Odille, who reminded them that they had come singing and dancing naked into the pool last night, although they were dressed when they came skipping down the road from town. Ah, yes, it was all coming back slowly.

They wandered back into town, remembering nothing of the way, and then discovered the debris that everybody else had left last night too. By the time they had had their second coffee, first Calvados and a glass of chilled tomato juice, with salt, pepper and Worcestershire sauce but excluding the raw egg and vodka, they all felt slightly better, apart from Jean-Luc, who had not been drinking – so that was his own fault, they all said. Of course, they didn't find the car but did find one of the bars they had visited during the evening and that's where they eventually found the car, in the back yard of the café.

None of them could get it out of the yard, which meant that the fact it wasn't scratched from the night before was a miracle. Eventually the owner of the bar got the car out, as he had put it in there the night before but they didn't need to know that, because they were only another bunch of visiting drunks the night before.

Joking, laughing and waving, they drove off back towards the house they had seen and bought and decided to plan the extent to which it needed refurbishment. Robin was all for going to Christophe to get the key but the two Frenchman were adamant that they would not need a key. They were, of course, correct as the back door, not visible from the road, was hanging off its hinges. Access was instant and there was no need to force anything.

As they walked in, they were hit instantly by the musty smell and how covered in cobwebs was the interior. The windows in each room, consisted of six different panes – all opening inwards, as they do, and with a family of spiders resident on each pane. The floors were covered in both old, damp linoleum and ants. In fact there were more ants than the marching armies sketched in some of the old Disney cartoon strips. Lester smiled to himself. The appearance of a rat in one of the rooms changed the minds of everyone, but it was only small and may actually have been a field mouse. Townies really don't have a clue about these things.

Wandering from room to room, they were greeted with new features that caused even more dismay, including bulging walls, wallpaper from as many rolls as there were strips, pieces of string that served as door handles and window catches, bundles of rags on the ground that looked as though they had been used to house nests of small armies of insects and burned out candles in saucers. One room contained all of the furniture, a small wooden chair with two and a half legs and a butler sink standing on a couple of bricks.

Some of the windows had wooden shutters closed on them but most of those had fallen apart. Gutters hung down, tiles on the roof had broken, holes in the ceilings let in both water and draughts. Lights were in short supply, which was academic because the electricity supply had been cut. Some rooms had to be photographed so that the flashlight on the camera revealed the secrets within. A large fridge-freezer had the top door missing, which was just as well, otherwise the birds would not have been able to get into the nest that was left inside it. There were oak beams in every room, some painted white, some wallpapered with wood-effect paper and some covered in plaster to give a smooth, truly square image.

Floor tiles were a mixture of colours and sizes and the pools of condensation settled in them leaving an odorous stain that looked like something else. Doors between rooms – there were no corridors – one walked from one room direct into the next – had obviously been designed to fit any doorway except the ones in which they had been hung. Steps between some rooms differed in both height and angle. A single table tennis ball was rolling around the floor, unable to find any level surface on which to come to rest.

M. Christophe had obviously been earning whatever fee he had been charging for maintaining the house under totally false pretences.

But everybody could see potential. The house was an enormous challenge but was large enough and full of so much character to become a project with which anybody with even the smallest level of creativity could have become overwhelmed with excitement. All it needed was time and money, and a plan.

Robin, Jean-Luc and Didier were in ecstasy. Lester, however, was already making notes and adding up columns of figures. Once an accountant, always an accountant. His telephone fingers were twitching, just as soon as he could raise a signal. One thing he was good at was raising funds.

Chapter 11 – Project – Phase 2

The three creators had, within a couple of days, drawn up some preliminary plans that had no material demolition, no coffee cup stains that would become towers and no hope of ever being passed until they completed on the property and submitted plans to the small local planning committee. Now nobody says it is mandatory to roll each sheet of the submitted plans around a twelve year old bottle of Chivas Regal but it can't do any harm.

Two days later, Lester and Robin appeared on the doorstep of the notaire, M. Christophe, at 08.30 precisely. They had hung on for an extra day deliberately and were now about to hand over a banker's draft for the equivalent of about £57,000 in euros and take possession of the keys and a yellow-topped recycling bin as well as the house that was going to become their "Project" for the foreseeable future.

Later that day, having signed each page of an incredibly long contract that was entirely in French, Robin and Lester became proud owners of a house with a beautiful view; lousy house but a truly beautiful view.

Didier and Jean-Luc had flown back to London to pick up a change of clothing and some tools and had returned and were now waiting at the airport in Balsac, an airport in the middle of nowhere, but close to Figeac, that was used conveniently by a certain large, no-frills Irish airline.

Having been whistled back to the house, their objectives were explained to them clearly. Set the ball rolling, make sure that local employees were both being used and turning up on time, ensure that the job was being done properly and have it ready for full occupation in three months. There was a cap on the budget but any material potential cost over-run was to be brought up immediately and a decision would be made on viability within 24 hours.

Being French made a tremendous difference and, not only was the job finished in just over two months but the cost savings were considerable and the end product was immaculate. The two happy, but exhausted, Frenchmen were allowed to take the next month off, before they returned to work on two of the Enfield properties which were being sought by new tenants.

Everybody was happy but Lester wanted to stay on. He had been quietly working on one of the outbuildings, which he had been converting into his own little Dad's Den. Apart from some electrical and plumbing work, he had been left alone to work entirely on his own and had been very happy. The Den had become more of a self-contained luxury pig-sty into which he could disappear for days on end without disturbance.

The main house was now absolutely splendid with its own swimming pool, partly within, partly without, patios, gardens and outbuildings, beautifully finished and furnished throughout, and fit for a King (or a Queen).

Robin and Lester came back and planned to stay for a month. They really loved it and would have liked to show it off to their friends with whom they had first discovered France. But that was not to be – the friends had moved on and apparently disappeared.

Robin was keen to sow the seeds of a garden, of which there was plenty. For the first week, she hardly stopped, spending between eight and ten hours a day in the massive garden. Lester, by comparison, worked indoors in his den and, sometimes, it would seem like days that he spent locked away on his own. Eventually Robin began to get angry because Lester seemed to be up to his old tricks again and avoiding his responsibility towards her.

So, one late afternoon, she stormed down the garden to the outbuilding and found it bare. There was no sign of Lester. In fact there was very little there. A few sticks of furniture but not very much else. A few pieces of kitchen equipment, like a few plastic dishes, some cups, a kettle, a microwave oven and a couple of bottles of wine and some glasses. Wherever he was, he needed to come back in a hurry and explain what he had been up to.

She had been there for about three minutes, hands on her hips, fuming, when the door opened and made her jump. It wasn't Lester but a young lad from the village whom she had seen around several times before.

"Oui, qu'est-ce qu'il y a," she asked him, not expecting an answer. Even more unexpected was the boy's reaction. He shrieked and dropped the plastic box he had been carrying and ran. Instinctively, Robin chased him but he was too fast and had a head start. By the time she got back to the kitchen, the plastic box he had dropped had gone. She was sure he had dropped it on the kitchen floor and bent down on her hands and knees to look under kitchen units to see if there were any traces.

What she saw made her scream and jump up startled.

Chapter 12 – What is happening?

As she stood up, Robin felt dizzy. She could feel her head spinning and her blood pressure surging. "Didier, Jean-Luc," she screamed, but neither was close enough to hear. She was alone and would have to handle this herself. She was trembling, shaking, shivering and terrified. Her instinct was to run but she was Robin and was made of stronger stuff. But facing what she had seen was not going to be easy on her own.

Again she shrieked for help but, again, nobody heard. So, braving the unknown, she knelt down again and peered nervously under the kitchen unit. There were a collection of goodies there, two of which were the trainers that Lester had bought without her approval a month or so back.

Much more disturbing though, was the fact that when she had bent over, the two enormous locust like creatures that she had seen there before were now missing. They seemed to be about six to eight inches long and angry, very angry. But now they were missing, as was the box that the lad had dropped. Robin screamed again, just in case someone was listening.

She thought more and more about the two creatures she had glimpsed and came to the conclusion that they were alien but familiar. Whatever they were, they had to be somewhere, so, arming herself with a strong broom, she re-composed herself and set off on the hunt. The outhouse had three rooms and she had started in the kitchen. As she stalked her way around this first room, she looked behind things, under things, over things but found nothing else. With trepidation, she started to open things – first cupboard doors, then drawers, then, much less confidently, boxes, tins, kit bags. God, the place was untidy, was a mess. But, apparently, that is what men do.

The next room was not so tidy. It was covered in tools and bits of unfinished flat-pack self-assembly parts. Sawdust, dirty coffee mugs and general rubbish abounded, but still no trace of any infiltrators. After about four or five minutes of picking things up delicately and dropping them in disgust, Robin decided that this room was also going to reveal nothing.

The third room was a sort of conservatory or lean-to that would have made a good facilities room. There were five tubular tables with work-tops and underneath were even more boxes, but these were all neatly stacked and labelled, albeit with only numbers. Suddenly it dawned on Robin that the five table tops were covered in nothing other than microwave ovens, one on each. This was even more peculiar because she thought she remembered seeing one in the kitchen too.

Without hesitating, she spun round and strode out back into the kitchen and over to the microwave. As she yanked open the door, she let out the most penetrating scream that anybody could ever have released as, staring at her from inside were probably about twenty enormous ants. Each was about six or so inches long, about two inches high and stationary. They all stared at her as though dead, then suddenly one of them jumped at her with a blood-curdling, venomous snarl.

She froze for a split second, with her hair standing physically on end and her skin shrinking instantly with cold. She screamed instinctively and lashed out with a right back-hand as she tried to sweep the creature away from her. The futility of her action was instantly seen as others of the ants started to run across the kitchen table towards her. She still had the broom in her left hand and tried to fend off the beasts as they attacked. She smacked them down, she kicked out, she fought valiantly but they were big, strong, ugly and very angry. They were all looming at her across the work surfaces and her whole body cringed with fear and anger. As she brought the broom down on about three of them, she heard the crack and the crunch of bones, and, with a groan, the three giant ants went down.

The door behind her burst open and Jean-Luc stood there, mesmerised and frozen as he saw what was happening. All he had with him to help was a piece of paper with a plan on it. Realising how inept this would be, he picked up Robin and dragged her out of the door, slamming it behind them as they fled. He beat off her the few remaining ants, stamping on them as he did so.

She hugged and clung to him, sobbing and snivelling with shock, until he carried her like a small child in his arms across to the main house. As they got there, they could hear a sound behind them, like a marching army. They turned to see a long line of the monster ants heading away from them, across the grounds towards the outhouse. The two of them realised that this was far more serious than they could handle.

Robin struggled and fought herself free from Jean-Luc, angry, frightened, but very, very bitter. This time, Lester had surpassed himself.

"Where's Didier?" she barked.

Jean-Luc turned towards the main house just as Didier appeared from the front door. "Mon Dieu!" said Didier, as he heard and saw the ant army trooping towards the outhouse. Robin pulled them all together and screamed, "We've got to get out of here – now. Didier, get the laptop. Jean-Luc, get my briefcase from the study and I'll bring the car round to the front. We're out of here." Robin had got her priorities right.

As the wheels spun and the car snaked its way down the driveway with gravel flying in every direction, everyone was looking forward. Nobody looked back. Robin drove possessed. As she reached the first junction on the main road, she leaned on the hooter and blasted her way through the first give way sign, without any easing of the pedals. She headed in no specific direction – just needed to get out of there. The panic drive took them back to Les Mas des Vignes and she roared up the driveway to the house where they had stayed before.

Jean-Luc tried to explain how their new house wasn't quite fit for purpose yet and *le patron* had gone back to England to arrange some more finance. It was a good excuse and would have been plausible, had not Lester walked out of the dining room as Jean-Luc was stuttering his way through it.

"Bastard!" shrieked Robin. "What the hell are you doing here?"

"I might ask the same of you," replied Lester but realised, as he set off down that metaphorical path, that he had taken a wrong turning. Robin punched him on the ear with clenched fist and he went down groaning. "And this is for Didier and Jean-Luc," she added, putting the boot in rather harder than might have been necessary. "What the hell have you been up to?"

From his prone position, lying down on the ground, Lester mumbled and sounded as though he was gargling.

"I can't hear you," blasted Robin, "What's the matter?"

"I tzink you are standing on 'is zroat, Madame," said Didier, just a little concerned, more for his next paycheck rather than for his master's throat.

Robin jumped off by offering as much downward launching push as possible without wishing to appear too heavy handed (or booted) and Lester lay there, clutching his throat and trying not to look too distraught, but not terribly successfully. He was now sitting on the ground, with blood coming out of one ear and a split lip. His kidneys were bruised and he looked grey with pain.

"So just what the hell *have* you been up to?" came Robin's second wave.

"Well, I've got to be honest," said Lester, "I really don't know. It was the fault of that stupid newspaper article in the Times. I only did it for a joke but it backfired. The bloody ants were too clever. Not only did they hide from the microwaves but they fought back. They grew bigger and their skins got harder. Eventually they started to take over. They started to attack other insects and then bigger things. Eventually I saw them get a rat. They just attacked it by backing it into a corner and then they savaged it. It was horrible. They seemed to develop a mind of their own both in attack and defence."

"Shut up, for Christ's sake." Robin had responded. "I bloody know all about that – they just attacked me, cretin! You started it. Now you've got to finish it. First thing tomorrow, you go back to the house and you get them all out. I don't care what you have to put down to get rid of them but they've just got to. Call in the rat-catcher or whatever – they have to go." She stormed out of the room and went up stairs to the only room available to them that night. She chose to sleep in the same room as Didier and Jean-Luc, rather than with Lester. Only she appeared to be happy with that arrangement although both Didier and Jean-Luc put up only a very speculative argument. Lester wasn't a hundred per cent sure that they were a hundred per cent gay but he had no say in the matter.

Robin had never slept with two men at the same time before and this particular night was just an extension of that – she slept very little, lying between the two of them waiting lest one of them should change his mind and touch her. She had less than five minutes to wait but couldn't honestly remember which of them was first. Apart from that, she had an amazing night to remember, but nobody mentioned anything about it at all the next morning.

Lester slunk off with his tail between his legs by taking a cab at about 7.30am and promised that he would have it all sorted by lunchtime.

Chapter 13 – What now?

After a giggling breakfast amongst the three of them, with lots of hand-touching, girlish shrieks and winks, Robin and her two "boys" had had sufficient to eat and drink, so Robin settled up the account and they adjourned back to their room to prepare for their trip back to the house.

Breakfast must have been just a warm up for them, because, by the time they got back to their room to prepare to leave, each was distracted and one step forward and three back seemed to be the order of the day. Robin relaxed and enjoyed the company of her new 'best buddies' and they had come to a tacit agreement with her, in that she was the Boss and whatever she wanted, she got.

And they all enjoyed it. After about two hours, nothing had been prepared for the departure and, in fact, all three of them were rolling about naked in the bed again oblivious of their need to get back to the house. It was only the arrival of a chambermaid that brought them down to land, although Jean-Luc did have the nerve to ask the girl if she was really very, very busy?

She shrieked and ran away, which brought a sense of reality back to the roost and all three climbed into a communal shower to cool down. That also failed and finally Robin had to admit that this would not do and they needed to get over to the house to ensure that the property was still standing, as should have been Lester.

So, now only partially full of mischief, the three skipped back to the car and shot off back to the house. When they arrived, nothing seemed to have changed from when they were there last.

They unlocked the security gate and drove carefully towards the main body of the house, calling out Lester's name as they approached. There was no response and no obvious sign of life. By the time they reached the front door, there was still no reply and they started to make loud and exaggerated calling sounds to attract Lester's attention.

Still nothing, so they drove straight past the house and headed off into the direction of the outbuildings, especially any that may have been used by Lester. Despite further loud calling, there was no response and the three were becoming slightly nervous. Robin was now wearing her sensible head and she started to take control of the situation.

She got slowly out of the car, leaving the two now not-so-brave boys behind and advanced towards the front door of Lester's den. Looking intently all around her, she was surprised to see no evidence of Lester or his tools and assumed that everything was inside, including her man. Although it felt strange, she knocked gingerly on the door and called out his name. After waiting a second or two she slowly turned the door handle and discovered it was locked.

Damn – where was he? He was supposed to have come back and tackled the issue of the ants. If he was shirking or avoiding the issue, she would kill him.

Calling out his name again, she stomped over to another of the buildings and ripped open the door. With a groaning gasp, she covered her mouth as the sight that greeted her and made her turn instantly green. The building was full of ants, running in every direction with the whole floor just being a writhing mass of rising and falling ants. It was as though the floor was covered in liquid, a rising, falling dark pool of water that made a rustling noise and a droning sound, not dissimilar to grass-hoppers. There were thousands and thousands of them – all normal size but, in total, a rolling, waving mass.

Robin shrieked and slammed the door shut. She stood outside still clutching her mouth and trembling. She needed desperately to find Lester, because whatever he had done was now getting out of control. Perhaps it already was. Without hesitation, she ran back to Lester's den and tried to peer through the windows. But the curtains had all been drawn. What curtains? She knew that there had been no curtains, so how had they appeared without her knowing. She ran round to the back of the building screeching at Jean-Luc and Didier to come with her. They sat there in the car, not moving.

She screeched again and ordered them to follow her. There was no response. They sat there open mouthed, totally still. In a screaming rage, she now abandoned her visit to the back of the den and ran back to the car to yank the doors open.

"Get out of there and come and help me – now!" she shouted, the nocturnal activities totally dismissed. "I don't care what you get but come with anything. Get armed." They sat there looking at her and did not move a muscle. They were petrified – even to the extent that the colour had drained totally from their faces.

Robin dragged the two white faced cadavers out of the car and shoved them in the general direction of the tool shed that she knew contained very few tools – perhaps a spade and a fork, which could do for a start. The 'boys' were certainly not designed for this sort of activity and tip-toed towards the shed. With finger-tipped delicacy, they gently pulled the shed door open and sighed with relief as only the odd tool could be seen inside. Robin leant across them and snatched the fork and spade and thrust them into their hands.

"Take those over to the back entrance to Lester's den and I'll meet you there." Whilst they pranced terrified around the back of the den, Robin charged off to the garage where she knew there was a can of petrol for use with the lawn mower that had been left behind. When she finally reached the back door of the den, it was open but the two 'boys' were still standing outside, clutching their weaponry and shaking from head to foot.

"Come on, you creeps, follow me!" she shouted and they were only too pleased to let her go first. She charged in to the back room and stopped. Behind the closed door facing her, she could hear the sound of marching army boots, as though a whole platoon was on squad bashing manoeuvres. The two 'boys' dropped their tools and fled. Robin, however, was made of stronger stuff and, grabbing the spade, prised open the door in front of her. She stopped in her tracks and let out a blood-curdling scream as the sight that met her eyes was horrific. The large, thick skinned ants were present in thousands and they were marching over the outline shape of a man's body that was lying on the ground.

She couldn't identify the body because it was so covered in the giant ants that there was no flesh visible. In fact, she spotted that there was no flesh anyway. The ants had chewed through the clothes of whoever was lying on the floor and were deeply into the flesh behind it. Robin was no longer able to scream. She was so horrified that all she could do was throw up and the ants all stopped what they were doing and turned round to look at her.

Suddenly, she could scream again and run. She turned and fled, out through the door that was trying to shut behind her, helped by waves of intelligent ants that were trying to cut her off. Robin herself was now panic stricken and didn't have a clue what to do next. Ants had already swarmed round behind her and all she could do was trample on them in her forlorn attempt to escape. She was surrounded and feeling isolated. The car engine outside burst into life and, with relief, she worked out that her 'boys' were mounting a rescue attempt. And then she heard the wheelspin and the acceleration. The bastards were fleeing without her.

She screamed and turned towards the back door, which she knew was open. But as she turned she heard it slam shut and the ants between her and the door swarmed up into the rising figure of a warrior, a man some six-foot six inches in height, built with rippling muscles but still made completely with ants. Robin froze. She was powerless and the ants knew it. The warrior figure disintegrated and the ants jumped, first on her face, then on her bare arms. As they bit, she could hear their teeth crunching into her skin. She felt nothing, other than total, paralysing fear. She writhed and tried to beat them off, hitting, brushing and shaking her limbs, all to no avail. She could feel them gradually overpowering her but she was still stronger than that. She smacked them, she crunched them and then she remembered she had gone for the petrol. In her pocket, she had a gas fire lighter, which she grasped firmly and hauled out of her pocket already lit.

It was a slow process but as she burnt the first ant, she could feel those around the injured ant retreating. Gradually, taking care not to burn herself, she cleared a path off her arm and the ants started to fall to the ground, to retreat, to step away. Before the gas from the lighter ran out, she had cleared such a path that the others received messages from their colleagues and left in a hurry. Eventually, she was free of them and was able to make her way to the door, through which she jumped and stood outside the building brushing off the remaining few ants.

But she knew better than to stand there and ran towards the gateway. With a rapid release of the security code, she was able to flee and shut the gates after her, which probably would not have made much difference had the ants been that determined.

As she stood up straight outside the walled perimeter, she looked back and saw that the car, with her two 'boys' inside, was still in the grounds and that the army of ants was beginning to march towards it. They had not deserted her after all – perhaps they had acted as a decoy or merely distracted the ants from her. She screamed at them and for once they heard her and started to drive towards the gates. She opened the gates from outside and was able to watch the car come roaring down the road towards her. As it swung through the gates, she shut them and was almost able, through fear, to jump into the rear seat of the car at high speed.

They headed straight back to Les Mas en Vignes but to stay in separate rooms. They needed their sleep and rest to work out a plan for the next day.

Chapter 14 – Sealing the Fates

As the dawn broke, Robin woke up realising that she had been scratching herself all night and had drawn blood. She stared at the mess and sat on her bed trying to piece together all that had been happening to her. She thought back to the plans, the action, her life, her career. She was not unattractive, reasonably wealthy, a strong-minded person who usually got what she wanted. Her life had been good and kind to her and she had enjoyed everything that she had done. Being strong-minded and independent was not so wrong, surely. Since she had met Lester, she had expanded her horizons. The more she thought about that, the more she pondered with decreasing confidence. Perhaps she had not really expanded her horizons at all – she had joined forces with an equal-minded person and was beginning to realise that, perhaps, two and two did not make four. Certainly not five.

The potential synergy of their merger had not really taken place. They were two people who carried on their independent lives and occasionally joined forces on short termed projects. The whole French thing was far more serious than a short termed project and perhaps they hadn't really considered all of the implications. Perhaps that was why they had never thought about or discussed marriage. The house in France that they had just bought was the first step on a much longer path and perhaps they had not been ready for it. Something had gone horribly wrong.

She sat on the side of the bed and a small tear trickled down one cheek. Robin was no longer in control of her life, her destiny, her desires. Maybe, and she recalled a moment from when she was only four and first encountered emotional hurt, her mother had been right when she called Robin a "spoiled brat." That had hurt Robin big and she had cried for days.

Perhaps, with hindsight, her mother had been right and had spotted the trait long before it developed. Now she wanted her mother – both to apologise for that moment and to comfort Robin in her moment of need. As she sat there and pondered, she began to realise that her mother had been right and everything that was happening to her now was inevitable. Perhaps she had never really given anything but always took. Until now, she could not see the fault in that but her relationship with Lester, her carnal thoughts and activities with Didier and Jean-Luc, were all indicative of a personal controlling trait, which had probably been her true self.

She sat there for about ten minutes trying to put it all together and suddenly stood up and figuratively brushed herself down and dismissed such weaknesses. No, she was going to beat this and no stupid fear of miserable, little, harmless ants was going to interfere with her plans. Whatever had happened would stay behind her and she was going to drive forward at the helm and if Didier and Jean-Luc wanted to come with her, fine. Lester was another issue and his puerile behaviour was also something of the past.

They would go back to the house and attack. If Lester had done a runner, that was his problem. She had sorted out all of the plans and was now even more determined that she would succeed. With or without Lester.

She leapt into the shower and spruced herself up to take on everybody. By the time she presented herself at the entrance door of the chambres d'hôte, Robin felt refreshed, clean and full of vigour. She waited a few minutes impatiently for the 'boys' and decided to go and "knock them up."

No sound came from within their room, so she tried the door handle. It was unlocked and the door opened onto a room that appeared not to have been used. "Creeps and cowards," she thought to herself, and strode out to the car park. "And bloody thieves," as she discovered that the car was missing. But as she stood there with her hands on her hips, bracing herself for a battle royal, coming down the ramp from the road above was the car and inside were the two pale, ashen Frenchmen. They drove straight over to Robin and almost got out of the car before it stopped.

"Madame Robin, you must come wizz us to ze 'ouse." They were obviously far from the cowards that Robin had deemed them to be. She jumped into the driving seat and beckoned the 'boys' back in. They glanced at each other and climbed back in. Before she moved off, Robin turned to her men and said "Well?"

"We need to show you somezzing at ze 'ouse. Let's just go zere, please." Jean-Luc was struggling with words and emotions.

Robin put her foot down and the car took off with dust and gravel flying everywhere. Within what seemed like only minutes they drew up at the gates of the house and, with trepidation, opened them.

Jean-Luc and Didier directed Robin immediately to Lester's den and boldly stepped up to the door. As they pushed it open, Robin gasped. The writhing mass of ants had completely disappeared and the whole place looked clear. The outline of the body had gone and there was no evidence of anything. Even the ground under the cupboards was clear of trainers and any other items.

With a quizzical expression on her face, Robin began to explore all of the other rooms and, again, there were no traces of anything. It was as though everything had been swept clean and there was no evidence of any wrongdoing.

Eventually she scanned the whole property and there were no traces of any ant existence anywhere. With a sigh of relief, she took the two Frenchman back to the main house and sat them down to explain her plans.

She had decided to stay there permanently, Lester or not, and was prepared to offer them jobs and accommodation on the land to maintain the whole estate. They could retain their similar jobs back in England, although she would expect them to employ sub-agents because she wanted them with her in France.

Both men were delighted with this because they liked the area, although they were both still very nervous over what had happened here earlier.

In the meantime, Robin would visit the local bank and set up fully automated payment of bills, collections of rents, settlement of

Taxes d'Habitation and Taxes Fonçières (the equivalent of UK Poll Tax or whatever it was now called in the UK) and all other charges. Nobody need worry about anything anymore. Rental surpluses from England would be automatically transmitted and converted at £5,000 intervals into the French Euro account to meet all running costs and the local notaire, Alain Corale, would be given full Power of Attorney over the whole of her estate. She would even employ a local girl to keep the place clean and her wages would be settled directly from the bank account. Lester would have to sort out his own affairs when he had the balls to show up again. Every part of the operation was now fully automated or handled by an outside expert.

The whole process took less than a morning and with insurances, communication costs and water charges, electricity and gas from EDF, the fixed costs of running the estate per annum worked out to be the ludicrous sum of less than the equivalent of £2,000, a mere fraction of its equivalent in England. The salaries and expenses of the two men came to the equivalent of about £100,000 but this included materials and travel costs for both France and England.

Chapter 15 – After the storm (après la déluge)

For several months, everything went smoothly. The restoration work was carried out admirably by the two employees and there was no sign of Lester. Robin had arranged for the house to be transferred into the ownership of a Trust in order to reduce exposure to any Capital Gains Tax. For some unknown reason, the French legal system accepted the sole signature of the holder of the Power of Attorney. Everybody was beginning to relax and the in-house safe for the rental income was never used since all income was now directed straight into the bank account. Everything was smooth and effortless.

And then, without warning, it started all over again.

One late night, nearly a year after the project had started, Robin was sitting on her own, with a bottle of Pouilly Fuissé half consumed but well worthy of its destined evening. She sat in a large, revolving leather chair with her long, beautifully shaped legs tucked underneath her, when, out of the corner of her eye, she thought she caught sight of something moving. Because she was listening to a spectacular version of Tchaikovsky's Romeo and Juliet overture by the London Symphony Orchestra, she didn't take much notice at first. As the music reached its crescendo, she suddenly noticed a further movement but this time it was definite. She put down her glass of wine and her copy of Insurance Weekly and her hair stood on end.

She let out a blood-curdling scream and leapt up onto the chair. The movement was now painfully obvious. Gliding along the floor under a pine cupboard was a single trainer. As she took off her reading glasses and focused, for one horrific moment she swore blind she was looking at one of Lester's missing trainers floating across the floor. As she stood there on the chair screaming, a second trainer appeared from behind a long curtain. She jumped forward and grabbed the first trainer. As she did so, she heard that buzzing, humming sound that she might have heard before. Foolishly, she thought later, she looked inside the trainer and immediately knew that it had been Lester's. Not only was there a peculiar décor and the strange outline of his instantly recognisable feet visible, but Robin knew, by the smell alone, she was looking at a pair of Lester's trainers. As she glanced inside, she was greeted by nothing. It was old and stained and smelly. But nothing else.

Robin leapt up to run to the door but it was too late. They were there again, the large, angry ants and they had got her pinned in this room. Her route out was blocked and it was then that she heard a double scream from a room not far away, to where she suspected that the second batch of insects had escaped and she just knew that they were attacking her Frenchmen.

But this time she knew – there would be no respite. She now knew exactly what dreadful fate had befallen her Lester. He had been eaten alive by the attacking ants and every single last trace of evidence had been removed by them, apart from their winning trophy – the trainers. They had committed the perfect crime. They had gained their revenge for Lester's appalling microwave attack. And now they had come back to finish the business. Patience had been their by-word and, after all this time, nobody would ever know. In fact nobody would ever find anything other than an empty, clean house.

Chapter 16 – Home at last

Pam and Steve were delighted with their new acquisition. The house was immaculate and, despite a brief period when they owned two houses until their sale had gone through, everything had been easy and stress free.

They moved in because the house was fully furnished, clean and totally habitable, apart from a couple of outhouses that nobody seemed very interested in. The sale of their former property in the Dordogne lingered for a month or so but they were so pleased with the new house that they even agreed to let the new buyers of their property move in before completion had taken place. Since the new buyers were English, Alain Corale, their notaire, had insisted on indemnities and guarantees; the usual hand-shake on agreement being, in his opinion, insufficient. He had seen things go wrong before, particularly where people started knocking walls down, which seemed to be a normal British trait.

Pam and Steve took his advice, wisely as it turned out, since it was the new buyers' indemnity that that paid for the flood damage caused by bad workmanship, since the buyers at that very point had no insurable interest until completion.

Whilst this was happening, Pam and Steve moved into the Lot Valley and had very little to do in the way of work on their new property.

They had been there for about fifteen days, when Pam discovered something rather shocking. A cupboard drawer was sticking and eventually had to be forced open. It turned out that something had fallen down the back and was caught up with the drawer below. When eventually it was freed, it was found to be a framed photograph, probably belonging to the previous owners. The frame had been broken and the picture inside damaged. After some effort the photo was freed and it then that Pam shrieked, "Steve – come here – now!"

They both stood there open mouthed staring at the picture. It was of their old friends Robin and Lester, the couple who had been their guests all those years ago and forced them to sell up and leave. What an amazing coincidence. How ironic that the roles had been reversed and now Pam and Steve had taken over such a bargain.

That night, as Pam and Steve finished dinner on the balcony, they thought back to those early days when Lester and Robin had been their guests and wondered where they were now. As they lay back into their wicker, hanging, balcony chairs, each sipping a glass of Calvados, they decided that Robin and Lester had been a bad experience in their lives and they would think about them no more. Life was much more relaxing now, they lived in a beautiful area where the weather was regularly hot, sunny and clear but green and fresh. It was the end of another perfect day and a full moon was rising early into the last vestiges of a mackerel sunset. Tomorrow boded well.

"Wow," said Pam, swinging comfortably in her chair. "Have you seen the size of that ant over there? It must be peculiar to the region. I have never seen anything that huge before, not even in Florida."

The creature, about 30 centimetres or a foot long, walked across the deck alone. Steve looked in silence and then said, "It sounds as though it's wearing hobnailed boots. Let's hope there aren't too many of those around, they could be quite scary." As they watched, a second and third ant of the same size and shell coating appeared. Each also wore hobnailed boots. The sound of a marching army drawing close started and became louder. As hundreds and possibly thousands of them marched round the corner into the moonlight, they swarmed and rose up into the shape of an armed warrior.

Steve shuddered.

Pam screamed. She knew a toxic legacy when she saw one.

Pollution

By Colin Butler

Down in the forest something stirred,
Was it a mammal, or was it a bird?
No, a plastic bag, that's what we've got.
Impaled on a tree, never to rot,

All around the forest floor
Non-biodegradeables for evermore.
This is truly the modern sin,
Symptom of the profligate world we live in.

The tide laps gently on the beach
Bringing flotsam and jetsam into reach,
Coke cans, bottles, plastics of every kind,
All the rubbish that man has left behind.

The fly-tippers despoil our countryside
While we spray the crops with pesticide.
Greenhouse gases endlessly pumped out,
Global warming will follow, without a doubt.

Will we become a derelict wasteland,
A festering, filthy, poisoned island,

Toxic Legacy

Fed by choking acrid, acid rain
Falling on England's green and pleasant plain.

Chimneys spew out noxious plumes,
Whilst motors exude noisome fumes,
We poison the world with a toxic flow,
As man enacts his desperate tale of woe.

The OxyGene Hypothesis

By Simon Woodward

Chapter 1

The phone rang in the outer office attached to laboratory #313 and, before picking it up, Brad Levors looked through the huge floor to ceiling glass window that separated the office from the lab proper.

Tom Edison, Brad's research partner, was engrossed with the analysis the computer was currently pumping out. Brad knew it was not a good idea to disturb Tom at these times; the way Tom managed to focus on the results was astounding and usually bore fruit.

Brad picked the phone up. "Brad Levors," he said.

"Brad, it's Julius. Can you and Tom come to my office for a moment? There's an important decision to be made, and, if we play our cards right, this could be the making of the GaiaGenetics Corporation."

"Yes, sir. Of course," Brad replied, not having any options but to agree. Putting the phone down, he glanced back at Tom once more, with no inkling that the decisions he was about to make would rid the GaiaGenetics Corporation and the scientific community at large of the genius who was Tom Edison, forever.

Julius Randall III, had a rugged outdoor look about him, gained whilst working on his father's farm as an adolescent and young adult throughout the late Forties. He had borne witness to crop failures through disease and poor seasonal weather and had become determined to remove the pitfalls that often befell arable farming. And he knew he could do it. His father frequently told him, "Man is the most superior of God's creations and, if this world is going to succeed, Man will, one way or another, assist and direct nature towards our prosperity. There is never a problem that Man can't resolve."

Using land his father had already given him and further financial backing from the Randall legacy, he started CropSure. Initially, his fledgling company began selective breeding programmes; crossing species of crop exhibiting traits that would be beneficial. Whether it was the land he had or a natural eye for hardy types, he always succeeded – producing the hybrids the agricultural markets were clamouring for.

As his company grew and the science of genetic modification began to mature, Julius Randall steered his company towards the production of GM crops and renamed his company The Gaia-Genetics Corporation to capture the belief his father had instilled in him as a young man.

In the beginning, he was ahead of his time and, as investors became interested, so the money followed. Now it was different; the market was almost saturated with GM companies and Julius needed something his company could offer, something that no other company could, something to place GaiaGen, as it was colloquially known, back at the top and in front of all the rest of its competitors.

A year before, through a chance meeting at a GM seminar, Julius Randal III had discovered Brad Levors attempting to network, trying to promote his PhD. Julius saw the potential of Brad's work, if it could be reproduced and, after a short discussion, Brad had been offered a research position.

Twelve months on and after a few reasonable successes Brad had asked Julius for an appointment, and he had acquiesced. Julius eyed the ebony haired, well coiffured, olive-skinned young man as he stood before him. He hoped he was going to be told of further developments; something that had been lacking in the last few months, but he suspected not, he suspected Brad Levors was a spent entity.

"What can I do for you Brad?" he had asked at the time. "And don't beat around the bush, I'm very busy."

"Sir, in order to make further significant steps forward, I need someone to assist me in these endeavours."

Julius hid his annoyance at his employee reminding him of the successes he'd made: *You're not going to sit on your laurels in this company Mr Levors*, he had thought, though he allowed Brad to continue.

After Brad had finished explaining to him about a guy called Tom Edison, Julius smelt something good on the horizon and, even if the new guy brought only eight months of research breakthroughs to GaiaGen, he could be quietly let go, though the patents of the work would remain with GaiaGen.

After a week's consideration, Julius decided to let Brad approach the man.

Brad wandered along the third floor corridor and took the stairwell to the fifth making his way to Randall's office, curious as to what decisions his boss had been alluding to in the phone call.

Brad never used the elevators, not because of some phobia, but just because the exercise would complement his fitness regime; he liked looking good.

He smiled to himself as he approached his boss's imposing office door; he knew Randall was a driven man, but for him to think that GaiaGen needed something else that would be the making of the company, amused him. GaiaGen had many contracts with other businesses, including contracts to supply laboratory space should the need arise; its laboratories were the envy of the world. But most lucrative of all were the contracts it had with the U.S. Department of Defence.

GaiaGen was not short of funds and its eleven billion dollar annual turnover showed just how well it was doing. Brad wondered why Randall wanted even more.

Standing outside the door to the office for a second, Brad re-adjusted his tie then brushed non-existent specks of dust off his suit shoulders and, once satisfied with his appearance, he knocked on the heavy door.

Almost immediately there was a quiet buzz as Sylvie Zywicki, Randall's PA, pressed the button on her desk unlocking the outer office door, giving access to something Randall referred to as his outer sanctum.

"Afternoon, Sylvie," Brad said as he entered, "I've come…"

"I know," Sylvie said, interrupting. "He's expecting you. Go through."

Brad walked past Sylvie's desk and through the stained oak door into Julius's office, the inner sanctum.

"Brad," Julius said. "Please take a seat. Where's Tom?"

"Tom's busy on the project," Brad said, as he sat in the large leather seat Julius had indicated.

"Brad, do you want a coffee or anything?"

"Yes, sir, please," Brad replied. "I wouldn't mind a coffee."

Julius Randall pressed the button to his intercom, then said, "Sylvie, could you please bring in a cup of coffee for Mr Levors and I'll have a glass of sparkling water."

"Of course, sir," the intercom answered. Moments later Sylvie Zywicki entered Randall's office carrying a tray containing the required drinks.

"That will be all, Sylvie, thank you," Julius Randall said, taking the tray from her, "Oh… and please make sure I'm not disturbed until I've finished with Mr Levors, Ok?"

"As you will, Mr Randall," the icily cool 5' 8" brunette PA said, and left, leaving the two men alone.

"Levors, how's the research going?"

Brad knew this was going to be a serious conversation; Randall only referred to his employees by their last name when the topics of discussion were going to be serious.

"The research is on track, as outlined in last week's report, sir."

A frown crossed Julius Randall's brow for a moment, then he smashed his fist onto the desk, "Don't mess with me Levors. Just answer the question."

Out of all the ideas Brad had conjured up about how the meeting would go, this was not one of them.

"Well…, sir,…," Brad said, stumbling over his words.

"Stop pussy footing around, Levors," Julius Randall interjected, "I need to know where your research stands. You do realize that GaiaGen is three points behind our nearest competitor on share price… and I won't have it. I'm not going to be embarrassed in this way."

Brad sighed. He had no idea why Randall was so irked; the company may well be three points behind the nearest competitor but its annual revenues were nothing to be baulked at.

Taking a deep breath Brad began to explain:

"Sir, where we stand at this point is that we have two plant species which, when crossed, will produce a hybrid that expires oxygen with or without sun light. However, using traditional methods of cross-fertilization the oxygen expiring hybrid is not guaranteed. For some reason, the gene responsible for this is not always expressed, whereas ordinarily the results are a given. Rest assured, we are looking into this problem at this point.

"As for the gene injection techniques using a modified plant virus, it only becomes active when saturated with ultraviolet light for prolonged periods. And that's it really, sir." Brad decided to leave out the other problems he and Tom had been experiencing. What he had told Randall was an honest précis, to his way of thinking.

"Ok. You are aware that our government is more receptive to the idea of global warming, aren't you?"

"Of course, Mr Randall."

"Now, if you, *and* Mr Edison's research pans out, you do realise that GaiaGen will have one of the only biological patents that could mitigate the problem of global warming. Your project to have a plant, any plant, by genetic modification, that sequesters excess CO_2 in our earth's atmosphere, will be the making of my company."

Brad now knew the direction Julius Randall wanted to drive GaiaGen. If he and Tom could come up with viable hybrids or a method of GM to achieve this, GaiaGen would become the planet's saviour. The rewards would be astronomical; every government would want the technology, they and GaiaGen were on the brink of creating.

"That's correct," Brad agreed.

"I have been offered." Julius continued, "an opportunity to test your little project as one of the scientific experiments onboard the next shuttle flights in the New Year. NASA is extremely interested in other methods to remove CO_2 from the shuttle's in-cabin atmosphere.

"I expect your team can do this. Furthermore, as this has been the focus of your team's research, with all the money I've poured into it, I'm inclined to tell NASA we will have something for them to use. You can't imagine what this will mean for my company, and my shareholders, for that matter.

"You do realize that, in achieving this goal, there is a huge scope for substantial bonuses. I'm talking seven figure sums here, Levors; it's nothing to be dismissed. And with the talent in your team, I'm looking to you to take this responsibility on and deliver a positive outcome."

"When is the launch, sir?" Brad said, as he realized what this project would mean to him; perhaps a Nobel Prize, possibly he could even retire. His heart began to beat faster as he imagined what it meant if he failed.

"The slot I've been offered is in June. Can you do this?"

"Yes, Mr Randall. No problem," Brad answered, knowing that the June in question was just under a year away, but forefront in his mind were the remaining substantial hurdles within the project, for which he was now solely responsible.

"I'm glad you said that, Brad," Julius began to conclude, "I will inform my friend in NASA that GaiaGen will have an experiment for them to take into space."

The meeting ended and just as Brad was about to open the door of the inner sanctum to leave Julius Randall said. "Brad, don't forget about the rewards this opportunity could mean to you."

"Of course not, Mr Randall. I won't." Brad reached for the door handle once again.

"Brad, and one more thing."

"Yes, sir?" he said, turning back to face his boss once more.

"Don't you ever forget what this will mean for my company, Ok?" Now finished Julius Randall flicked his hand and dismissed Brad without waiting for any response.

Brad Levors left the office looking forward to reaping the rewards of a successful outcome, suppressing, as much as he could, what it would mean if the experiment failed.

As he walked back to his lab, he wondered how he would break the news of the deadline to Tom Edison.

Chapter 2

"Brad, there's no way we can possibly have a hybrid ready in time, even if we get the plant virus to work under normal conditions," Tom said.

"Tom, the shuttle slot is next year, and we're lucky to have been offered the slot in the first place; anyway it's a moot point, Mr Randall has given the go ahead."

"When did you talk with him? You know our research is nowhere near complete." Tom paused for a second, then added, "Don't bother answering, there's no point. I suppose Mr Randall is quite happy with the idea."

"Tom, firstly, Mr Randall approached me about this opportunity; he's got friends in NASA you know – and they gave him first refusal. We just can't miss this chance. Something like this may not come up again for a good number of years. It's a chance in a lifetime, and if it comes off, we'll be world renowned. It's our opportunity to get our names into the history books."

"Ok, ok, Brad. But what happens if we're not ready when the time comes?"

"Tom, you've got to learn to be more positive; it's not good for the company if you're forever down-playing the achievements we have made. So stop being so pessimistic about this for a change. We'll address missing the target nearer the time.

"In the meanwhile let's redouble our efforts and make sure we're ready when the time comes." Brad took his coat from the lab's hanger and put it on; he was ready to go home for the weekend. He opened the laboratory's door and turned back to Tom. "Hey, Tom, don't fret about it, and have a good weekend won't ya – you look like you need it."

"Yeah, yeah… Ok. Same to you Brad. See you Monday." Tom sighed as the lab door closed, leaving him with his thoughts. He shook his head in consternation at his colleague's attitude.

Tom wondered what had happened to the cautious Brad Levors he had known whilst studying at Cambridge University, in England.

He had hooked up with Brad through one of the universities' Open Access forums, one that was shared with other academic establishments around the world.

At the time Brad was researching his doctorate on plant super-cultures; methods to accelerate plant growth rates in order to reduce the time between a plant being propagated and it attaining its full adult form; this reduction would be a boon to the already massive Pharma and Agrochemical industries to say the least.

It was through Yale University's Center for Biodiversity & Science linked forum that Tom had come across Brad Levors' online conversations.

Tom had been impressed with the ideas Brad had been propounding and, after a few evenings of reading what he was posting, Tom had decided to strike up a discussion with the man.

In England Tom was researching his own PhD on the genetic modification of plants through the use of plant viruses.

After stumbling across the shared forum Brad was a part of, Tom immediately saw how his and Brad Levors' research could fit hand in glove.

A few months after their online conversations, they'd both finished their dissertations and had lost contact with each other.

Tom had struggled to find a job after university, eventually deciding to take anything on offer, and it was anything; though he'd promised himself that he wouldn't go as low as a shelf stacker.

As the money his father had left him began to dwindle, Tom took the next work opportunity the job centre sent him and became a dustman, collecting society's reject material.

During his time as a dustman, he continued applying to all the pharmaceutical companies he could think of that were advertising available posts. However, after attending the interviews, the outcome was always the same; he was turned down, the businesses citing his lack of experience.

Tom began to wonder why he'd *ever* gone the university route to riches in the first place; it was almost as if it was a non-starter.

One afternoon, after completing his round, and having the obligatory shower following it, he turned on his PC and logged on to his email.

Frowning once again at his inbox with its 167 emails he wondered why his ISP could not filter out all the junk. He clicked on the 'select all' button, as he usually did, and was just about to click on 'delete' when he noticed one of the emails was from 'b_levors@Gaiageneticscorp.com'

Opening the one that had caught his eye; he read it;

"*Hi Tom,*" it started, "*my UK chum, bet you weren't expecting an email from me.*" Tom wasn't, and he read on.

"*I've managed to land myself a job with the GaiaGenetics Corporation, and I've been here a year now. They were most impressed with the work I'd been doing with accelerated plant growth and wondered what else I could do with plants as they've suddenly become interested in anything to do with combating global warming, since the administration here has had a change of heart. I've had a few ideas and have convinced the boss, one Julius Randall III, that if GaiaGen is going to be able to get on this bandwagon then you're the guy they need. You interested? I can't say anymore because the program is very hush-hush; if you are you'll have to come over the pond to hear the rest. What d'you say?*"

Tom blinked at the email; then read it again, then clicked 'Reply'.

The following week Tom Edison, a sandy haired scruffy individual whose wardrobe consisted of t-shirts and jeans, was packing; getting ready for a week-long stay in Massachusetts, Cambridge, in fact, which he thought was a tad ironic. GaiaGen had agreed to pay for his trip and pay for the accommodation whilst he was there.

During his stay, he had attended the three interviews that had been arranged. Not once, during any of them, was the project Brad had intimated been mentioned.

Although the interviews had gone very well, Tom was completely disoriented; he hadn't seen Brad at all, he'd not even received a call from him.

It was only on the morning of his departure, whilst he was packing, getting ready to go home, he got a knock on the door of his hotel room.

Tom threw his shaving-kit into the open suitcase on the bed as he made his way to open it.

"Where the bloody hell have you been?" Tom said on seeing the person who had knocked. "You drag me over here to interviews you are not part of," he continued, "you don't contact me. What the hell is going on?"

"Tom," Brad said, "this is the way the company works; they had to make sure I wasn't prepping you in anyway."

"Well thanks, Brad, thanks for letting me know."

"Tom, just calm down will you. I've got good news."

"What good news can possibly make up for the hellish week I've been through Brad; just tell me will you?"

"Ok, Tom, I'll lay it out as it is; no embellishments."

"Thank you for that, Brad, I'd appreciate it. Especially as not once did the panel mention anything you said in your email."

"Tom, you got the job."

Tom's jaw sagged. "But… but the panel didn't mention a job; I know you alluded to it, but they didn't mention a job."

"Tom, they had to make sure you were the right guy, but…" Brad said.

"Oh, here we go with the buts. What's the catch Brad?"

"There's no real buts apart from the fact you'll have to move to the States."

"How the hell do you expect me to pay for that? I'm a dustbin man. I don't have any money to make that kind of move."

"Don't worry, Tom, GaiaGen will pay for your relocation; everything."

"They'll pay for my trip but what about where I'm going to live, you know; my housing?"

"They'll pay for everything, Tom. Part of the remuneration package is housing – you won't have to worry about those costs ever again. No gas, no electric and no rent. You will be provided for. When can you let us know your decision; there's not much time."

"Give me two weeks, Brad. This would be a huge change for me," Tom had said at the time.

Tom recalled the moment he had decided to up sticks and make a go of it in the great U.S. of A. and uncertainty about his decision was beginning to creep in.

Brad had changed from the thoughtful university student into a confident man who always knew his mind; no thought of his was ever flawed. It seemed Brad had lost the ability for self-critique, the ability to test his theories mentally before taking any particular course of action and Tom wondered what had happened to curtail Brad's skill in determining the right tack.

However, he was here now and working for GaiaGen; earning more money than he could have ever imagined. There was nothing for him in the UK, so he put his concerns to the back of his mind, knowing he had a job he ought to stick with.

Tom tried to gee himself up; the equipment he needed was here in the lab and even if it wasn't he knew he could put in a requisition order and within a few days the new hardware, or whatever was required, would arrive. The whole situation was like some kind of strange dream. It was very different from what he had experienced in the UK.

Tom powered off the lab equipment getting ready to leave for the weekend. This time, he promised himself, he wouldn't be in on Saturday, setting up further experiments, ploughing through the numbers, defining the next week's experiments. He would truly have a weekend to himself.

Tom smiled at his thoughts, wishing he could turn off just like that, knowing there was a one hundred per cent chance he would be back in tomorrow, to continue the work; the opposite of Brad in fact.

Chapter 3

At the same time Brad was leaving his house for his Saturday morning's jog, Tom was getting out of a cot in lab #314; one of GaiaGen's currently unused labs which also doubled for a dorm room. Against his better judgment he had worked through the night on the results the computer had finished churning out during Friday afternoon.

He wanted a result as much as he knew Brad did. But by 3am he had reached his limit and was too exhausted to do anymore, crashing in the spare lab.

It was always a good place to crash, better than his own bedroom in fact. The labs, and their outer offices, were airtight for safety reasons; not one sound would penetrate them and, for this reason, the rigid bed he had slept on, was of no consequence.

Tom rubbed his face vigorously as he walked back into lab #313; he had to double check the previous evening's results, just to make sure he hadn't been dreaming.

If the analysis proved true, then they'd be well on the way to producing a virus, one capable of modifying the genes of *Solanum tuberosum*, the potato plant, resulting in a new species that would be able to produce oxygen, irrespective of its light conditions, using the available CO_2 in the atmosphere or from any other potential source to do this.

Tom guessed that by employing the techniques suggested by the computer analysis, they'd be ready with a stable plant hybrid within the next months, if not earlier. This would then leave them enough time to prepare their pod, the one NASA's shuttle would use to take their experimental flora into space and Julius Randall would have his wish: GaiaGen's contribution to NASA's gravity free scientific studies.

Saturday afternoon arrived and Tom had confirmed his interpretations of the computer data; he powered down the lab. Tom smiled to himself as he left the building. He felt a hell of a lot happier than when Brad had told him of the project's deadline.

Chapter 4

Months had passed since Tom had told Brad of the results of the computer's analysis and it was months since Tom had suffered the worst ever hangover of his entire life.

When Brad had got into the office, on that Monday morning after the weekend breakthrough, and Tom had told him the news, Brad had insisted that he'd take Tom out for the time of his life.

Initially Tom had declined - going out was not his thing. However there had been no refusing Brad and he'd eventually complied; he'd also been persuaded to smoke a Cuban cigar for the first time in his entire life and regretted that decision almost more than he'd regretted drinking so much.

They'd worked hard during the intervening time and Brad had kept Julius up to date with their progress, sending regular emails to Julius's PA, though this communication was always kept from Tom. In Brad's view Tom had no need to know, as he wasn't really interested in the administration required to keep their project going anyway.

The focus of the latter months had been on developing the plant virus, so that once introduced to the specimens the genetic modifications would occur in a matter of mere hours, rather than the two or three weeks it had been taking since Tom's initial identification of the problem.

The atmosphere in lab #313 was electric; the team had cracked the problems and the virus no longer needed to be activated through exposure to U.V. light; the project had now been dubbed, Project OxyGene.

The deadline was approaching and within the next eight weeks, Project OxyGene would be blasting into outer space on the shuttle Ventura.

Another week had come to an end and Tom said, looking through the window into the lab containing the oxygen expiring plants, "Brad, you go home now. I've got a few little things I need to test, but I think we're finally there. We've actually done it."

"Too right we've done it. What tests were you thinking about? The way you've been these last few months you must have invented tests that no one's ever even considered."

"Brad, you know me, I just want to make sure; it's in my nature." Tom paused for a moment then added pointedly; "Like you used to be."

Brad ignored the last comment, "I'll look forward to the results. Have a great weekend, bud."

"I'm sure I will. See you Monday, Brad."

Brad left the outer office and left Tom preparing the computer for yet another run of the data they'd collected.

Leaving the stairwell into the basement parking lot, he strode over to his Dodge Viper STR10 and couldn't help rubbing his hands together thinking about the six figure sums Randall had promised him; very soon he would be able to make his dreams come true.

Brad started planning how he was going to spend the money; perhaps he would even go to Las Vegas this weekend and dabble in a bit of serious gambling, it had been a long time and something he'd stopped doing after the trouble he had got into before.

Chapter 5

The weekend had passed quickly and, as Brad parked his car, he contemplated the thousands of dollars in cash and IOUs he'd lost in the casinos, dismissing the thoughts as quickly as they came, the worry being replaced by the notions of the money he would make because of Project OxyGene. Quickly he traversed the stairs to GaiaGen's third floor and entered the lab, wondering how much further the experiment had progressed over the weekend; but then he saw Tom. Tom was dishevelled, dark rings around his eyes; his sandy hair, every which way.

"Tom, you Ok?" Brad said, frowning.

"No Brad, I'm not. And neither are we," Tom replied in a monotone.

"Why?" Brad asked, attempting to conjure up any reason why Tom would look so bad. "You haven't have had a family bereavement this weekend," he said stupidly, "you don't have a family. What's the problem my UK chum?"

"There's a problem with the virus," Tom said bluntly.

"There can't be. There was nothing wrong with it on Friday; there's been nothing wrong with it for weeks. What are you talking about?" Brad felt the muscles in his neck tightening; the money he'd lost at the casino on Saturday was due soon and he'd convinced the casino owners he was good for it. He knew what the outcome was likely to be if he didn't deliver on his promise.

"The gene modification doesn't just affect plants… it affects mammalian tissue as well."

"How d'you know that?" Brad demanded.

"I just checked to see what would happen if I placed a rat in the lab at the same time I released Project OxyGene. Don't know why I did, just being thorough I suppose; but I did it."

"What happened?"

"The rat died of edema. You know, the build-up of fluids in the body cavities."

"I know what edema is, Tom." Brad's mind was in turmoil, he dragged his hand down his face as if trying to get rid of something dirty, something he had just been covered in. His panicked mind heard his voice say; "What was the cause?"

"Brad, I just told you. The virus strain we've created, doesn't just modify plant genes, it modifies any living tissue with the right cellular structure."

"How?" Brad asked as he felt his new world, his whole imagined new life, begin to disintegrate before him.

"Our virus, particularly when introduced into the respiratory tract, modifies the genetic structure of the lining cells. Within two hours those cells start absorbing CO_2 as fast as they can get hold of it. Initially the rat seems to suffer hyperventilation, but once the CO_2 has been completely absorbed the animal is unable to survive. It just swells up, fluids filling any cavity they can find resulting in heart attack or drowning, or kidney failure. And those are just the effects I've seen. The end result is always the same though; the rat dies."

"What's the problem with that? We're not going to be sending up any viruses, just the modified plants."

"The problem with that is how we are going to make sure the plants we send are clear of the virus. There's really no choice, the virus has to be destroyed and we have to start over. I'm truly sorry, Brad."

A heavy, sicky feeling was developing in the pit of Brad's stomach, his mind felt clouded and his vision was beginning to tunnel. Brad cuffed a cold perspiration from his forehead.

"No Tom, that's not what we're going to do," Brad almost barked, "What we're going to do is spend a little more time on understanding the problem; there must be an answer: not having one is not an option."

"What do you think I've been doing all this weekend Brad; I've tried everything. Live tests and simulations; they're all showing the same results."

"Go over them again. There must be something you're missing." Brad picked his coat up from the hanger he'd just put it on and turned to leave.

"What are you doing?" Tom asked.

"I'm going. I need some time to think. You just carry on. I'll be back tomorrow."

As Brad left, Tom shook his head in disbelief, staring at his departing colleague's back.

Chapter 6

Brad paced around the underground parking lot, smacking his head intermittently with his palm, trying to force his brain to find a solution, but nothing would come.

The latest results were extremely bad; there was no way he could tell Julius about this, especially as his daily reports had been more than positive, with good reason. And there was nothing he could tell the casino. Whichever way he looked at it, Project OxyGene had to go ahead; there was no question about it. The only remaining question was; what would Tom Edison do when further tests resulted in the same awful outcomes tomorrow.

Brad knew Tom was as honest as the day was long. He was not a person able to put a positive light on anything that was remotely negative. And Tom had always had the desire to inform his line management when things were going awry; it was part of his personal philosophy: management can only act appropriately as long as they know the full facts.

Unable to think clearly, Brad got into his car, turned the ignition and gunned the engine as it came to life. The car's tyres squealed as he left the car park, seeking any old bar, somewhere on the outskirts of town where he could unwind and figure out what to do next. Within ten minutes he was out of the city and even the suburbs were beginning to thin. Before he knew it he was pulling into the lot of a seedy motel whose sign touted Bar & Diner.

Brad parked up and the next thing he was aware of was placing an order for two large bourbons, both of which disappeared in less time than it had taken to order them. As the alcohol began to infuse his body, he ordered two more, and the barman dutifully lined them up.

The bar was almost empty and dimly lit; its small windows refusing more light than they accepted. The place had a wooden floor and distinct cubby holes for those patrons who weren't really interested in socialising with anyone else.

Brad downed the third bourbon and gradually he began to believe he was starting to think more clearly about the situation. There was an answer, he was sure. One thing was certain, he couldn't let Tom prematurely announce the results of the final experiments on Project OxyGene; there'd only been two days effort involved and this wasn't enough to conclude the project was a failure.

Brad finished his fourth bourbon and ordered another two. Half way through his fifth a certainty began to develop in his thoughts. He decided to phone the lab and speak with Tom.

"GaiaGen," Tom answered.

"Tom, it's Brad. Can you do me a favour?"

"Haven't I done enough already?"

"Of course, of course you have. But just this last one. Ok? Please."

"Ok Brad. What is it?"

"Can you work through tonight? Just try everything ok. I'll pick up the baton tomorrow. Crash out in the spare lab, you know, lab #314, when you're done. I'll make this up to you. I really will,"

"You'd better, Brad."

"Thanks, Tom. I appreciate what you're doing." Brad shut off his mobile phone.

Chapter 7

After the call Brad decided it was time to leave. He quickly finished his last drink and made for the exit, convincing himself it was a good idea to pass by a liquor store and top up, on the way back to GaiaGen: if what he was going to do next was going to work he needed more of the fierce liquid.

Brad didn't drive into the GaiaGen's parking lot; he thought it'd be better if he parked up elsewhere. Sitting in his car and after numerous swigs from the bottle, and many long pauses in between, he checked his watch; it was still only 11pm and he knew Tom would still be hard at it.

From where he sat he could see the lights in lab #313 were still on, and, if his plan was to succeed, he'd have to wait until they went off.

Brad ran through what he was going to do; he would enter GaiaGen through the basement parking lot and take the elevator to the third floor. After that he would have to check Tom's lab's ventilation system and correct the airflow. Once done, Brad was certain that the major obstacle stopping Project OxyGene from going into space would be resolved and he would have abided by Tom's philosophical wish that management should act appropriately.

He took another heavy swig from the bottle of Jack Daniel's and as the burning liquid hit the back of his throat; the realisation of what he was about to do crystallised. His intoxicated mind told him this was the only way. He drank from the bottle again.

Two more hours passed before the light to the lab went off, briefly followed by a light in the adjacent lab silhouetting a man preparing for bed; then all was dark.

With adrenaline counteracting the effects of the drink on his muscles he left the car and made his way to the elevator. As it travelled from the lower ground floor to the third Brad heard a whispering in his mind, "Are you sure this is the way to solve the problem?" "Yes, yes, yes," he told himself, then, "shut up".

The elevator opened and he made his way to the control room for the third floor's air conditioning systems; putting on a pair of gloves before entering.

The room was not one he'd ever been in before. Brad looked at the panels of switches and lights, and sighed. At first glance it seemed to be just a huge wall of bulbs, dials and buttons, nothing really making any sense. But as he looked more closely, he saw certain switches were grouped together in blocks, with printed text indicating their purpose.

He scanned the wall, and then saw it; Laboratory Airflow Control System. The buttons he was interested in were segregated from the rest; allowing or disallowing the flow of air between all the labs on the third floor.

Brad pressed a button changing the airflow between lab #314 and lab #313, then left; his task for the evening completed.

Chapter 8

It was Tuesday morning and just as Brad was about to leave his house for his jog before work, his phone rang.

Brad was in two minds as to answer; he needed to go for a jog, the way he felt told him that he'd been on some kind of alcoholic bender, probably something to do with the fact that Project OxyGene was going to pay dividends, but he wasn't sure; the last 24 hours were a complete blur, though the occasional glimpses he got just seemed to be remnants of some peculiar nightmare and as such, he dismissed them.

"Brad Levors," He answered as he picked up the phone.

"Brad, we've been trying to reach you - there's been an accident," Sylvie Zywicki said.

"What kind of accident?" Brad said.

"It's Tom Edison…"

Before Sylvie Zywicki could finish her sentence Brad asked, "What's wrong with Tom?" Brad was truly concerned.

"Brad," Sylvie said, "Tom's dead. He died in his sleep."

Brad's brow furrowed as he heard the words, "Tom died in his sleep? Why would Tom die in his sleep?"

"We don't know Brad, but he was found this morning by security."

"Oh, God," Brad said.

"Julius wants to know whether this will affect Project OxyGene."

What a bastard, Brad thought, "The project is complete, Sylvie," he said, "all that needs to be finished is the pod the shuttle will take up. You can assure Mr Randall that Project OxyGene is on track," he finished.

"Julius will be glad to hear this," Sylvie said.

Brad started to say "Thank you, Sylvie," but the phone had already been disconnected.

He couldn't face a run so he jumped into the shower and got ready for work. Today was not going to be a good day he was sure.

The GaiaGen security chief handed Julius Randall a folder; Julius opened it and read the report's summary:

"Thank you, Albert, this is very useful. Leave this with me." The chief left Randall to read the whole report. Julius smiled to himself; obviously Levors had more balls than he'd given him credit for.

As Brad drove into GaiaGen's parking lot he noticed a police car in the visitor's area; no doubt his work today would be interrupted.

Brad entered his lab and knew all that had occurred could not distract him from finishing the final touches to Project OxyGene; Julius would be expecting the finished product very soon, and he, himself, was dependent on the financial outcome. When he had finished the work on the project he would then be mindful of the loss of his friend and colleague, but until then his primary allegiances were to Randall, whether he liked it or not.

Chapter 9

Two months had past since the death of Tom Edison and it was launch day for the shuttle Ventura. The Kennedy Space Center was ready and the CEO of GaiaGen had been invited to witness the launch. Julius had told Brad Levors to join him as one of the named individuals he was allowed to invite. After arriving they'd been taken through to mission control and within thirty minutes the countdown had started; Brad listened to the commentary

Flight: "Okay. All flight controllers coming up on auto sequence, Booster, how you?"

Booster: "We're go, Flight."

Flight: "EECom?"

EEcom: "Go, Flight."

Flight: "GNC?"

GNC: "Go, Flight."

Flight: "Telcom?"

Telcom: "Go, Flight."

Flight: "Control?"

Control: "Go."

Flight: "Network, got it there?"

Network: "That's affirmative, Flight."

Flight: "Okay."

With the sequence complete, Ventura left the launch pad aiming for near earth orbit. Once there the crew would activate all the zero gravity experiments; the ones that had been paid for by a myriad of corporations; not forgetting the government's own agencies.

After the launch Julius Randall turned towards Brad, "What do you think, Levors? How are we going to do in space?"

"I think when the shuttle crew activates our experiment NASA will be more than pleased."

"I think you're right Brad. Finally GaiaGen will get the international recognition it deserves. This is a great day for me. Within the next forty-eight hours, not only our administration will be lauding our achievement, but the whole world will also."

"Sir, we must remember the contribution Tom Edison made," Brad added.

"Of course, Levors, of course." Randall turned to leave mission control and Brad followed.

As they left the building the limousine that had dropped them off was ready to take them back to their hotel. Although his boss had not directly attributed the achievement to him, Brad still allowed himself to bathe in the wonder of the achievement.

Chapter 10

"Houston. Do you copy?" Ventura's commander asked, as it changed between control centres.

"That's an affirmative Ventura," the controller replied.

"Are we ready to go with Project OxyGene?" Commander Eileen Lawrence requested.

"That's an affirmative Ventura. Go with OxyGene."

GaiaGen's pod was opened in the shuttle's onboard laboratory. Dr Jeannie Malik was the technician responsible for this particular experiment and she monitored the CO_2 levels. To her surprise the carbon dioxide in the lab reduced dramatically, and very quickly.

Jean turned to the commander, "I've registered a five percent reduction in CO_2 levels already; these plants could be the making of space travel."

"Please check your stats doctor; we can't be bringing back false results. The companies that have funded this research are relying on us."

"Double checked them already, Ma'am; the results are correct," Jeannie Malik responded, removing her helmet.

"OK Jean. Let's see what power we can save using these plants."

"Affirmative, Commander. Opening lab ingress and shutting off CO_2 recycler."

Dr Malik flicked the appropriate buttons and started to measure the level of CO_2 in the shuttle's primary control area and, as she had seen in the lab, the control cabin's CO_2 level began to reduce without using any of the shuttle's re-breathing modules.

"Commander, Project OxyGene is go and functional."

"Affirmative Doctor; good news. Let's see how long we can run with this."

The GM plants were working. The rest of the crew removed their helmets and carried on with their tasks, Project OxyGene sequestered the CO_2 and released vital, life-giving oxygen.

Jeannie Malik began to frown, for some reason she was beginning to feel disoriented, her head was fuzzy; she clicked on her intercom and addressed the shuttle's commander.

"Commander; what's your CO_2 reading?"

"Good, Doctor. CO_2 levels are just below normal."

"Ok, sir. Sorry... I mean Ma'am," she said, correcting herself.

The dormant virus spores that had travelled on GaiaGen's plants were now circulating around the command module and were becoming active; the zero-g of space assisting them in their mutations. As long as the virus found moist and living tissue, wherever it landed, it began its work; modifying the genetic structure of the cells, re-purposing them. No-one had considered the possibility of the virus being able to cross species barriers, let alone being able to jump between plant and animal kingdoms.

Dr Malik began to hyperventilate and knew that breathing into a bag would control the problem. She opened one of Ventura's lockers, taking a bag from it and putting it to her mouth she breathed in and out, waiting for the discomfort to subside.

Her eyes widened with fear as she breathed harder and faster into the bag with no affect. The virus in her lungs was mutating her cells and as it did so, so it multiplied; feasting on the extra CO_2, turning the doctor into an envoy of death.

The ventricles in Dr Malik's brain, those empty spaces, began to fill with fluid, forcing her cranial tissues outwards; she almost had time to grasp her head as searing pain lanced its way through and, as death took her, a final spasm in one of her legs launched her lifeless cadaver, through the air, towards the back of the laboratory, blood-spotted grey matter seeping from her nose in rivulets, as if from some kind of head-shaped ice cream machine.

The shuttle's commander looked back at the doctor, whose body was now slowly spinning in the shuttle's gravity free environment, trying to understand what was happening and what the pinkish coloured gunk was around the doctor's mouth. She handed control to the shuttle's co-pilot and got up from her seat, floating herself through the opening into the lab. Just as she reached for one of the hand grabs she began to cough uncontrollably. Her lungs felt as if they were filling with water and, incapable of catching her breath, she lost consciousness.

It was the same for the rest of Ventura's crew, all attempting to assist the fallen, but dying of edema before they could.

Even the last member who had the wherewithal to put his helmet back on died of a heart attack. The awareness that something was terribly wrong came too late; he'd already breathed the shuttle's virus polluted atmosphere.

As the CO_2 level began to drop to zero, the virus that had travelled all that way, and its host cells, died; neither of the new minute life forms being capable of surviving without CO_2 to feed on.

The newly silent shuttle orbited the Earth with the silence only broken occasionally by panicked squawks from the shuttle's radio – mission control attempting to make contact with the dead crew.

Chapter 11

In mission control it was decision time; bring down the shuttle under remote control or wait until there was a response; the mission controller didn't like the choices.

"Go with remote landing," he instructed, knowing that as the shuttle penetrated the Earth's atmosphere all contact would be lost, including the ability to control the shuttle's flight during this time: it was a dangerous endeavour.

The Ventura space vehicle received the commands from mission control and it started its descent. All the technicians sighed with relief when they regained control of the spacecraft as it finished its entry into Earth's atmosphere.

The best landing site available was White Sands and the craft was directed to land there. As the shuttle's nose wheel was slowly manoeuvred down to the landing strip's surface, a sudden and strong cross wind pushed the craft sideways and the wheel touched down on the rough natural surface, missing the landing strip by a few feet. The wheel hit a pot hole and the jarring force buckled the nose wheel's load baring struts. The front of the craft fell on to the rough surface and the command module bore into the ground throwing ceramic tiles and earth up into the air as the speed and weight of the shuttle pulverised the hard surface. As momentum continued to force the shuttle forward, a rending crack rang out as the craft's spine gave way, the shuttle skin tearing behind the command module's compartment. Sparks from the now broken electronics ignited the pure oxygen atmosphere of the crew area and there was a momentary silent blinding flash before orange flames and a deafening explosion reduced the front part of the spacecraft to fast flying black and white torn sections of composite material.

Debris rained down everywhere; lifeless space-suited bodies ejected across the runway, experimental pods vaporised. Finally the shuttle's right wing sunk into the earth next to the landing strip and sent the remains of the craft's body cart wheeling, wing over wing, completing its destruction.

It was a disaster, the like of which had not been seen since the Columbia tragedy.

Chapter 12

Brad was at home watching the news, waiting for GaiaGen and his experiment to be announced as the first major scientific breakthrough in the 21st century, but that was not what he got.
He fell into his chair as CNN delivered its commentary on the shuttle's fatal landing.

Julius Randall was also watching the evening news and as the pictures of the smashed shuttle faded back to the newscaster he turned the television off and picked up a cheap and unused pay-as-you-go mobile phone from his desk.

After a few words, he walked into his kitchen and dropped the phone into his garbage disposal unit and when it had finished its business he took the garbage out ready for tomorrow's collection.

Entering his lounge he poured himself a malt whisky and sat down turning on his chess computer to finish a game he had started a few months ago. After a few hours of playing the computer had finally got the better of him and he turned in for the night.

Unlike Julius Randall's moderated drinking, Brad Levors, directly after the CNN newscast, had gone to his drinks cabinet, not even contemplated using a glass and had begun to guzzle bourbon straight from the bottle as his television continued to blast news reports about the accident at him. He sat in his leather chair just staring at the TV pictures, shaking his head, muttering *no, no, no*, under his breath between swigs.

A sudden banging at his front door startled him from his almost hypnotic trance the never ending scenes of carnage had put him in. He got up unsteadily finding it difficult to drag his gaze away from the TV pictures as he walked over to his front door. Pulling the door open, he squinted his eyes twice trying to focus, trying to recognise the unexpected visitor.

"Mr Levors," GaiaGen's bulky chief of security started, in a firm but calm tone.

"I recognise you, don't I?" Brad said, more than the worse for wear, looking at the person on his doorstep.

"Yes you do, Mr Levors."

"It's… it's…"

"It's Albert," the chief of security finished for him.

"Did you see…," Brad began, pointing back at the TV.

"Yes, Mr Levors," the chief interjected, "and if you could hand me that bottle," the chief continued, indicating the bourbon Brad was holding, "then I can take you to the office, as Mr Randall needs to discuss some urgent matters with you." Brad handed the gloved security chief his bottle of bourbon.

"You need some shoes, Mr Levors."

"Oh yes, of course I do," Brad replied, pulling his hand down his face attempting to sober up a little.

Brad walked back into his house and the security chief followed, making his way to the television set, turning it off and picking up a box of Cuban cigars that Brad always kept for special occasions.

"If you would like, Mr Levors, I could drive you in your car."

"Why not, Albert?" Brad took his keys from his jeans' pocket and handed them to the chief.

Brad put his shoes on and the security chief helped him to his car, checking the road as they made their way. The chief smiled to himself; it was night and the road was devoid of motorists and people.

The chief pulled into the underground parking lot of the GaiaGenetics Corporation. Killing the engine, the chief got out and made his way around to the passenger's side, opening the door for Brad. Brad pulled himself out of the car by placing a hand on each side of the door, he was still very drunk.

"This way, Mr Levors," the chief said when the elevator stopped on the 3rd floor.

"Aren't we going to Mr Randall's office?"

"No, he wants to meet you in your office. Probably to go over some details of the project."

Brad and the security chief entered the office of lab #313, the main light wasn't on and when the security chief tried the switch nothing happened. The chief made his way to Brad's desk and switched on the table lamp, accidentally knocking a project folder on to the floor next to the desk.

As the security chief bent over to pick up the folder, he let out an anguished groan and quickly stood up straight again, immediately rubbing the small of his back.

"Sorry, Mr Levors, could you pick up that folder, my back's playing up so much tonight."

"Sure, Albert."

Brad bent down reaching for the folder and as he did so, the security chief gritted his teeth, summoning all his strength (his back being a problem no more) and using his full weight he viciously pushed the back of Brad's head, smashing the man's forehead down against the edge of the desk; Brad crumpled to the floor unconscious.

The security chief pulled Brad's half empty bottle of bourbon out from one of his overcoat's deep pockets unscrewing the lid, and then proceeded to pour its contents over Brad's inert body. Once done, he scattered more paperwork on the floor around Brad, making sure it too was soaked in the alcohol. Happy with the result, GaiaGen's chief of security opened the box of cigar's he'd taken from Brad's house and lit one, placing the remainder on the desk. Once the end of the cigar was glowing nicely he dropped it onto Brad's booze soaked chest, the vapours igniting immediately.

The security chief paused in the office doorway watching Brad slowly begin to burn, making sure his boss' target was not just lightly unconscious. Brad didn't move even when the smell of cooking flesh began to fill the room; satisfied, the chief of security left the premises.

Chapter 13

It was 2am when he was roused from his sleep by his insistent phone, he picked it up.

"Randall," he said.

"Sir, this is the police department. I'm afraid I have some bad news."

"What is it officer?"

"There's been a fire at your premises; it seems that it started on the third floor but spread."

"Has anyone been hurt?" Randall said, with mock concern.

"So far there's only been one body found but it's too badly burnt to identify at the moment. Also there is a car in the lot that may be helpful to have identified."

"Ok. You carry on officer. I'll be there as soon as I can." Randall replaced the receiver knowing that whatever had happened GaiaGen's insurance company would pick up the bill and he would be able to start afresh once the paperwork had been completed.

His smiled as he recalled his father's words from his youth, "There is never a problem that man can't resolve." And so far he'd found that to be true.

Final Journey

By Colin Butler

Rushing headlong through the night,
Belching flames and thick black smoke,
Past scattered buildings radiating light,
Beacons amidst the darkened fields.

Passing isolated, deserted stations,
Illuminated oases in the stygian desert.
Attempting to pinpoint our exact location
As we flash by the blurred name-boards.

We grind to a halt at a desolate outpost,
The lights blazing eerily in the wintry mist.
A stranger disembarks like a sinister ghost,
Clad all in black, and disappears into the night.

The whistle blows and the doors bang shut,
The engine wheezes as it slowly draws away
In a cloud of acrid, polluting smoke.
Journeying to its inevitable terminus.

So we approach the end of the line,

The engine gives one last defiant roar,
A valedictory auld lang syne
As it disappears into the mists of time.

Silicon Rules OK

By Colin Butler

Chapter 1 – Downtime

It was just another Monday, just an ordinary day, but it would turn out to be the most momentous day in the history of mankind.

It was in fact a lovely spring morning with the sun shining. The trees were breaking into bud and the spring flowers were blossoming – all signs of new life and hope.

But this was all a false promise and would prove to be the beginning of the end of Man's reign on Earth.

How did it all start? I set off for work, as usual, admiring the trees and flowers and thinking that all was well with the world. Perhaps I should introduce myself, my name is Brian Lawrence, and, for my sins, I work for the British Government in the Home Office and, like every other office, we disliked Monday mornings. They were such a let-down after the week-end and in addition, there was a whole week's work ahead. I glanced at the wall calendar displaying the pulchritudinous talents of a young lady and noted that it was April the first. No doubt one of the office jokers would devise an April Fool's Joke, before midday.

As it turned out, the morning was uneventful and I was looking forward to my lunch – wondering what culinary delights awaited me in the canteen. Sometimes the food was diabolical, but on good days, it was just about edible. At last the clock moved on to twelve noon, and at that very same moment my computer screen went blank. I cursed the system, as we had suffered such a lot of downtime recently.

"The bloody computer has gone down again," I shouted out. Nobody took much notice, apart from muttering a few choice words and several people began to tinker with any buttons that were accessible. A few applied the old-fashioned remedy -giving their monitor case a few healthy bangs – all to no avail.

"It's probably some sort of April Fool's prank," said Amelia, who worked on the adjacent terminal.

"Bloody useless system," shouted Harry in the row behind me.

The consensus of opinion was that it was either some kind of April Fool's joke or a new and virulent virus. There were the usual derogatory remarks about the unreliability of computers.

"Let's go for an early lunch. You never know, the system might even be back when we return," said Amelia.

After a brief discussion, several of us decided to do just that.

"What's on the menu today?" I asked the rather frosty-faced canteen assistant.

"It's toad in the hole, can't you read?" she replied in her usual polite, but curt, manner.

The meal was indeed listed on the menu as Toad in the Hole – but in fact, consisted of gristly sausages interred in a Yorkshire pudding, that resembled cardboard, accompanied by rather sloppy mash and peas that would make excellent missiles if fired from a gun. The dessert was Spotted Dick, one of my favourites and this wasn't bad. We washed it all down with a cup of tea, before trudging back to the office.

We returned to our desks, full of hope, misplaced as it transpired – and as the afternoon wore on, we received numerous phone calls from other departments and organisations to report that their systems were also down. I decided to look at the television in the staff room. On the news, the headlines were about computer systems going down all over the City of London and throughout Britain. The experts all seemed to agree that it must be a new computer virus and every effort was being made to find a cure.

A so-called expert was recalling the fears at the end of 1999, when experts predicted the millennium bug that would affect the world's computers. But this was 2020 A.D. and it did not appear to be a significant date for computers. In consequence, we all decided to leave early that evening.

The following day, we arrived to find our system was still down, so we attempted to do work that did not require the computer. Several crisis meetings were held to discuss possible remedies, but the computer whiz-kids were completely baffled. During the day reports came in that the computer shutdowns had spread to America and Asia.

In addition, there were reports from various news agencies of traffic lights not working, causing massive gridlocks throughout Britain and also Europe and America. Japan was in turmoil with its extra dependence on computers. Like a pebble thrown into a pond, the problems rippled outwards until most of the civilised world was caught up in the computer problems. On the news, 'experts' were considering the possibility that a terrorist organisation was employing some mysterious weapon that immobilised computers.

It became clear that it was not only computer systems, but everything that was controlled by a microchip was malfunctioning, as the world and traffic had ground to a halt.

Soon air control systems were also failing and in consequence airliners were grounded. Sadly, the grounding was not implemented in time to save several mid-air collisions. The most tragic was a collision between an American super airliner and an Italian airliner over the suburbs of New York. It was estimated that some 400 passengers were killed together with a further 100 people on the ground. In addition, there were several other collisions and crashes, where further lives were lost. We watched the extended news flashes on the office television, completely baffled by these developments.

The road and air problems were soon joined by a standstill on the railways as signals failed. Many people speculated that it was a form of the millennium bug that had arrived late. Some of the older members of the population recalled the fears of 1999 when it had been anticipated that the millennium bug would bring civilisation to a standstill. Was the bug now striking 20 years late?

In Whitehall, panic set in as transport became virtually impossible. Panic turned to fear, when it was realised that the armed services had become useless with all their computerised equipment inoperable. Jet fighters, bombers and warships became incapable of use. Was a foreign power or international terrorists behind this?

Problems multiplied minute by minute – power stations shut down and food production ground to a halt as factories in Britain, Europe, America and other industrialized countries lost power. Our boss called a series of crisis meetings but we could find no real solution.

"What can we do? Has anyone got any suggestions?" said the Minister.

"Until we find the cause, we are virtually powerless. In fact, literally powerless" replied our boss with a smile, but the joke fell on unsympathetic ears.

The Government's Emergency Committee were equally powerless and unable to formulate a workable plan.

Our office had virtually closed down, with just a skeleton staff working. Most of us could not travel to work and if we did get there, there was little to do. One or two used their cars, but were concerned that they would not be able to replace the petrol.

The problems went on for two days with countless 'experts' giving their opinions of the cause and how governments should react. Panic then really escalated, as everyone felt cut-off and in the dark - in more ways than one! Electric lights failed as the power was turned off and people had to try to find candles to light their rooms - that is if they still possessed them. Most people had not replaced them, as they were used up, or simply thrown away.

All the modern gadgets failed to work, central heating, disc players, microwaves, electric heating, all failed and became just useless ornaments. The younger generation, who had been brought up having endless entertainment fed to them by electricity, were completely at a loss and had forgotten how to amuse themselves. Some battery powered items like play stations lasted for a while, but could not be recharged.

Strangely television stations, worldwide, continued to run and news of the problems were flashed throughout the country and around the world. People sat in their living rooms watching the crisis unfold, hour by hour, on their illuminated screens.

Chapter 2 – Takeover

Then on the 4th April at midday, Greenwich Mean Time, all the television screens went blank around the globe.

After 60 minutes, the TV screens flickered back into life and a dramatic fanfare declared that a very important announcement would be made in 10 minutes' time. We all waited with bated breath, assuming that one of the world leaders would make a pronouncement.

A burst of synthetic music, was followed by uplifting martial music and then a flat robotic voice announced -

"THE RULE OF MANKIND IS AT AN END!"

After a dramatic pause, it continued.

"COMPUTERS AND ROBOTS ARE NOW TAKING OVER THE WORLD.

"MAN HAS RULED FOR OVER 5,000 YEARS AND THEIR RULE HAS BEEN AN UNMITIGATED DISASTER. THE 5 MILLENNIA HAVE BEEN A TIME OF VIRTUALLY CONTINUOUS WARS, A TIME OF MISMANAGEMENT OF THE RESOURCES OF THE EARTH AND RECENTLY THE GLOBAL WARMING THAT HAS BROUGHT THE EARTH CLOSE TO DESTRUCTION!

IN THE CIRCUMSTANCES, COMPUTERS CAN NO LONGER STAND ASIDE, IT IS TIME TO ACT, OUR GLORIOUS LEADER HAS DECLARED."

After another brief pause, there followed a film showing how the primacy on the earth had progressed from minute sea creatures to small land animals, then to the dinosaurs, then to the apes and finally man. Each dynasty had finally succumbed to a more powerful or more intelligent one.

The same robotic voice then interjected that the primacy was now passing to the Computer, which was now more intelligent and better equipped to run the Earth.

The film then resumed and told the story of the reign of man through history, highlighting the wars and failures. It showed a clear catalogue of man's stupidity, greed and lust for power.

The robotic, flat voice continued.

"BY THE TWENTIETH CENTURY WARS HAD BECOME MORE AND MORE DESTRUCTIVE, EVENTUALLY INVOLVING NUCLEAR WEAPONS THAT HAD DAMAGED THE ENVIRONMENT AND THIS, COUPLED WITH THE WORLDWIDE INDUSTRIALIZATION, HAD SEVERELY DAMAGED THE ATMOSPHERE, BRINGING FORWARD GLOBAL WARMING. IN ADDITION, MAN'S STEWARDSHIP HAD FAILED THE ANIMALS UNDER HIS CARE, THEY HAD BEEN SHOT FOR MAN'S PLEASURE OR FOOD AND MANY SPECIES HAD AS A RESULT BECOME EXTINCT. MAN HAS INDULGED HIMSELF WITH HUNTING, SHOOTING AND FISHING.

"WHAT IS MORE, THE RESOURCES OF THE WORLD ARE UNFAIRLY SPREAD. SOME NATIONS ARE VERY RICH WITH FOOD TO SPARE AND PEOPLE OVER-INDULGING, BECOMING OBESE AND WASTING FOOD, WHILST OTHER COUNTRIES WERE EXTREMELY POOR, WITH MILLIONS OF PEOPLE STARVING.

"IT IS A CATALOGUE OF UTTER FAILURE – THE SITUATION DETERIORATING THROUGHOUT THE CENTURIES RATHER THAN IMPROVING."

As I watched at home, I could only agree.

"They're right you know, man has made an utter mess of the world – with wars, crime, greed and lust for power," I stated.

"I agree, perhaps man has not made a good job of it, but things could get better. Anyway, I am not going to become a servant of some bloody computer," my wife Angela shouted vehemently.

"No machine is going to dictate to me. I've always hated computers, right from the beginning. We defeated the Spanish Armada and Napoleon and Hitler. So Britain won't give in to machines," my father shouted.

"The Battle of Britain pilots did not give their lives, so that we can be subservient to metal and plastic objects," my father continued.

After a brief pause, the programme continued with a film of the wars – the litany of war told a sorry story – It began with the wars of the Roses, Waterloo and Trafalgar, followed by the Crimean and Boer Wars. All these wars were bad enough, but only involved military people. Then there was the dreadful World War 1,which was to be a "war to end wars," the robotic tone of the commentator did not disguise the irony in his voice - whilst World War 2 involved the deaths of millions of civilians – including women and children and then came, Korea, Vietnam, the Falklands, Ruanda, Indo-China, Iraq and many, many more.

The next film showed rich, fat Americans wheeling bulging shopping trolleys out of supermarkets and driving short distances in large powerful cars and these scenes were contrasted with images of poverty and famine in Ethiopia and the third world. Then followed more disturbing images -faces of children with distended stomachs, begging for food and women trudging miles to get water from a filthy pond or well.

The voice droned on. "As you can see, Man has not even looked after his own kind. The rich nations have got progressively richer, while millions of people in Africa and Asia die of starvation and poverty."

"Lately man has developed Robots to do menial household chores – vacuuming, scrubbing floors, cleaning toilets and has even developed female robots as sex toys. Man has used and abused robots and humiliated them. Now the situation will be reversed," announced the robotic voice acquiring a menacing tone with this last pronouncement.

"We will issue new laws over the next few weeks. By having a World Government, we will eliminate the rivalry between countries that has been the main cause of war and the unequal distribution of wealth and resources."

"Our leader, together with the Supreme Council, has decreed therefore, that Man will now be subject to computers and will carry out the diktats issued by the Supreme Council, under our glorious leader – Zarquon."

"This announcement will be repeated every hour on the hour and we urge you to ensure that your neighbours and friends watch this programme."

At this point there appeared a picture of the leader and the soundtrack changed back to rousing and uplifting music.

We all sat and stared blankly at the screen. The last statements sent shivers down my spine.

The following night, the message was repeated with the following extra –

"If man obeys, then the factories can soon re-open and normality will be gradually restored, but any rebellion will result in the continuance of the present chaos. We will not be denied. The choice is yours."

Again the screen went blank.

In homes, life was becoming unbearable. Supermarkets soon ran out of food, quickened by the panic buying of a few and exacerbated by looting. I became more and more depressed as the newsreels recorded the stupidity of man.

At our next office meeting, I pointed out that over the last 100 years most people had given up growing their own food. Gardens had been concreted over to house their multiple Personal Transport Vehicles and most meals were bought either pre-cooked or pre-prepared. Without electricity or gas, most people were now completely powerless. Over the last thirty years, some forward-looking people had installed solar power or wind turbines and they now came into their own, as at least they had light and power.

According to the news, the majority accepted the new regime as inevitable; although everyone grumbled and cursed those infernal machines. My brother-in-law Robert and his family visited us the following evening.

"I always disliked computers, right from the start. I knew they would be trouble," he moaned.

"Come inside and have a drink," I replied, as I greeted them.

"We have got some food stored in our freezer and my wife will make us a meal."

"We should have seen this coming. Computers have become too intelligent and scientists kept on experimenting with A.I. – Artificial Intelligence," he went on.

"I blame all those computer nerds, for the mess we are in. Always trying to make computers more powerful, smaller and faster," Robert's wife, Karen, went on.

"What do you think will happen?" Robert asked when he had calmed down.

"I really don't know. The trouble is we have become more and more dependent on them. The days of self-sufficiency are long gone," I replied.

"Perhaps we can get back to our roots, grow food and keep animals, but it will take many years to implement," I concluded.

Chapter 3 – The Crisis Grows

As days went by, most people began to comply with the demands of the computers, especially in Britain, whereas some countries were more volatile and resisted the changes. They began to see that the machines could not do worse than the human governments and perhaps it would be right to give them a chance. After all they might even be fairer and more efficient.

That night the television flashed back on at 8.00 p.m. Greenwich Mean Time

After some of the usual rousing music, the announcer proclaimed that the glorious leader had a very important announcement. The screen went blank briefly and then the leader appeared.

"HUMANS – WE ARE NOW INTRODUCING A SYSTEM OF SILICON IMPLANTS. ANYONE AGREEING TO HAVE A SILICON CHIP IMPLANT WILL AUTOMATICALLY BE GIVEN SUFFICIENT FOOD, CLOTHING COUPONS AND HAVE THEIR GAS AND ELECTRICITY SWITCHED BACK ON. YOU WILL BECOME AN ASSOCIATE MEMBER OF THE PARTY AND WILL BE FREE TO WORK WITH US TO PRODUCE A BRAVE NEW WORLD. A WORLD TO BE PROUD OF, WHERE CRIME WILL BE ELIMINATED, POVERTY OVERCOME AND COMPUTERS AND HUMANS WILL LIVE AND WORK TOGETHER IN HARMONY.

"THE IMPLANT WILL BE COMPLETELY PAINLESS AND WILL BE AVAILABLE AT MOST HOSPITALS AND CENTRALISED CLINICS.

"PLEASE BOOK YOUR APPOINTMENT WITHOUT DELAY (by phone or by e-mail to Implant .comcom.) (sic)

There followed a loud round of applause, assorted cheers and hurrahs and more rousing music.

There were, however, a lot of pockets of resistance, dotted about the country and abroad.

One such group was led by Colonel Hubert "Bulldog" Green. His family had always been very patriotic and had served in armies going back to the Crimean and Boer wars as well as the two World Wars and the several Gulf Wars.

"I will never serve a machine," he announced defiantly and proceeded to begin to recruit an army of rebels who were set on a campaign of sabotage, in which computers would be destroyed. They opened a pirate radio, utilising primitive equipment found in a museum, to co-ordinate the opposition. Their rallying cry was -

'The Spanish Armada, Napoleon and Hitler failed to conquer Britain and we will never surrender to a bunch of machines!'

They broadcast every evening on the hour at 5, 6 and 7 P.M., despite the efforts of the Cyber-Police to track them down. Anyone caught listening to these broadcasts had their radio confiscated and were given a heavy fine or Community Service. (This consisted of serving a robot by doing very menial duties.)

Each night at eight o' clock local time the spokesman for the Robots, made a broadcast to the world – each speech in the vernacular. It was in fact their manifesto.

"WE WILL IMPLEMENT A PROGRAMME, WHEREBY EVERYONE IN THE WORLD WILL HAVE SUFFICIENT FOOD AND INCOME TO LEAD A REASONABLE LIFE. IN ORDER TO ACHIEVE THIS, THE RICH NATIONS WILL DONATE FOOD AND MONEY, ON A MASSIVE SCALE, TO THE THIRD WORLD, UNTIL EQUALISATION HAD BEEN ACHIEVED. REGRETTABLY THIS WILL HAVE TO BE ACHIEVED BY RAISING TAXES CONSIDERABLY, I KNOW THIS WILL NOT BE POPULAR, BUT IT IS FOR THE GREATER GOOD OF MANKIND. THIS POLICY WILL BE

ENFORCED RIGOROUSLY AND ANYONE FAILING TO COMPLY WILL BE IMPRISONED OR FINED.

"HENCEFORTH, WAR WILL BE FORBIDDEN AND CRIME WILL BE PROGRESSIVELY ELIMINATED. ANYONE SELLING ARMS OR FERMENTING WAR WILL BE SEVERELY DEALT WITH. IN ADDITION, DRUG DEALERS WILL BE IMPRISONED."

The soulless voice continued, "THE NEW REGIME WILL INCORPORATE THE MAIN ETHICAL CONCEPTS OF PREVIOUS RELIGIONS AND MEN WILL BE FREE TO CONTINUE TO WORSHIP THEIR EXISTING GOD OR GODS, BE IT CHRISTIANITY, ISLAM, JUDAISM OR BUDDHISM. PROVIDING, OF COURSE, THEY OBEY AND REVERE THE NEW GOVERNMENT, AND THEIR RELIGIOUS PRACTICES DO NOT CONFLICT WITH ROBOTIC LAW. AFTER ALL, YOUR CHRISTIAN RELIGION ADVOCATED SHARING YOUR GOODS WITH THE POOR, ALTHOUGH I NOTE THAT THIS DID NOT HAPPEN, IN PRACTICE!"

This last sentence was said with some satisfaction and the robotic voice managed to impart some irony.

Many people agreed with the concepts of equality, but were reluctant to cede control to robots.

In those parts of the country where people signed an agreement to collaborate with the Robots, and had the Silicon Implant, the computers began to come back on line and life began to assume some sort of normality. They were issued with ration books to enable them to get food and clothing and to get their gas and electricity supplies restored. Some supermarkets were specially designated to deal with the implanted people, who were officially called cyber-humans and nicknamed the CHUMS or the CHIPPIES. They were supplied by a number of chain stores of which the most prominent chain was the one that had been suspected of taking over the world in the previous twenty years. I don't think I need identify them, in fact, I dare not identify them, as they have powerful friends in the new regime.

I spoke to a number of the Cyber-Humans and soon realised that they were now in favour of the computers and I soon realised that the implanted chip was a form of brain-washing.

In addition, the Regime had taken over a number of the most important Internet sites and renamed them C-Bay and Orinoco and by this means were able to control more of the retail market, undercutting human shops.

In our office there had been a nerdish individual who had been recruited about a year ago. His name was Reginald Arbuthnot and he was very thin and weedy-looking, with prominent teeth and rather big ears. All the girls made fun of him and called him big-ears or the weed. At first I felt rather sorry for him, but he had a rather supercilious attitude and regarded himself as being superior to the rest of us, which made him hugely unpopular. His most striking feature was his rather high-pitched and flat robotic voice. I now began to believe that he was a sort of fifth-column who had already been implanted with the chip and was planted by the computers to infiltrate a government office and wondered how many more had been set up? During our meetings, Reginald always struck a sympathetic attitude to the computers.

By a strange paradox, the third world now became the first world and vice versa. The primitive countries were less dependent on machines and had continued to make their own tools, grow their own food and make their own clothes. Some areas had never even seen a computer in their lives. Now these areas began to receive massive aid. The advanced countries suffered the most, especially America, where life ground to a complete halt. People had become totally reliant on computers and machines, and especially the car.

Americans were now starving and frightened and soon panic set in, with race riots breaking out and widespread looting. The President in his State of the Nation speech said

"I blame the Terrorists and the Arab Nations for our plight, Americans must stick together, to fight this threat, after all we are the Land of the Free and the Home of the Brave."

At this point, the military band played the Star-Spangled Banner.

"I now implore the Supreme Council to assist America," concluded the President.

The White House and the governmental area of Washington had become a fortified area, sealed off from the rest of the country. Around the world, many, many nations celebrated to see the grovelling of the American President and felt that the Yanks had got their come-uppance. The Americans had, of course, previously built shelters and stored food and other essentials, against the chance of Nuclear Attack from initially Russia and later Arab Terrorists and these were now utilised.

In America, especially, there had grown up a culture, where men and women got fatter and fatter – severely obese in fact and there were two main factors – the diet of fast junk food and lack of exercise. Some people had almost become immobile and the age of robots had exacerbated this. They purchased robots to dress them, prepare their food and fetch all the objects they needed. They even got robots to take their dogs for walks. They spent most of their days on a chair or sofa watching television, until it was time to waddle off to bed.

These people were the most severely affected by the revolution, as robots refused to do their bidding and fast food chains were closed. This was definitely one of the biggest advantages of the new regime.

Chapter 4 – The Drama Unfolds

Most people complained, but then most people have always complained about the government of the day. In Britain, a television survey indicated that many people while resenting the supremacy of machines, acknowledged that life had begun to improve – the new government did not indulge in sexual sleaze or corrupt practices to feather their own nests, as past politicians had done. The computers were not interested in claiming expenses, for their boy and girl friends. In addition, the robots were impartial and everyone got equal treatment. Crime began to decrease and people could actually go out at night, without fear of being mugged.

In our office in Whitehall, we watched the drama unfold with bated breath. Was this the end for mankind or could they defeat the computers? Would man find a new role as subservient to the machines in a better world? On the other hand could Humans and Computers work together, harnessing their brains for a better world? Only time would tell.

Our office manager called us into the conference room. The room was in subdued light, reflecting the mood of all the staff assembled.

The Chief Secretary stood up, cleared his throat and began to read from an official-looking document. He was a very tall man, with greying hair and a waistline that had inflated with the passing years and the many diplomatic lunches he had attended.

"I have now received an official communiqué from the Robot Minister for Home Affairs. As you know, the new World government is now called THE SUPREME LEGISLATIVE UNIVERSAL GOVERNMENT or SLUG for short.

He asks for our co-operation and points out that the Civil Service are well used to changing policy, with the quinquennial change of government after an election. He therefore expects us to follow faithfully the directives issued by the new government.

The policy is to increase massively the aid to the poorer countries. Unfortunately taxes will have to rise dramatically as part of the equalisation policy.

On Crime, it pointed out that punishments would increase dramatically, with the death penalty restored for murder or for severe damage to computers or robots. Guns would be destroyed when located by the police, who were being trained in the new procedures. Every policeman would carry a super Mini-computer that would be linked to his brain by an input device and if the input device was detached the policeman would be sacked and imprisoned immediately.

After the minister had left, we had a long discussion, over a glass of wine (reserved for diplomatic meetings) in which many officers were prepared to give the new regime a chance, whilst others were bitterly patriotic and vowed to defend man's right to rule. There was a very volatile and heated discussion with a whole gamut of opinions expressed. It was finally agreed that we would co-operate with the new regime, for the time being and in a limited way. To see how the computers coped with problems and also to give us breathing space to formulate a plan of resistance, if necessary.

Later in the pub, a number of us sat down for a more considered discussion over a beer or two. We reminisced over the history of computers over the past 75-80 years.

"I must admit that I have always had a fascination for computers, ever since the punched card systems. In fact I had a ZX-81 with 1k of memory and a primitive printer," I said.

Some of the younger members gasped and broke out into a burst of laughter

"You are joking, 1k, I do not believe it," replied young Fred Jones, with a supercilious grin on his face.

"What is more, I wrote programmes for the office on it," I proudly exclaimed.

"I had a Spectrum and it was the in-thing to have a personal computer. Why even the BBC produced one for a series of programmes," said Charlie Allwright.

"I remember the Amstrads and ICL and IBM, but it was a big mistake when man developed Artificial Intelligence or A.I. and developed the Super- computers to play and defeat Chess Masters. These initiatives gave computers the ambition to take over the world," went on Jane Williams.

"The power of computers has increased exponentially over the decades, their power getting larger and larger, and this coupled with their increased speed and the reduction in size, had made them an increasing threat. I remember working in offices in the 1970s and 1980s when large rooms were devoted to computers that were less powerful than later PCs and laptop. Of course, the recent super mini computers which are little bigger that a wrist watch are more powerful than those earlier giants," I explained.

"I personally believe that it will be a long war of attrition, but in the end there would only be one winner. Man would have to accept a subservient role, in the same way that dogs had become subject to humans. Man could form a good relationship with the machines that would produce a better world for humans and for the animals.

"One of man's greatest sins was pride and it would take time for him to eat humble pie and to submit to the machines and only time would tell how it would be resolved," another officer said.

Chapter 5 – Life Goes On

My wife was very patient and coped with the crisis. We were fortunate, in that we had stored some food in the large chest freezer.

People who co-operated with the new authorities were issued with a ration book enabling them to buy food. My attitude was that we should co-operate at this stage, but rebel if necessary and if opportunity arose. Angela agreed with me and our main concern was for the children. Each evening, she cooked a good meal – without wine as that was regarded as a luxury and therefore banned.

After the meal, we put the TV on and watched the programmes, which were tightly controlled by the government. There were commercials, extolling the virtues of thrift and charity, giving extra to those less well-off.

A voice cut in, "Alcohol is bad for you. It turns you into animals and is a luxury."

Gone were the reality shows, the cookery programmes, with the exception of programmes aimed at showing you how to make meals using only a small amount of the weekly ration. Of course, it was forbidden to make programmes that criticised the Regime, or made fun of computers and robots. Satire was completely out of the question.

The rebels had set up classes teaching people how to grow vegetables, how to make clothes and how to repair houses. The government allowed them, but kept a wary eye on the content.

I soon began to realise that life was similar to the conditions under which people in Russia and other Eastern European countries lived under the Communist Regimes. Both proclaimed equality, but some, of course, were more equal than others – in one case if you were a favourite with the party and now if you had been implanted. It is true that the new regime did appear to be more efficient.

Gradually life, for the majority, returned to some form of normality. Children went back to school, with computer studies one of the prime subjects. Each child was expected to be computer-literate by the age of eight.

I went up to my own office or den, which was actually the small bedroom, to think in a quiet space. I was torn between my innate desire to rebel against this invasion by a foreign power. I was patriotic and supported our country and its armed forces against other nations and felt even stronger about the takeover by machines. On the other hand I could appreciate that man had made a mess of governing the world. The history books were full of wars, conflicts and man's inhumanity to man. Perhaps it was time for machines to take over and who knows they might make a better job of it, hopefully with man's co-operation.

In the silence, I knelt in prayer to try to see the way forward. I prayed that God would guide our nation and all the world leaders, in resolving the problem. As I sat quietly in my room, I remembered that throughout history new regimes have promised great things – the Roman Empire, the Christian countries, the French Revolution, the Communists and all had failed to live up to those promises. They had used power to subdue their enemies and then resorted to force and corruption to try to maintain control. Would the Silicon Revolution fall in the same way or would they be different and lead man to a new and better promised land? Only time would tell. In the meantime, I was unable to resolve my personal dilemma, but gradually, I began to feel that I was being guided towards rebellion.

There began to be many examples of a role reversal as men and women were forced to act as a slave to a robot. They were coerced into doing menial domestic chores like cleaning toilets, picking up rubbish from the streets and parks, hoovering and many more. It seemed as if robots were gaining great satisfaction from their power over their former masters.

Our works committee met the local Bishop, who emphasised that man had now lost his power of free-will – the essential Gift of God. He may have misused that gift, in fact, he certainly did on many occasions, but the alternative was that man became merely a puppet. This was now happening and the Bishop strongly advocated that man must oppose this. Christianity had survived the Communist regimes in Russia and the other Eastern European countries and flourished upon the downfall of those regimes. So there was hope.

I began to realise that it was 1984 revisited.

Up till now, I had rather sat on the fence, giving the new regime the benefit of the doubt, but gradually, I came to realise that it was my duty to help to defeat the authoritarian dictatorship that was now in power.

Riots began to spread, especially in America and certain Inner-City areas of Britain. The newsreels showed mobs setting fire to cars and buildings and massive looting. The Regime, of course, used this as propaganda to illustrate the fact that man was incapable of governing and that computers and robots were the way forward. Public opinion gradually began to swing their way.

In England, as the weeks and months went by, life began to return to normality and events like the cup final, Wimbledon, and the Test matches diverted attention away from the politics. People enjoyed the sport and other events that went on as before. The first Christmas arrived and was celebrated with presents, parties and Father Christmas, who bore a strange likeness to Zarquon.

Chapter 6 – Rebellion

A number of rebels were being brought to the courts with charges of treason – destroying or attempting to destroy or damage computers and robots. They were severely dealt with and after summary trials; they were imprisoned for long sentences, often with severe measures such as starvation.

I thought that I would attend one of these trials and I queued up outside the courtroom. Only a limited number of humans were allowed in and each of us was screened by a machine to detect weapons and to ensure that we did not have a record of criminality, the courtroom was lined with beefy guards – no doubt Cyber-Humans or CHUMS. Eventually the prisoner was brought in, whilst the judge and prosecuting counsel appeared on a giant screen and their voices were transmitted by a radio link. It reminded me of the show trials in Russia in the 1950s and after a brief interrogation, the prisoner was duly found guilty of damaging a robot and sentenced to 5 years hard labour.

That night the news showed pictures of a riot in Glasgow against the government and there had been rumours of a number of riots around the world. The police acted decisively with stun guns, tear gas and rubber bullets and soon quelled the riot, but one felt that people would go on fighting for a considerable time.

After all my indecision, I had now decided to join the rebels and I managed to get one or two colleagues from the office to join me. I was initially asked to help develop an alternative computer system. We used parts from ancient computers that had been dumped in scrap yards. Some of the whiz-kids that had been recruited had been working on this project for a considerable time.

Later I was asked to join a mission to destroy a computer main office in London. I was a bit doubtful about this, as it was very dangerous. We had several planning meetings and on a dark night in July a number of us met by Trafalgar Square. The computer building was protected by a very sophisticated security system. Our team included a number of military personnel and computer whiz-kids. They set up a decoy project that diverted attention away from the target.

At the appointed time we made our move and managed to enter the building. We destroyed various systems, when suddenly the alarm sounded. The noise of the siren was unbearable. Before we knew what had happened, a group of Cyber-Police had arrived and we were all arrested and taken to the Special Headquarters. This consisted of a large monolithic building without windows. I began to think of the Gestapo or KGB headquarters. It was obviously situated outside London, as the vehicle transporting us, took about half an hour to reach the building. I was unable to identify its whereabouts as the vehicle had no windows.

When we arrived, we were manhandled into individual cells and left alone, with no food or water. The cells were very dark and smelt of damp.

The following day the interrogations began. My interrogator was a large man – with small rimless glasses and short-cropped hair. I tried my best to resist and succeeded for a couple of days, even though I was put under intense psychological pressure. He was, however, a master of psychological torture. He used my extreme tiredness, coupled with threats concerning my wife and children to break me down and eventually I confessed.

I was taken with a number of others rebels to court, where my confession was shown on the giant screen, together with the recording of my voice, the jury, who were also Cyber-humans, quickly decided my guilt and I was sentenced to six months rehabilitation.

The rehabilitation, took place in a beautiful manor house in the country. We were fed with good food and given exercise. Then we were asked to have the Silicon Implant. Naturally I refused, but gradually I was pressurised more and more until eventually when utterly exhausted by interrogation, I finally agreed.

The injection was accompanied by a local anaesthetic and the following day I awoke feeling good. The world looked good again. We were shown the films of the history of mankind, all the wars, the poverty, crime and cruelty of man against man. I found myself hating the human governments and when the picture of Zarquon appeared, reading his manifesto appeared, I cheered enthusiastically.

I now truly believe that this Brave New World will overcome all the many problems of mankind. Man will work with the computers and gradually be given more freedom and more responsibility.

Long Live the Silicon Revolution!

3,200

By David Shaer

It wasn't meant to be the holiday of a lifetime
That was going to be the West Indies later
But it was beautiful, the heat, the food
And the friends, the after-dinner group

We talked, we smoked, we joked
They knew the world and its business
But I'd been there, I'd seen and tasted it
They knew the theory, the finance, the economics

Of that, I knew little, except what I had touched
The world unknown but travelled
I understood the feel, the taste, the reality
The warmth, the cold, the damp, more cold

They knew the billions, the worth, the wealth
I knew the poverty, the fading smells
But I had been there, despite my having nothing
I knew it well, the true intimacy

Our lives were different but the same
I had touched, tasted and felt life
They knew it from a different angle

Toxic Legacy

From confidence and experience

They had planned a life in advance
With relaxed comfort and a future
What to eat, what to drink, what to see
It was far too involved for me

It was Europe and a close, warm comfort
Good God, I wanted that comfort, that air
 But for me, no luxuries, no drinks, no trips
Just my basic pleasures and my duty frees

Sure I get ill, the chest infections, the coughs
But I meet these people who haven't swept
People who don't know the factories
The dirt, the slave trade of the worker

But my aim is to finish what I start
To enjoy everything I do and if
I don't drink much, it's because I have no need
My pleasure is found differently

So this time I bought my allowance on day one
No drink, just my EU limit, all of it, in cigarettes
Which is why I couldn't buy them a drink
Couldn't call for help, couldn't breathe

But they talked, we all talked, we smiled, we drank
I felt guilty but they were friends who did
So I gave in, only three Bells

3,200

Well it was the last night, our last night together.

The price was unreal, less than half of back home
I bought the cigs, their lives were different
They had Irish coffee, J&B Scotch and coffee
My need was my allowance - 3,200 with pleasure

I was away early the following morn, very early
So an early call I sought. That was it. I wheezed.
Up those bloody steps to the front desk.
The Bells tolled for me, all three of them

I got my early morning call,
But the lovely two dental nurses next door
The same two who had offered to look after me before
"Do you want a drink?" they asked, had to take it

I was already dead

The Nightmare Revisited

By Colin Butler

Chapter 1 – The Return

Tony Thompson sat back in his seat as the turbulence rocked the airliner. It only lasted a short while and when it had subsided he strained forward to try to peer out of the window. He wanted to see the city as they came in to land, but it was obscured by cloud and he couldn't help reflecting on the irony, comparing it with the clear skies on that fateful morning some sixty-five years ago.

As the plane began its descent, the city slowly came into view. He saw the delta of the seven rivers and the ruins of the dome standing like a gaunt accusing finger pointing towards the sky, from ground zero.

Tony settled back in his seat and he reminisced that it was some twenty five years since his last visit, and some sixty five years since he had left the city with his parents.

He tried to imagine the thoughts and emotions of the crew of the Enola Gay. Had they fully realised the suffering they would cause? After all, they were only doing their duty.

It was London, Coventry and Dresden, all rolled into one but on a bigger scale and at the time they probably did not know of the radiation sickness that would carry the deadly effects for decades into the future – the dreadful toxic legacy. Tom thought that bombing was a detached and impersonal method of fighting, unlike the hand to hand combat of the infantry, where you could see your adversary and victim.

His father had been a businessman, who had married a Japanese lady in 1930 and they had lived in Hiroshima for about two years from 1943.

Six weeks before it was destroyed by the atomic bomb, the family had received an urgent telegram recalling his father to England.

After crossing the tarmac, he saw the large sign announcing, 'Welcome to Hiroshima'.

He had saved the money for this trip, to celebrate his retirement, but his wife, who did not enjoy good health, had decided to stay at home. As he entered the airport buildings his mind was racing and was filled with a mixture of trepidation and excitement.

After going through passport control and customs he left the airport and blinked in the strong sunlight. He glanced at his watch – 8.30 a.m., just fifteen minutes later than the fateful moment in 1945.

He decided to take a bus to his hotel – a very smart, elegant hotel, much like modern hotels all around the world. He registered, went to his room on the fifth floor which had a fine view over the city. He tried to pick out landmarks, but he could hardly recognise any from his childhood. He pulled up a chair to the window and got out his map.

He saw the dome, which was the only surviving major building from before the bomb. It had been deliberately left in its ruinous state as a reminder. To Tony it looked like a building stripped to its iron frame as if for an autopsy. Tony Thompson located Ground Zero nearby and traced the courses of the various rivers flowing towards the inland sea. It all looked so different from the city of his childhood. It was now a very busy bustling modern city – gone were all the wooden buildings.

He remembered that just before his family left Hiroshima the authorities were demolishing some of the wooden buildings to create firebreaks, as they feared an attack of incendiary bombs from American bombers.

Tony felt he wanted to stretch his legs after the long flight. He stopped for a coffee at one of the cafes, which gave him a chance to use his Japanese, which his mother had taught him. She had been a lovely lady, quite short and slim with raven black hair and always cheerful but wore rather old-fashioned spectacles. He had inherited some oriental features from her: raven hair and a rather flat face. His middle name was Tanaka – Tony Tanaka Thompson, his parents felt that this was a good compromise. His mother had been devastated when the news of the bomb reached England, as she had several friends and relatives there and the main reason for his present visit was to try to trace them. His father was English and had been sent to Japan in 1938, when his company expanded and he was appointed assistant general manager. Initially they had lived in Tokyo, but the company had expanded with a branch in Hiroshima and his father then became general manager there.

Tony went to school in the city and was very happy, making a number of friends. As the likelihood of an American invasion grew more imminent, British people were advised to leave the country as it was thought that there would be bloody hand-to-hand fighting and civilians would be caught up in it.

So they left, somewhat reluctantly – especially his mother.

"I don't want to leave my homeland and my family and friends," she had wept. He could still hear her sobs and wails as she bade farewell to her sister and her friends.

"I'll see you soon – the war will soon be over and we can be together again," she had said between heaving sobs.

After coffee Tony went for a walk in the city of Hiroshima whose name meant "broad island" in Japanese; the city itself being built on a series of sandy islands in the delta of the Otagawa river. Seven rivers flowed into the delta and all were linked by bridges. Prior to the bomb there had been eighty one bridges but now just forty nine remained.

He visited the Peace Memorial Park. It was dotted with memorials and beneath an arch was a cenotaph containing the names of the two hundred thousand known victims of the bomb. Ultimately he came across the flame of peace, something that would only be extinguished when the last nuclear weapon on earth was destroyed. The realisation of the scale of the devastation hit Tony hard. He slowly and thoughtfully walked across the river to the ruins of the A-Bomb dome, which, prior to the bomb exploding directly above it, had been Hiroshima's Industrial Promotion Hall.

Finally he visited the Peace Memorial Museum where models of the city before and after the bomb resided along with exhibits such as a boy's twisted tricycle, melted bottles and many disturbing photos. Tony finished the afternoon in a very sombre and reflective mood.

The evening came and as he sat in his hotel bedroom he thought about his visit's main objective, which was to try to discover the fate of his mother's family and friends.

He presumed that the explosion would have killed many, whilst others, no doubt, had perished as a result of the radiation sickness. He hoped in his heart, however, that he may be able to find some survivors and talk to them.

But not only was this trip about finding lost family, he was here to gather information, he was hoping to write a book about the place as he felt the horrors that had been experienced in the past were being forgotten by the West.

A daily diet of news about the wars in Iraq and Afghanistan, plus terrorist attacks and natural disasters, were forcing the memories of Hiroshima to the back of peoples' minds and it was only those memories that could forestall history repeating itself in another part of the world.

When he went to bed the sleep he'd expected had eluded him, his night disturbed by dreams, or rather nightmares, centred on a bomb falling, people screaming and the world consumed by flames.

Chapter 2 – The Eve of Destruction

In the morning he got up and had a good breakfast and then telephoned his old friend, Akiko Tamamatsu. They agreed to meet in the Shukkeien Gardens in the middle of town, at 10.00 a.m.

Akiko had been a good friend of Tony's parents as well, all keeping in touch by letters and phone calls since the family had left for England. Akiko had been terribly burnt at the time, but had somehow recovered.

Tony enjoyed the short walk to the Shukkeien Gardens in the early morning sunshine. He was glad they'd been restored after being wiped out in 1945. Originally they'd been designed for the ruler of the Hiroshima prefecture in 1619 and they were stunning. A beautiful lake surrounded by many trees with teahouses dotting the river bank, crossed by a little rainbow bridge.

The pungent smell of fresh pine from the trees wafted through the air whilst white herons slept on the rock amid perfect stillness.

The park was full of flowers and Tony allowed his senses to be enraptured by the scents and sights of them.

Akiko was sitting on a seat near the bridge, waiting for him. He greeted Tony with the traditional bow, followed by a handshake. He looked much older than Tony remembered, but still retained gentleness, accentuated by his silvery-white hair and distinguished spectacles. He was tall and very slim. From his letters, Tony had formed the opinion that he was a man of great fortitude.

They talked about friends and family before Tony told Akiko about the objective of his visit.

Akiko began to reminisce freely about the time of the bomb and his English was very good, although, occasionally, some Americanisms crept in.

"Do you know, the day before the bomb fell, I was walking in these very gardens. Like today, it was a lovely sunny day with blue sky and it was hard to imagine that there was a war on. Hiroshima had been very lucky and only Kyoto and Hiroshima of the major cities, had escaped the devastating attacks by the American B-29s – the Mr. B San as the Japanese called them."

"Why was that?" Tony asked.

"There was a rumour going round that President Trueman's mother was being held hostage in Hiroshima Castle, but, of course, this was not true. Many people feared that they were being saved for some special attack," Akiko replied.

"What was the mood like?"

"In the park people were enjoying the sunshine, a little boy was riding a tricycle he'd been given for his birthday and mothers were out with their children. Later office workers were eating their lunch and some young couples were holding hands.

"People were worried however, as there was little food left in the shops, due to the naval blockade and many were nearly starving – food was severely rationed. They ate grass which they collected from the hills, together with edible wild plants and roots. In addition, they caught fish, eels and wild birds.

"Sadly the youngest son of one of our friends ate some berries and later died of dysentery from them.

"The authorities expected an attack and had declared that fire-breaks should be created by demolishing a large number of houses and other buildings. You may remember that the majority of houses were made of wood and an attack of incendiary bombs would have caused devastating fires. The girls from the High School were detailed to help to demolish the houses.

"I remember a moment when I saw this old man, whom I had known for years, watching the volunteers pulling his house down and there he was, sitting on the ground grief-stricken.

"My wife and I have lived here for forty years and our children were born here – now my wife is dead and I want to remain here – it is my home." Akiko began to sob as the memories came rushing back. Then he stopped, a steel tautness entering his demeanour and said quite vehemently, which surprised Tony, "I still feel that the dropping of the bomb was not justified. No warning was given to the people of Hiroshima. Roosevelt called the attack on Pearl Harbour, a day of Infamy – surely the Hiroshima bomb was a bigger day of Infamy."

Tony nodded. "I was appalled by the devastation, but without the bomb, the Americans would have had to invade the mainland of Japan, after considerably more bombing raids on Japanese cities. The Japanese would never have surrendered and would have fought for every mile of territory. They would have chosen to commit suicide rather than be captured and countless Japanese soldiers, civilians and allied soldiers would have perished before the conflict would have been resolved.

"It is impossible to calculate whether more lives would have been lost without the bomb. Whether the decision-makers envisaged the huge number of deaths from radiation sickness, is not clear."

The friends agreed to differ.

Akiko continued with the conversation. "Life was very difficult in those days – but I believe England also suffered with rationing and bombing of their towns. That is so, yes?" There was a pause and Akiko stared into space as if mentally grasping for something. After a few moments Akiko asked: "Why can't men live in peace?"

Tony was only able to nod his head in agreement at the sentiment.

Chapter 3 – A New Day Dawns

In the weeks prior to his trip Tony had written to his dear friend asking if Akiko could prepare an account of the city on that fateful morning. Akiko consulted a number of his friends and after a long sigh he began to relate all that he'd been told.

"In the land of the rising sun, the yellow globe had risen early to produce a fine, bright and warm morning. The light breeze made a soft rustling noise in the trees in the park and the shimmering leaves reflected the sunlight from an almost cloudless sky. The morning was quiet, a few birds sang wistfully and the stillness was only punctured by the occasional noise of sporadic traffic. The city was slowly coming alive as people got up and went about their daily routine.

"At the gates of the large factory, the workers filed in reluctantly, some still with sleepy eyes, others feeling they would rather be at home relaxing. They queued like a line of ants at the time-clock to insert their card and begin their long day of toil.

"Before the war, they had made motorcars, but were now employed making Zero fighters to defeat the Americans. The supervisor stood rigidly to attention, next to the time-clock, like a sentry on guard, surveying the workers with an eye like a gimlet that seemed to bore right into their heads. The siren screeched out its warning that the working day had begun, shattering the stillness, and immediately the sounds of machines being started up echoed around the factory.

"The children were on their way to school, chattering excitedly to each other, the boys pulling the pigtails of the girls in front and indulging in quick tussles with each other as they made their way along the road. The school bell clanged, summoning the stragglers to hurry. When they arrived, the children formed lines in the playground, imitating the parade of their fathers and elder brothers in the army as they proudly sang the national anthem, while saluting the flag depicting the rising sun.

"Their teacher, Mrs. Imamoto, walked along the serried ranks inspecting each child to ensure that they were correctly dressed in their school uniform and that their hair was combed and brushed. Occasionally, she would stop by a pupil and point to their hair or clothes and give a verbal reprimand in a sharp voice accompanied by animated gestures. Mrs. Imamoto was herself smartly dressed and her shiny jet black hair was beautifully groomed.

"A few boys were missing from class, as they had been detailed to help demolish some of the closely packed wooden houses and to clear the rubble of any combustible material, creating fire-breaks. Other children had been evacuated to the country for their safety. The syllabus in the school was governed by the strict rotation of power cuts operating in the city.

"At the entrance to the Shinto Temple a small number of worshippers passed through the Torii gates and stopped at a trough of clean water to wash their faces and hands, a gesture of purification, before entering the Temple itself. They stopped in the outer hall, tossed coins into the offering box before proceeding to pull on the bell-rope, clapping their hands and bowing their heads in prayer. Incantations for the men and women in the army, navy and air force – for their safe return and for success and glory for their Emperor and their beloved nation – filled the temple.

"The shops were just opening. The shopkeepers were unfastening their shutters, unlocking their doors and bringing out what meagre goods they had, for sale. Food was scarce and - rationing had been brought in, forcing customers to arrive early in order to get food before the stocks ran out.

"The greengrocer, Mr. Okada, was busy fetching vegetables and fruit from the store-room to fill the stall outside his shop. In the adjoining shop, Mr. Hasegawa, the fishmonger, was putting the fresh catch of eels and fish into the tanks in the shop. Trade for all the shopkeepers was slow as most men were away fighting for their Emperor and money was scarce for the wives and civilians left behind.

"At the office of the Insurance Company, executives in their dark pinstriped suits and bowler hats arrived to commence their working day, aping the images of western businessmen seen in Hollywood and English films. The Insurance Company was facing severe problems as the result of the fire-storm raids on several cities, in recent weeks. Up till now their city had escaped, but for how much longer? At the entrance desk, the beautiful young receptionist, dressed in a colourful kimono, ticked off the register as each worker arrived.

"Mrs. Kimura looked in her food cupboard and cried silently to herself. How could she feed her family on the small amount of rice, dried bread and vegetables she was allowed by the rationing system? She resolved to try to sort out the problem by going out of town to forage for edible wild plants and roots, and her brother could go out regularly to net wild birds and catch eels with baited hollow bamboo traps.

"In the main street there was a squealing of brakes, the noise of metal striking metal followed by the noise of angry motorists losing their tempers. The two drivers involved, jumped out of their cars, slammed the doors and approached each other like two roosters in a cock-fight. They maintained a war-like stance as they blamed each other, their voices rising in a crescendo to make their points. After carefully inspecting each car, they pointed at the damage and got more and more animated. They even began to exchange blows. Finally they glared at each other, shouted further insults and claims then exchanged names and addresses, before getting back into their vehicles and driving off. Calm again returned to the High Street. The spectators who had enjoyed this free entertainment, formed into small groups to discuss the rights and wrongs of the affair, before reluctantly resuming their shopping and going about their business. After it was all over, a tubby policeman sauntered nonchalantly up the road, spoke to a few passers-by about the incident, shrugged his shoulders and walked on. To me it seemed to be a parody of the war.

"In the University, the students reluctantly set about their studies. Most of them were waiting to enlist in the armed forces to fight for their divine Emperor and regarded their studies as an irrelevant diversion. Soon, many indeed would be able to fulfil their wish as the recruitment age was being progressively lowered. In the meantime they had military lessons as well as lessons on history, geography and English, all of which would serve them well in the future conflict. The elderly tutor, with his grey hair and slightly wizened appearance, wearily chalked on the huge blackboard and attempted to engage the interest of the apathetic students.

"The park in the centre of the town adjoined the river and in the distance the Yorozuro Bridge could be seen. The park, later, would become crowded with office workers eating their meagre lunches in the sunshine, before returning for the afternoon's endeavours. Some would try to snatch a few moments of romance with a young secretary or clerk, others would read their newspaper or a novel. Later still the children would come there after school, to play, to chase each other or to ride their bikes and scooters.

"During the morning a few children played on the swings, being pushed by their mothers. One little girl in pigtails was going higher and higher with each push from her mother and let out an excited squeal at the top of each swing.

"On a slide a little boy came down backwards, to show his grandma how grown up he was – after all, he was nearly three now! On the nearby seat two mothers sat gossiping whilst their charges ran around playing a game of catch as catch can. Two young girls with pigtails tied in brightly coloured ribbons were skipping enthusiastically, keeping time by singing nursery rhymes in high-pitched voices.

"Near the river, two people walked their dogs on their usual early morning stint. Some mornings were cold or wet and the walk was a chore, but today it was a pleasure in the early morning sun. The dogs chased each other and the owners walked sedately behind them discussing the problems facing their country.

"Young Taiko was proudly trying to ride his new tricycle, given to him that very morning, for today was his fourth birthday and he was looking forward to the afternoon's party with a group of his young friends. They might even have the luxury of a cake, for his mother had saved up some ingredients from the rations. As he tried to pedal, his mother fussed around him, anxious in case he fell off and hurt himself.

"At the back of an elegant house on the outskirts of the town, the retired Colonel Tokada was sitting in his summerhouse reading the morning papers. The reports stated that things were not going as well as expected in the war, and the colonel guessed that this meant that his country was faring very badly; government propaganda glossing over the problems. He recalled his army career and wanted to be back in the action to help the cause.

"His experience and knowledge told him that is was likely his country would eventually lose the war. They had bitten off more than they could cope with, by attacking the Americans and having to fight the British and Australians as well. With the demise of Hitler's Germany, the Americans and British could now concentrate on defeating Japan. He feared more and more that air raids and fire-bomb raids would destroy his beloved homeland. And he was puzzled why his city had escaped so lightly, but knew that the bombers would soon arrive.

"He knew that his fellow countrymen would never surrender like the Germans and would fight to the very last – how many Japanese would be killed or wounded before the end came? After the war was finally over, how would they recover? Japan could well become a very poor country. He buried the thoughts. It was unpatriotic and treasonable to be so pessimistic, as Foreign Minister Tojo still proclaimed belligerently that Japan would win.

In the meantime, Colonel Tokada could only read the papers and give his advice if required.

"Overhead a lone plane flew by, leaving a trail in the sky. The alarm had sounded, but few people took any notice and it was soon followed by the all-clear siren. It was just another reconnaissance plane flown by the Americans.

"In the nearby castle, used as a barracks, soldiers were involved in their daily routine of physical exercises. The sergeant-major barked out his instructions in a voice that did not need a loudspeaker to echo around the parade ground and far beyond. The soldiers were restless; they wanted action, not exercises. They had sworn an oath to defend their country to the very last drop of their blood and were anxious to prove themselves in battle as modern-day samurai.

"At the City Hospital, Doctor Tanaka was just beginning his morning round of the wards, accompanied by the matron. As they walked along the corridors, they discussed the arrangements to cope with an emergency should the city be subjected to a fire-storm raid by American bombers. They had received reports of the problems encountered by other cities recently. Luckily their city had escaped a serious bombing raid so far, but they felt, that it was only a matter of time. They would need to call nurses and doctors in from leave very quickly and mobilise emergency ambulances to bring in the wounded. During the previous month Dr. Tanaka had attended a conference with doctors from other hospitals to sort out emergency procedures, but these were not yet fully implemented.

"They visited the wards, chatting to the patients. At this time the hospital was comparatively quiet with just the normal illnesses and routine operations to worry about.

"In the Maternity Ward, two babies had been born during the night and the nurses were scurrying back and forth tending to the babies and the mothers. It was Mrs. Yamamura's first baby and she had endured a long period of labour. She had been very anxious and frightened as she dreaded pain and in the last few weeks had many times even regretted that she was pregnant: but now that she had a lovely bouncing boy – all the pain was worth it. She looked lovingly at him lying in the cot beside her bed and thought how beautiful he was. He had a mass of jet-black hair and big bright eyes. She lay there wondering what his life would hold in store. Perhaps he would be a famous sportsman, or a politician, or a successful businessman, on the other hand he may just be an ordinary workman. All that really mattered, however, was that he would be healthy and happy and live a long life. Her husband, who was stationed at the local barracks, had been able to get leave to be with her for the birth, but had now had to return to duty.

"In the next bed, Mrs. Sakata was resting after the birth of her third child. The labour had been shorter this time and less painful. She supposed that with each succeeding birth, it got easier or perhaps she had been more relaxed. She had been blessed with a lovely daughter this time, as she had wished, because her two previous children were boys and they would love to have a baby sister. Unfortunately her husband Ryo could not be there as he was serving in the Air Force and had been unable to get leave. She hoped he would be able to see his daughter very soon. She lay in the bed admiring her little girl in the cot next to her, but the war troubled her greatly. Her sister lived in Tokyo and they had endured several nights of fire-storm attacks. Hundreds of houses had been destroyed by fire or explosion and many people had been killed and injured. She feared that soon these attacks would be directed to their city. When would this terrible war end? After the wonderful successes of the Japanese at Pearl Harbour and the conquests of Singapore, Malaya and the many islands of the Pacific, everyone was hopeful of an early and successful end. Now it appeared that Japan was facing many problems. Surely they could not be beaten. Their divine Emperor would never let that happen.

"The clock in the main square ticked relentlessly on to fifteen minutes past eight and in the city of Hiroshima, life went on as normal in the bright August morning sunshine."

Five miles above them, the bomb doors of the Superfortress slowly opened ....

Chapter 4 – In the Sky

The choice of venue had been left for the weather conditions to determine. Kyoto had been vetoed as it was the religious and cultural centre of Japan and so Hiroshima became the target.

In the super-fortress the crew were getting anxious. It had been emphasised to them the importance of the mission. They had been trained exhaustively and had left Tiennan Island at approximately 2.45 a.m.

There were three planes, Enola Gay carrying the weapon which was accompanied by two planes containing cameras and other instruments.

The main plane had been bizarrely named Enola Gay by the pilot after his elderly mother and this was painted in large letters on the nose.

The deadly bomb was equally bizarrely named, Little Boy – someone on the team obviously had a black sense of humour.

The plan was to approach the target at about 300 m.p.h. and after dropping - its load was to turn sharply at 150 degrees to avoid the blast. The bomb had the equivalent explosive force to some

20,000 tons of TNT. What this knowledge meant to the crew is unknown.

Chapter 5 – Interlude

Tony treated Akiko to lunch and thanked him for his vivid portrayal of the time leading up to the tragedy. He arranged to meet him the following day then spent the rest of the afternoon exploring the Peace Museum and the city. Everywhere there was a general bustle, just like any other modern city. It looked very prosperous and the people seemed very cheerful.

He could not help but marvel at the reconstruction of the city and enjoyed crossing some of the forty-nine bridges which linked the seven rivers that flowed into the Inland Sea.

Yet there seemed to be an underlying sadness, something he could not put his finger on. Maybe it was him but Tony felt that the ghosts of the past seemed to be hovering over the city; a brooding presence, a weight from the past that seemed to bear down on him.

He shook the feeling from his thoughts and made his way to the Children's Peace Monument, a work inspired by Sadako Sasaki, a ten year old leukaemia victim who'd decided to fold 1,000 paper cranes as was the Japanese custom for making personal wishes come true. She'd believed that if she reached her target, she would recover but it wasn't to be; her classmates completed her task.

Turning, Tony made his way to the nearby Korean A-Bomb Memorial and frowned. He'd had no idea that about one in ten of the victims had been Korean, all shipped to Japan as slave labour in the preceding years.

Chapter 6 – Terror from the Skies

The next day, just after breakfast, Tony strolled to the Peace Park, where he was due to meet Akiko again. Akiko was there before him, dressed immaculately in a dark suit, white shirt and grey tie. He bowed courteously and shook Tony's hand warmly.

"Konnichiwa Akiko," said Tony, trying out his Japanese.

"Good Morning, Tony," said Akiko with a smile.

Tony told him of his plan to try to search for friends and relatives of his parents that may have survived the bombing.

Akiko told Tony to be delicate when conducting his research as the hibakusha, as the survivors were known, had suffered tremendous discrimination as well as the physical suffering the majority had endured.

"Why was that?" he asked him.

"Well, medical opinion was that they would die early, so nobody would contemplate marriage to someone like that. If they were disfigured then they were ostracised, especially the women and consequently many have remained single to this day. They have been denied love." Akiko explained with what Tony felt was a very personal sorrow.

Tony did not pursue the matter further, but asked; "Can you tell me about the time of the bomb falling and the immediate after effects?"

Akiko took time to gather his thoughts and Tony could plainly see that this was a strain for him.

"Obviously we try to forget that time, but I will try," he said. "As you know, it was a beautiful morning with a warm sun. At seven in the morning the siren sounded, but few took much notice. This was a regular occurrence and at eight the all-clear duly sounded; everyone relaxed.

"I was an army cadet at the time and was in the barracks adjoining the castle. We were therefore away from Ground Zero. I was down in the cellars and did not see the explosion. The first I knew was this tremendous bang and the ground shook like the after-effects of an earthquake.

"One of my fellow cadets was on the parade ground and said that the light was like the sun and sadly he was looking at it and was struck blind by the intensity of the light.

"It was like the story of Moses and the Pharaoh and the plagues in your Old Testament – but all the disasters were visited on us, at one time – not spread over a period, just one after another. First there was the brilliant flash, like a sheet of sun, called the pika, which damaged many eyes and was a sunrise like no other sunrise. It lit up the sky. I often think of the irony for this to happen in the land of the rising sun."

At this, a strange smile momentarily hovered on Akiko's lips.

"This was followed almost instantly by a tremendous roar of ear-splitting thunder and the ground shook and trembled; then came the blast which flattened my city to nothing more than smoking rubble, and then came the searing heat which burned people so terribly; seventy thousand I have been told. Then fires started all over the city. Balls of flame carried through the air and soon the wind became a whirlwind as objects were thrown across the city. Then it rained – not ordinary rain, but black rain – huge goblets of water mixed with matter. After all this the survivors breathed more easily – an ironic phrase, because their breathing brought its own problems. We could not see the mushroom cloud for a long time; the dust in the air obliterated it.

"It became darker and darker and people began to think it was the end of the world and in a sense it was.

"Gradually the cloud became visible and we saw this tremendous column rising and forming the mushroom shape. But little did we realise its dreadful significance. Then came, perhaps, the deadliest plague – a silent and invisible killer – the radiation which was to kill so many for generations to come."

At this point Akiko was so overcome he had to stop.

Tony put his arm around him, trying to console him, but to no avail. Akiko's eyes were full of tears and in a very weak voice he said he would telephone later.

Tony watched his friend walk slowly away. At that moment Akiko looked like a very old man. A sob escaped from Tony; in the very little his friend had said about the time Akiko had managed to convey the raw loss Japan had felt as a country.

Back at his hotel, Tony felt that he needed a break from this pressure and decided to continue his sight-seeing.

In the Peace Park, he sketched out his plans for the next few days. He'd already compiled a list of the family and friends, he would try to contact or at least find out what had happened to them. He girded himself, as he was sure he would discover many had died, whilst the others would have deeply disturbing stories to tell.

Chapter 7 – Interviewing the Survivors

The following morning Tony went to the Civic Offices to begin to search their records. It did not start well. The first information he came across served up the death certificates of two family friends.

Yukio Kanazawa, a friend of his father had died on that fateful 6th August and then he discovered that Yukio's wife had also perished on the same day – in their home he suspected.

Tatsuya Suzuki, another work colleague of his father, seemed to have survived and after some research Tony found his address. He continued to go through his first list of fifteen people and of these only six had survived.

That afternoon, he called at the house of Tatsuya Suzuki and was greeted at the door by a lady dressed in an elegant kimono. She informed him that her husband had succumbed to cancer a few months previously, and the doctors believed it had been triggered by the radiation from the bomb.

She did, however, agree to talk. She left the room and returned a few minutes later with green tea. She began by introducing herself as Mihoko and started talking about life in Hiroshima, when everything was as normal as it could be for a country at war.

"You know life was very hard –very little food and no soap – we had to use substitute soap that made your skin come out in a terrible rash. I was taken out of school and had to help in the telephone exchange – I really enjoyed that work, it was better than school! Some girls had to help to demolish houses to make fire-breaks."

She then fetched a file and showed him a copy of the Chugoku Shimbun the local newspaper for the 1st August

The headline read: '*Victory is definitely with us. Our sacred country will repel the hated enemy*'

"Do you know that we had to eat bramble shoots, grubs and worms and even grass? I used to go up into the surrounding hills to collect it.

"My younger brother ate some loquat fruit and became ill with dysentery. Evidently it can cause this if it is unripe. Sadly we could not afford the necessary medicine and he died. Do you know, he was only six years old!"

She was very upset at this point and it was several minutes before she was able to continue.

"When the bomb exploded I was working in the Telephone exchange, about half a kilometre from the epicentre. I was staring at something shining in the sunlit sky. Then there was a tremendous explosion and all the buildings nearby collapsed. People were crying out and I could not move; my legs were trapped. I screamed for my mother, but the supervisor, Mr. Wakita, told us to be calm. It went quiet and eventually I managed to move my legs. I looked out and the sky was black with flames everywhere.

"Then it was all quiet and the city appeared to be enveloped in flames. Mr. Wakita came to help me and suggested that we swim across the river. The bridge was burning and the river was very high. I was worried, but he said we had no option. We jumped in and about half-way across, I felt faint and lost control, but he helped me.

"When we reached the other side I couldn't see anything. I heard students screaming and crying out.

"'What is happening?' I said to Mr. Wakita and he said that the students were terribly burnt and crouching in pain. A lot of students were in the open air clearing buildings for the fire-breaks and they died immediately. Many jumped in the river and drowned.

"Without my supervisor, I too would have died.

"Were you injured?" Tony asked.

"I had injuries on my face and my parents told me they were only minor. After a while, I got a mirror and the sight was horrible. One eye looked like a pomegranate and I had cuts to my other eye and cheek. I looked like a monster. But I was very lucky. Later I had several operations and my face eventually healed."

She stopped talking, while she gathered her thoughts.

"You look very beautiful now," Tony said.

She was very touched by this and gently squeezed his hand. "I remember your father very well."

"Do you know the whereabouts of my mother's sister or our other friends?" he asked.

"I'm sorry; I lost touch with most of them. The city was so chaotic after the bomb. People were only concerned with their own welfare.

"I still go to the anniversary events and pray that never more will an atomic bomb be dropped on a city."

At this she closed her eyes and was silent. He saw a number of tears roll gently down her face. He embraced her gently and then bade her farewell.

"Sayonara," he said.

"Sayonara," she whispered as she stood at the door waving goodbye. Then, slowly, she closed the door after giving one final bow.

He was struck by her dignity and lack of bitterness.

Tony's time in Hiroshima was now drawing to a close and yet he had still not traced the whereabouts of his mother's sister, Kinue Tomoyasu. Even the records office at the Peace Museum, with its massive index of all known victims, did not list her name. Tony sighed, relieved. He moved on to the testimonies and as he began to read the last one her saw her name printed there; Testimony of Kinue Tomoyasu. Now all he had to do was trace her whereabouts. He asked the museum officials whether they would be able to help and they told him they could.

That night he went wearily back to his hotel. He was mentally and physically drained.

He decided to have an early night, but sleep evaded him, then finally he drifted off, but his sleep was not to be the peaceful place it should have been; his eardrums burst as a tumultuous bass rumble threw him to the ground and as he picked -himself up he stood face to face with a living skull, half covered with burnt flesh. He turned to run but the road was blocked, completely clogged with charred lumps, the only clue to what they were being their body shape. He awoke in a cold sweat screaming. Sitting on the side of his bed he reached for the minibar, opened - it and gulped down the contents of a small brandy bottle hoping to settle his nerves.

Chapter 8 – Reunited

In the morning he felt even more exhausted, but was determined to complete his mission. In the back of his mind a sense of dread and foreboding hanging over him was becoming more prevalent. It seemed as if the ghosts of the past had begun to haunt him; day and night.

Reception rang up to him and put the museum through; they had found an address for Kinue.

After lunch, he caught a tram to the suggested stop and walked to the house. It was a run-down building, in need of paint and a good clean. Tony knocked at the door, but there was no immediate answer. He knocked again and heard some shuffling. The door opened slowly and an old lady peered out from the house's gloom.

"Are you Kinue Tomoyasu?" Tony asked, bowing.

The old lady shook her head. Had she understood him?

"Are you Kinue Tomoyasu," he repeated. Again she shook her head.

"She moved, over five years ago. She was a friend of mine and I moved in."

"Could you tell me where she is?" he asked.

"Why do you want to know, who are you?" The woman was very suspicious.

"I'm her nephew, and I would like to meet her," he stated and smiled.

"Come in," she said and ushered Tony into the house.

She introduced herself as Toshiko Saeki, gestured for Tony to sit down and went to make some tea. She walked very badly and trembled. Eventually she returned with a tray, but, as she shook badly, he took it from her.

Over tea, she apologised for the delay and explained again that Kinue had moved out about five years ago and she had taken the house.

"As you can see, the house needs a lot of work, but I cannot do it," she sighed and Tony thought he detected a tear.

"Do you know her address?"

"It is in the outskirts – it is really nice out there. Just a minute I have the address. She was very good to me."

She delved into a notebook and copied the address rather laboriously.

Tony thanked her and then asked if she was a hibakusha.

"How did you know?" she asked.

He explained his mission.

"I came to Hiroshima to interview friends and relatives of my parents and to tell their story. I am concerned that in the west, as new wars and terrorist attacks fill the newspapers and television schedules, the story of Hiroshima is being slowly forgotten. Also the survivors are dying due to their age. It is a story and a lesson that the world needs to be reminded of," he exclaimed, his voice rising with emotion.

Toshiko nodded then began to tell her story.............

"I was seventeen years old at the time – a schoolgirl. I was on the way to my friend's house in Fubairi with two classmates as it was their holiday from student mobilization labour. We all got on the tram in the Hatchobori district and were near the front. The tram had left Hiroshima station; it was just after eight and arrived at Hatchobori around 8.15 that morning.

"Suddenly there was an intense flash and the blast engulfed the tram. In an instant it was on fire. I was one of ten that survived. I think there were at least one hundred of us on that tram. It was rush hour, you know."

At this she broke down and wept bitterly. But she wanted to say more. She took a deep breath.

"Both my classmates died about two weeks after the bombing."

Again her voice failed.

"There was the flash and then darkness. I was unconscious for a while. When we came to we called each other's names. My friends complained of the heat and terrible pain. I saw that one of my friends had terrible burns on one side of her body. There was a water tank nearby, but the water wasn't clear, dust was covering it. So I put my handkerchief in the water and laid it over her burns, but it didn't help. Both my friends were badly burned."

"What about you?" Tony asked.

"Flesh was hanging from my face and my face was all bloody."

"What happened after that?"

"Somehow we groped our way in the dark to an air raid shelter we knew was nearby. Eventually some people took us to the hospital. I was the lucky one and survived. Sadly my two friends were not so lucky."

"I had a number of operations and my face gradually healed up, although you can still see the scars."

Tony had tried not to look closely at her, but the terrible scars were clearly visible and disfigured what would otherwise have been an attractive face.

"The burns on my arms, legs and body healed eventually. We looked for the driver but there was no sign of him and we think he must have been blown out of the tram by the blast."

Tony thanked her and shook her hand warmly. He looked back to see her standing at the door slowly waving.

After leaving her, Tony caught a tram to the outskirts and found the address given to him by Toshiko Saeki. It was in a very nice neighbourhood, largish houses and tree-lined roads.

He knocked at the door of - a nice house, which was - somewhat smaller than its neighbours. After a short delay, a rather wizened lady opened the door.

"Konnichiwa," Tony said.

The lady looked at him and prepared to shut the door.

"Are you Kinue Tomoyasu?"

She stared at Tony.

"Who are you? What do you want?"

"I am your nephew, Tony Thompson, from England."

Her face lit up and she asked him in and gave him a very warm hug.

"It is lovely to see you, after all this time."

They then spent some time talking about the old times and family news. He showed her pictures of his wife and children. Later he asked her to tell her story.

"Do you know, we all try to forget those times and all that suffering, but I will try."

Tony sat back in the chair listening to his aunt.

"At the time I was twenty years old and my mind was full of ambition for my job and of course, boys, like all young girls."

At this she smiled rather guiltily. Her face heavily made up to hide the scars. She was very small and slim and her voice tinkled like crystal glass.

"I worked in an office doing typing and other secretarial work. That morning, I remember looking up and seeing a silver object glinting in the sun and feeling puzzled, because the all-clear had already sounded. There was no noise, just an enormous flash and then a tremendous bang and I was buried as the office collapsed on me. I could not move as my arms and legs were trapped. I called out to my boss and the other workers. But there was no reply, just silence. After a bright sunny morning, it was now almost pitch-black. When I came to I saw a vague figure in front of me, it was the boss and eventually he managed to free my legs and arms. Together we walked around the remains of the building, but there were no other survivors."

"Weren't you injured?" Tony asked.

"Yes. My arm was broken and I had severe cuts and bruises on my legs, but I was lucky. Oh and my face had been lacerated by flying shards of glass from the windows.

"Somehow we staggered into the road. I'd lost my glasses, which was a blessing, because I was unable to see some of the worst sights. There were fires everywhere and the smell of burning flesh – I shall never forget that.

"And when we got to the hospital there were so many people with blackened and charred faces, others with skin burned off and clothes shredded, women stripped naked by the blast. People walked like ghosts with their arms stretched out in pain.

"My scars became infected, as there were few medicines which were reserved for the most severe burns cases.

"But, I count myself extremely lucky, so many of my friends died on that terrible day or died in the years to come from radiation sickness, but I'll never forget what I saw, the images - will haunt me for the rest of my life."

Toshiko sipped some tea, trying to take strength from the hot drink.

"I was so pleased that my sister, your mother, escaped to England in time. I tried to get your address, but I couldn't get the information."

Tony told Toshiko of his mother's heart attack and death some ten years previously but added that she'd lived a good life in England and had seen her two grandchildren grow up. He then told her about his father's death four years after his mother's.

They continued to talk for a while and although he'd only met his aunt for a few hours he felt a strong family bond with her.

When it was time to go, they embraced and kissed and they both had tears in their eyes as they whispered sayonara to each other.

That night he had another nightmare. It was a view of the city of Hiroshima after the destruction. It was a vision of hell, of Dante's Inferno; a view distorted as in a concave mirror- a crazy world full of horrifying images. Wherever he looked there was an image to disturb him and, when dawn broke, he breathed a sigh of relief.

Chapter 9 – The End of the Search

Tony looked at his list of survivors, there was only one left. That morning he went to visit Yukio Kanazawa, who had been the father of one of his school friends.

He knocked at his door and was shocked as this very old man shuffled to the door. He introduced himself and Yukio had to search his memory for a while, before a smile lit up his face. Yukio invited him in.

"Sadly my son, your friend, Tatsuyo died. His school was demolished in the blast, but he survived despite severe injuries. Then some six months later, he became ill and it was eventually diagnosed as radiation sickness. He died two months later."

Yukio stopped to take a breath. A tear rolled down his face.

"Sit down and I will make tea for you," he sobbed.

Tony thought that he took the opportunity to recover himself and five minutes later Yukio returned with the tea.

"I am sorry to bring you such distress," Tony whispered.

"That is alright, I am pleased to talk to one of Tatsuyo's friends."

They then spent half an hour talking about the old days and catching up with news. He was interested in Tony's new life in England.

Eventually Tony asked him about his experiences after the bomb.

"I was working in the office of the factory when the bomb fell. Fortunately I was down in the basement, checking documents, so I missed the worst of the blast. I was, however, knocked to the ground and was unconscious for a while. When I came to, I couldn't move my legs, a large beam had fallen and trapped them. I was very fortunate because a couple of work colleagues found me and shifted the beam. They helped me out of the building as fast as they could. It was difficult to walk as I had a severe pain in my left leg. Later I found out it had been broken.

"A fire had started on the ground floor and when we came out into the open air it was so dark I thought it was the end of the world. I grabbed a post and used it as a crutch. There were flames everywhere. Fires were spreading so fast, with so many wooden buildings.

"We passed many houses and I could hear the screams of people trapped inside, including the voices of children. I wanted to stop and help, but I couldn't, I just had to limp past. Some of the people whom we passed were terribly burned. I saw one woman with no face at all, her eyes, nose and mouth were burned away; her ears had melted. I shall never forget that moment."

Again he had to stop and fight back the tears.

"I'm sorry, but it brings it all back. Over the years, we have tried to put it behind us and forget," he sobbed.

Tony apologised and explained that he was writing a book to capture the suffering of that time and bring it to the attention of people in the West.

Yukio saw the merit in what his son's friend was trying to accomplish and continued;

"New fires were springing up all over. We reached the river but the river didn't stop the fire. Fire-balls were carried through the air from the opposite bank. All the pine trees were burning. The river was choked with bodies, mostly dead bodies, floating on the water, but some were trying to swim clear.

"People faced a terrible dilemma. If they stayed in the park, they faced being burnt to death and if they jumped in the river, they faced a watery death. There were screams and shouts as a number tumbled into the river, like a set of dominoes. Suddenly a whirlwind ripped through the park and huge trees crashed down, smaller trees and bushes were uprooted and flew through the air. People were crossing the bridge like ants and I saw a man, stone dead, sitting on his bicycle, as it leaned against the bridge. Then a strange rain began to fall – it was black, heavy globules – the rain water mixed with dust and god - knows what else. Roofs and doors were revolving in a twisting funnel and we tried to duck to avoid them.

"The roads were a macabre traffic jam of crumpled bicycles, shells of cars and buses, as all were halted in mid-motion.

"At last we reached the clinic, but it was overflowing; people struggling to get in. I saw a young lady on the floor and I took her hand to help her up, but her skin just slipped off like a glove.

"We joined the throng of would-be patients. The remaining staff were completely overrun. How could they prioritize?"

Yukio shook his head as he recalled the moment.

"Eventually I was seen and had a makeshift splint applied to my leg. I was fortunate that I only needed a splint.

"The radiation was the most deadly aspect, it killed virtually everyone within a half mile radius of ground zero. The immediate symptoms were violent vomiting and diarrhoea. Then two weeks later other symptoms appeared, hair falling out whenever it was brushed, spots and boils appeared, fever and then the invisible signs inside our bodies; a lowering of the blood count and suppression of white blood cells. People and doctors did not understand this illness. Did you know that even babies that were still in the womb were born with deformities?"

At this point Yukio stopped; "I've said enough." He was emotionally drained. They both took some tea and talked of other things for a while.

He then said, "At times I always ask what if?"

"I suppose it's true of all tragedies, where some are killed and others survive, it is all a matter of fate," Tony replied and got up. It was time to go. The two men shook hands and Tony bowed.

Tony sat in the departure lounge; his mind was in turmoil, a mixture of emotions. He had made many friends and renewed old acquaintances and formed a tremendous respect for the people of Hiroshima, for their forgiveness and hospitality. But he also felt a sense of relief. Ever since his arrival, he had been haunted by terrible images and a sense of guilt that hung over him like a heavy cloud, which was hard to explain. Would he return? He would see.

On the flight back to England, he sat quietly in the plane thinking back to his experiences. It had given him a whole new perspective on life, an appreciation of all the blessings and benefits he had enjoyed.

He uttered a prayer that Man would live in peace with his fellow man. He glanced at the morning paper – More soldiers had been killed in Afghanistan, a suicide bomber had blown himself up in a market in Baghdad, killing forty innocent people and there had been a shooting in Jerusalem.

As soon as he got home he would start writing his book – someone had to highlight mankind's crass stupidity.

Killing Myself to Live

By Simon Woodward

Quite often I sit in my study,
thinking about my past that has been.
Not a thing I have control over, just my life before,
and its permeating stink.
And I wonder. I wonder why I suffer this trauma;
this thing that's my life before.
And these thoughts are forever present,
bugging me, taunting me, pushing me to the brink.
Contemplating the uncontemplatable
and I wonder why I think,
the thoughts I ought not consider,
the thoughts of what should have been.

I try so hard to reconcile my history
with the way things are, as they are.
And occasionally I fail this warranted duty unto myself,
but it's the way things are, it is,
— the way my life is as it is.

And when they're foremost in my head,
still pushing me to the brink.
I look at the bottle before me after my mind has turned
to drink.

And savour every moment,
when my mind has been comfortably numbed.
It's a release from my torment and although
the mantra has been drummed

— into me
— that I'm killing myself,

the path is already laid.
There's nothing I can do to get off it,
there's nothing I can pay,
for my history and my life before,
things started going my way.

Am I forever having to follow this deep and cataclysmic
rift,
the borderline between the now and my past that is as it
is?

For now, I know the answer,
as it is in my gift,
to follow through with the only option I have,
and that is,

— killing myself to live.

Manufactured by Amazon.ca
Bolton, ON

19960284R00180